W9-BJZ-509

The First Mountain Man: Preacher's Bloodbath

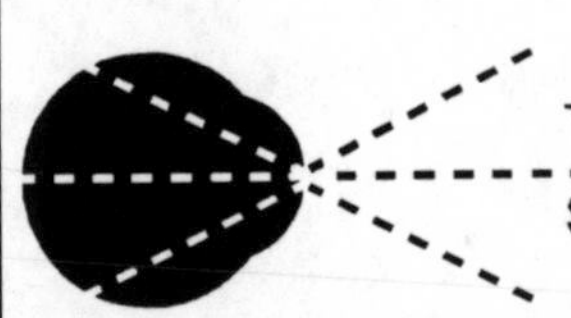

This Large Print Book carries the
Seal of Approval of N.A.V.H.

THE FIRST MOUNTAIN MAN: PREACHER'S BLOODBATH

WILLIAM W. JOHNSTONE
WITH J. A. JOHNSTONE

THORNDIKE PRESS
A part of Gale, Cengage Learning

Farmington Hills, Mich • San Francisco • New York • Waterville, Maine
Meriden, Conn • Mason, Ohio • Chicago

Following the death of William W. Johnstone, the Johnstone family is working with a carefully selected writer to organize and complete Mr. Johnstone's outlines and many unfinished manuscripts to create additional novels in all of his series like The Last Gunfighter, Mountain Man, and Eagles, among others. This novel was inspired by Mr. Johnstone's superb storytelling.

WWJ steer head logo is a Reg. U.S. Pat. & TM Off.
Thorndike Press® Large Print Western.
The text of this Large Print edition is unabridged.
Other aspects of the book may vary from the original edition.
Set in 16 pt. Plantin.

LIBRARY OF CONGRESS CATALOGING-IN-PUBLICATION DATA

Names: Johnstone, William W., author. | Johnstone, J. A., author.
Title: The first mountain man : preacher's bloodbath / by William W. Johnstone with J. A. Johnstone.
Other titles: Preacher's bloodbath
Description: Large print edition. | Waterville, Maine : Thorndike Press, 2016. | Series: Thorndike Press large print western
Identifiers: LCCN 2016019239 | ISBN 9781410488329 (hardcover) | ISBN 1410488322 (hardcover)
Subjects: LCSH: Large type books. | GSAFD: Western stories.
Classification: LCC PS3560.O415 F5727 2016 | DDC 813/.54—dc23
LC record available at https://lccn.loc.gov/2016019239

Published in 2016 by arrangement with Pinnacle Books, an imprint of Kensington Publishing Corp.

Printed in Mexico
2 3 4 5 6 7 21 20 19 18 17

The First Mountain Man:
Preacher's Bloodbath

CHAPTER 1

The man burst out of the brush, eyes wide with terror as he ran, arms pumping, legs moving so fast they were almost out of control. Every few steps, he twisted his head to glance wide-eyed behind him as if Ol' Scratch, the Devil himself, was behind him, closing in.

Might as well have been.

Based on his appearance, the terrified man looked like he shouldn't have been scared of anything. He was tall and rugged, with broad, powerful shoulders that strained the buckskin shirt he wore. His bearded, weather-beaten face showed that he had spent a lot of time on the frontier. He had two flintlock pistols, a tomahawk, and a sheathed knife tucked into the sash around his waist, and he carried a long-barreled rifle. A powder horn and a full shot pouch bounced against his hip as he ran. He was armed for bear, as the old saying went.

But it wasn't a bear that was after him. Even as terrible an engine of destruction as one of those creatures could be, what pursued the trapper was worse.

As he started up a bare, rocky slope, he lifted his frenzied gaze and saw a clump of boulders above him. If he could get in among those rocks, his pursuers couldn't come at him all at once. At least he would be able to put up a fight . . . for a while, anyway. His heart slugged harder as he increased his pace.

He heard them howling as they crashed through the brush behind him. Like a pack of wolves, they were. Sometimes he could face down wolves and make them retreat, if he didn't show any fear. That wasn't going to work. His pursuers were worse than wolves.

With enough of a lead, he lunged into the clump of boulders and turned. His pursuers had reached the edge of the brush, charged into the open, and started up the slope after him. They wore buckskin leggings and tunics and had large necklaces of thick leather decorated with small, shiny rocks draped around their shoulders. They carried war clubs and spears and looked like they knew how to use them.

A man in the rear of the party, urging the

others on, was dressed similarly but also sported a headdress styled to look like an eagle's beak. A pair of actual eagle's wings, stiffened so they would remain spread out, was attached to a harness strapped to his back. He carried a spear and shook it in the air as he shouted at his companions.

The trapper flung his rifle to his shoulder. He would have liked to ventilate that eagle-wearing varmint in the back, but he couldn't get a clear shot at the man. He settled for drawing a bead on one of the warriors in front and pressed the trigger. The rifle boomed, and the target went over backwards as the heavy lead ball smashed into his chest.

The war chief or whatever he was yelled louder.

The trapper set the empty rifle close enough that he could snatch it up again and use it as a club, and drew both pistols. Already loaded, all he had to do was pull back the hammers as he planted himself in the narrow opening between two boulders.

Three of the attackers flung spears at him. He ducked one, and the other two bounced off the rocks. The leading edge of the charge was only about twenty feet away.

He leveled both pistols and pulled the triggers. The barrels gushed smoke and flame. Two more attackers went down, and the thunderous explosion of the shots made the others pause for a second — long enough for the trapper to dart back a few feet, drop the pistols, and snatch the knife and tomahawk from his belt.

The gap between the boulders was so narrow only one man at a time could get through it. Of course, the attackers could stand off a ways and chuck spears at him, but the odds of hitting him were small and soon they would be weaponless.

Through the opening, he saw his enemies hesitate, even though their leader was still behind them, exhorting them on.

A grin stretched across the trapper's whiskery face. He had already killed three and was confident he would take more of them with him when he crossed the divide.

A faint scraping sound behind him was the only warning he got. As he turned, he caught a glimpse of a figure hurtling at him from the top of one of the rocks. Somehow, at least one of his pursuers had gotten around him.

The warrior crashed into him, the impact driving him against a boulder. He felt something snap and knew he'd probably broken a rib. Pain shot through him but it didn't stop him from swinging the tomahawk. He felt bone shatter as he smashed it against the attacker's head. The man collapsed.

More warriors crowded around the trapper. He slashed back and forth with the 'hawk and the knife as he tried to clear a space around him, but there were too many of them. One thrust a spear into his right thigh. The trapper yelled in a mixture of rage and agony. Then a war club caught him on the head and dropped him to his knees as the world began to spin crazily around him.

It was no use. They ripped his weapons away from him, along with the shot pouch and powder horn, and bore him the rest of the way to the ground. He writhed and tried to strike out with his fists, but strong hands gripped him and held him down.

He had never been a religious man and hadn't set foot in a church since his ma had made him go back in Pennsylvania, long before he headed west to the Shining Mountains. But he had never considered himself a heathen. Knowing that his tormentors were about to kill him, he begged forgiveness for all his sins — and there were aplenty.

Instead of skewering him with spears or bashing his brains out with their clubs, the warriors picked him up and carried him out of the boulders. The fellow who wore the eagle headdress and wings stood with his arms folded across his chest as he regarded the captive with a look of haughty hatred. He spoke harshly in his gibberish of a language.

The trapper knew half a dozen Indian dialects but had never heard that one before.

The man made a sharp gesture. Several of the warriors swung their clubs, but instead of aiming the blows at the trapper's head, they broke his legs and arms, snapping bones with great precision. He howled, and the cry resounded along the valleys and wooded slopes.

With the trapper completely helpless, the warriors picked him up again and carried him over to a low, squarish rock that had split off the mountain from above and toppled down in ages past. They laid him out on the rock and stepped back.

The war chief moved up beside the rock and sneered down at the trapper. He gestured again, and an old man the trapper hadn't seen before came into view. The old man's face was as brown and wrinkled as a nut. He placed a long cloak made of eagle feathers on the war chief's shoulders and handed the chief a knife.

It was not the sort of hunting knife the trapper carried. The blade was made of flint chipped down to an edge. The handle, also made of stone, had been fashioned into the shape of a man kneeling far forward. The war chief grinned as he ran the ball of his thumb along the blade. A drop of blood welled from the cut as he leaned over the captive.

The trapper's eyes widened and bulged from their sockets until it looked like they were going to pop out.

The war chief slashed the trapper's buckskin tunic and ripped it aside, baring the man's hairy chest. The trapper screamed as the chief began sawing with the blade.

The screams didn't stop until the chief pulled the trapper's bloody, still quivering heart out of his chest and thrust it aloft with a strident, triumphant cry.

CHAPTER 2

Two men moved through the woods, each very different from the other. One was a Crow Indian, tall and muscular, with a rugged, middle-aged face that looked like it might have been hewn out of a redwood tree.

The Crow's companion was little more than half his height, a white man in buckskins and coonskin cap. Despite his diminutive stature, he was broad-shouldered and brawny, too, with the upper body development of a much taller man.

As far as his weaponry was concerned, he carried a rifle with a barrel somewhat shorter than usual so he could handle it better. That was the only concession to his height. The two flintlock pistols at his waist were full-sized — as was his fighting heart.

"I don't wish to cast aspersions on the acuity of your hearing or the veracity of your declarations, old friend," the little man commented. "So I have no doubt that you actually did hear shots and screams from this direction a short time ago. But we've found nothing so far, and I begin to wonder if our search might be fruitless."

The Crow regarded him gravely. "Umm."

"Yes, I share your concern over Rawley. He was headed in this direction when last we encountered him, and the man's notorious for his predilection for impulsive, reckless behavior. He easily could have waltzed right into trouble, just as you point out, friend Nighthawk."

The trappers who operated in the Rocky Mountains, from above the Canadian border to the Sangre de Cristo far in the south, knew the little man only as Audie. His full name, the name he had used when he was a professor at one of the most prestigious universities back east, was a mystery. He had given up the academic life and come west to live a much simpler existence on the frontier. As he liked to put it, the dangers of grizzly bears, mountain lions, and hostile Indians were nothing compared to what lurked in the hallowed halls of the Ivy League.

Soon after his arrival in the mountains, he had won friends far and wide because he was able to recite from memory the complete works of Shakespeare and many other poets. Men who spent most of their time alone in the vast wilderness were desperate for any sort of entertainment, so Audie was a popular figure around the campfires.

Somewhere in his travels, he had fallen in with Nighthawk, a deadly, taciturn Crow warrior. An unshakeable bond had formed between the unlikely friends, and they had been trapping together for several years.

Nighthawk pointed.

Audie nodded his agreement. "Very well. We'll continue in this direction for another half hour, and if we don't find any sign of Rawley, we can turn back and return to our camp."

As they moved through the woods, being cautious out of habit and taking advantage of the cover they found, Audie thought back to the previous evening, when Jacob Rawley had shared their campfire.

"There's somethin' mighty odd goin' on in these parts," Rawley said. "You recall Mike Dickinson? He vanished a couple weeks ago. Said he was gonna check some of the streams up there in Shadow Valley, toward Sawtooth Cliffs, and nobody's seen hide nor hair of him since. Jack Phillips found some bones in the valley yonder, though. Human bones, he claims."

"Did you see these skeletal remains with your own eyes?" Audie asked.

Rawley shook his head. "Naw, Jack claims he give 'em a decent burial, even though he couldn't find all of the fella they came from. But he found what had to be a leg bone, and you recollect that limp Mike had on account of he busted his leg when he was a boy? Well, Jack said that leg bone he found had a place on it that looked like it'd been broke and then healed up years ago."

"That's hardly conclusive evidence some misfortune befell Michael. Besides, I'm not sure Jack Phillips has the necessary skill to positively identify human bones, let alone evidence of a previous fracture."

"I'm just tellin' you what he told me, Audie."

"Anyway, even if the bones *did* belong to Michael Dickinson, their existence doesn't necessarily indicate foul play. We both know there are a myriad of methods a man can confront his mortality in these mountains."

"Lots of ways to die, you mean?"

"Precisely. And it would require only a few days for scavengers to strip the bones clean."

"You're right about that," Rawley admitted. "But Mike ain't the only one who's disappeared around Shadow Valley and Sawtooth Cliffs lately. There are three or four other fellas I ain't seen in a good long while, and I've heard rumors that even more trappers are missin'. I think it's Injuns." He glanced at the Crow. "No offense, Nighthawk."

"Umm."

Audie frowned. "The tribes in this vicinity have been on the peaceful side in recent years, Jacob."

"Yeah, well, you never can tell when something'll get 'em riled up," Rawley insisted.

"Besides, I don't recall hearing of any tribe that actually lives in Shadow Valley."

"They could've moved in from somewheres else. I reckon the best thing to do is head up yonder myself and have a look around."

"Do you think that's wise? I mean, if there is some sort of unusual depredation going on . . ."

"Mike Dickinson and me was trappin' partners for a couple years. If he ain't dead, maybe I can find him. And if he is" — a grim cast came over Rawley's face — "maybe I can settle the score with whoever done for him."

"You'll do what you think best, of course —"

"I always do," Rawley declared.

And now it appears that Rawley's stubbornness might have led him into more trouble than he bargained for, Audie mused as he and Nighthawk climbed a ridge. *That is, if Nighthawk is right about what he heard earlier.*

Audie had great faith in his old friend.

They paused at the top of the ridge. To the west as the landscape fell away was a broad valley, and on the far side of that valley, forming its western boundary, were the Sawtooth Cliffs.

It was actually the first time Audie laid eyes on them. Despite their wanderings, he and Nighthawk hadn't been *everywhere* west of the Mississippi.

He had heard of the Sawtooth Cliffs numerous times, though, and usually when anyone spoke of them, it was to mention how ugly and sinister they looked.

That was true. The cliffs ran roughly north and south as far as the eye could see in either direction. They were at least two hundred feet tall, and the rim rose and fell in a jagged pattern that made it look like the teeth of a saw.

They look like the lower jaw of a gigantic predator, thought Audie. Teeth poised to rend and chew until there was nothing left of their prey . . .

Nighthawk swept a hand out to indicate the valley in front of them. "Umm."

"Yes, Shadow Valley is a good name for the place," Audie agreed. "It definitely has a gloomy atmosphere about it. Do you think Rawley is out there somewhere?"

Again, Nighthawk lifted an arm and pointed. Audie spotted what the Crow's keen eyes had already taken note of. Dark shapes were circling lazily in the sky some distance away, closer to the cliffs.

"Carrion birds," Audie murmured. "Never a good sign. Do we turn back or do we ignore those black-feathered, foreboding auspices and press ahead?"

Without answering, Nighthawk started down the slope. Audie went after him, catching up easily despite his short legs. He possessed a nimbleness few of the full-sized could match.

In the several hours it took them to cross the valley, the buzzards disappeared. That was a bad sign. It meant the birds had descended to feed. Whatever had caught their attention was no longer alive.

They had reached a point where the cliffs loomed over them when Nighthawk grunted, started moving faster, and climbed a bare slope toward a nest of boulders. Audie hurried to keep up with the Crow's long-legged strides, following him.

Before they reached the rocks, Audie saw what had caught Nighthawk's eye. Buzzards formed a dark mass as they fed on something lying on a rock slab. The ugly birds rose into the air, squawking in protest as the two men approached.

"Merciful God in heaven," Audie breathed as he saw what the buzzards left behind.

It had been a man, and enough of his clothes remained to recognize what Jacob Rawley had been wearing when he'd visited their camp the previous evening. It was the only way Audie could tell who the dead man had been. Not much of his face remained.

The buzzards had been at his chest, too, and that was rather odd. Rawley's buckskin shirt wasn't torn open raggedly as the birds might have done to get at his flesh. It looked like someone had cut a slit in the shirt, then ripped it back. The straight edges of the cut remained, indicating that a blade had been used.

Rib bones were visible through the bloody, shredded flesh. Nighthawk leaned forward, studied the mutilated trapper for a moment, and then pointed at Rawley's chest.

Stepping closer, Audie grasped instantly what had caught Nighthawk's interest. "Good Lord. It looks like someone reached in there and *pried* those ribs apart. Why in the world —"

"Umm." Nighthawk clenched a fist and thumped it lightly against his own chest.

"Yes. Oh, my, yes. Even if the buzzards had picked it apart, there would be *something* left." Audie swallowed hard. "The conclusion is inescapable. Someone cut poor Jacob's chest open, pried those ribs apart, reached in there . . . *and ripped out his heart!*"

CHAPTER 3

Preacher heard singing in the night, somewhere up ahead of him. He reined his rawboned stallion to a halt and told the big, wolf-like cur who padded alongside, "Stay, Dog."

The mountain man swung down from the saddle, looped the pack horse's lead rope around a nearby sapling, and took his long-barreled flintlock rifle — already loaded and primed — from its sling attached to the saddle. He moved forward through the darkness with his thumb curled around the rifle's hammer so he could cock it in an instant if he needed to.

The men he heard sounded peaceful enough, if a mite tipsy. Carrying on like that at night wasn't the best idea — drawing too much attention to oneself never was, on the frontier — making Preacher suspect some jugs of tanglefoot were involved.

No one could ever accuse him of drawing

attention to himself. On the contrary, the big mountain man was famous for his stealth. On several occasions during his longstanding hostilities with the Blackfoot tribe, he had slipped into the enemy camp in the middle of the night, cut the throats of several, and then slid back out without ever being noticed. None of the survivors had even known he was there until the bodies were discovered the next morning.

Because of that, some of the Blackfeet had taken to calling him Ghost Killer. Others called him the White Wolf because of his deadliness.

The song's ribald lyrics ended in laughter as Preacher saw the glow of a large campfire up ahead. The party that had made camp had to be a large one. The men didn't seem to care about the size of the fire or the loudness of their singing. The fire would keep animals away, and a large, well-armed group of men didn't have to worry much about being attacked.

Still, such boisterousness went against the grain for Preacher. There was a time and a place for everything and nighttime in the wilderness wasn't for loud singing.

He was close enough to pause and call out, "Hello, the camp!" A fella didn't just waltz in unannounced at night. That was a good way to get shot.

The men fell silent.

After a moment, someone responded. "Who's out there?"

"They call me Preacher."

"Preacher!? Well, the saints be praised! Come on in, you old he-coon!"

The voice was familiar. "Is that you, Miles?"

"Aye, 'tis!"

Preacher hadn't seen Miles O'Grady since the previous year. He had always gotten along with O'Grady and figured if the Irishman was part of the group, they were all likely to be friendly, but he kept his thumb on the flintlock's hammer just in case as he strode forward and stepped out of the trees into the circle of light cast by the campfire.

A quick head count told him there were fifteen men in the bunch. He looked around, saw several familiar faces in addition to O'Grady's broad, ruddy one, and nodded to his acquaintances. It seemed a little odd to him, seeing all of them together.

Most fur trappers were, by nature, solitary creatures, content with their own company except on those rare occasions when they attended a rendezvous. If they partnered up with anybody, only two or maybe three would be in a group.

In the early days of the fur trade, large parties had been common. But like anything else, the customs had evolved over time.

O'Grady moved toward Preacher and stuck out a hand. "Last I heard, you were over in the Wind River country."

Preacher shook his hand and drawled, "Yeah, but I didn't have much luck there. Decided to see how the plews are over here. Looks like you fellas had the same idea." He paused, then added meaningfully, "At the same time."

O'Grady's mouth quirked. "Well, that's not exactly why we're all here together like this. It's because of what's been happening over in Shadow Valley."

Preacher frowned and shook his head. "I hadn't heard of anything goin' on over there."

"Well, it seems like 'tis not a very healthy place to be these days. Sit down, warm your bones by the fire, and I'll tell ye all about it."

"Let me get my horses and my dog," Preacher said. "I left 'em back in the woods a ways . . . until I found out what all the celebratin' was about."

" 'Tis not celebrating we are," O'Grady said with a sigh. "More like trying to hold off the darkness with the power of song."

Preacher thought about the situation as he fetched Horse, Dog, and his pack animal. O'Grady, like most Irishmen, was given to bouts of melancholy. Whiskey would just make it worse. Maybe that was all that was going on.

Preacher brought his trail partners back to the camp, unsaddled the big gray stallion, and took the supplies off the pack horse. He picketed both animals, although he knew from long experience that Horse would never willingly stray far from his side. Neither would Dog.

He joined the other men and sat down on a log with several of them. O'Grady offered him a jug.

Preacher shook his head. "Not right now. I'd rather hear about whatever it is that's got you fellas spooked."

One of the men said, "I ain't ashamed to admit I'm a mite scared. You don't know what's goin' on in this part of the country, Preacher. It ain't safe no more."

Preacher grunted. "Shoot, I don't think these mountains were ever all that safe. If you don't have Injuns wantin' to kill you, bears and cougars and lobo wolves are always around. Not to mention avalanches and floods and forest fires. Seems to me like there's always been a million ways to die once you get west of the Mississipp'."

"Yes, but this is worse than usual," O'Grady said. "Nigh on to a dozen men have disappeared around here this year."

"What do you mean, *disappeared*?" Preacher asked with a puzzled frown.

"Just that. Vanished. Dropped off the face of the earth like they never existed. Most of us know someone that's happened to, and the rest have heard stories."

The men sitting in a circle around the campfire nodded solemnly.

"That's not the worst of it, though. We've found bodies" — the Irishman shuddered — "and the things that had been done to them."

It must have been pretty bad to affect O'Grady, thought Preacher.

Although he hadn't been in the mountains as long as Preacher had, Miles O'Grady was a veteran trapper who had been in his share of fights.

"Indians have been known to torture captives," Preacher pointed out. "Hell, one time a bunch of 'em planned on burnin' me at the stake."

"Yeah, I've heard the story," O'Grady said. "Reckon we all have."

"I haven't," one of the other men said.

Preacher didn't know him, couldn't recall

ever having seen him before. The stranger was young, probably in his early twenties. Of course, Preacher couldn't hold youth against a fella. He hadn't even been shaving yet when he lit a shuck from his family's farm and headed off to see the elephant.

"Then you don't know how Preacher got his name." O'Grady seemed glad for an excuse to change the subject. "By the way, Preacher, this youngster is Boone Halliday."

Preacher reached over to shake hands. "Boone's a pretty well-known name back in Kentucky."

"I know. That's where I'm from. In fact, my ma named me after Daniel Boone." The young man grinned. "I reckon that with a name like that, I couldn't help but turn out to be a trapper and a long hunter, right?"

Preacher wasn't sure Boone Halliday could make that claim just yet. He appeared to be pretty wet behind the ears, which in his case stuck out rather prominently from the sides of his head. Boone had a shock of brown hair falling down over his forehead under the wide-brimmed, brown felt hat he wore. Actually, he looked more like he ought to be behind a plow somewhere instead of wandering around the high country.

But every mountain man had to start somewhere, Preacher supposed.

"Tell me about your name," Boone went on.

Preacher shook his head and waved a hand. "I disremember how it got hung on me."

"Well, I don't." O'Grady leaned forward eagerly.

CHAPTER 4

The Irishman launched right into the story. "Preacher was just a sprout, maybe not even as old as you yet, Boone, when he got himself captured by some Blackfeet who had a powerful grudge against him. They tied him to a stake, piled wood around his feet, and were all set to burn him the next morning, but he started preaching to them instead."

"Preaching?" Boone repeated. "Like in church?"

O'Grady nodded. "One and the same."

"What made you decide to do that, Preacher?" Boone asked.

There was no getting around it, so Preacher said, "While I was back in St. Louis, I'd seen a fella standin' on a street corner goin' on about the Gospel whether anybody was listenin' to him or not. He kept it up for a long time, and when I came back after doin' some other things, he was still at it. That stuck in my mind, so when the Blackfeet had me, I commenced to doin' the same thing."

Preacher warmed a little to his topic as all the men looked on with great interest, even the ones who had already heard this story many times. "You see, Injuns take a keen interest in killin'. It's not exactly a sport to 'em, although there's a little of that in the way they feel. It's more like, hell, I don't know, an art, I guess you'd call it. They want to kill their enemies in the way they feel is right. But if you can distract 'em with somethin' they find even more interestin', they'll hold off on the killin' for a while. That's what I figured to do by preachin' at 'em."

Boone smiled. "It must have worked, since you're still here."

"Oh, it worked, all right. When the sun come up the next mornin', they didn't set fire to all that dry wood they'd heaped around my feet. They just sort of gathered 'round and stared at me, and I kept on preachin'." A wry smile appeared on the mountain man's rugged face. "I was a mite wound up by then. I'd gone on all night, so I just kept goin'. I was pretty hoarse and worn out by then, but I'd figured out that my life depended on it."

Boone leaned forward, enthralled by the

tale. "What happened?"

"Well, they didn't kill me. You're right about that. They decided I was crazy." Preacher tapped his temple. "Touched in the head. And since Injuns believe the spirits watch over folks like that, they didn't dare kill me. Wasn't nothin' else they could do except let me go."

"So it was the Indians who first called you Preacher because of that," Boone said.

O'Grady said, "No, that was other trappers, once the story got around. A bit before my time, but I heard all about it, let me tell you. And the name stuck, didn't it, Preacher?"

"Seems to fit me," the mountain man drawled.

"Do you even remember what your real name is?" Boone asked.

Preacher just shrugged. As a matter of fact, he knew good and well that his given name was Arthur. He'd gone by Art when he was a youngun. But that time was so far in the past that it didn't matter anymore.

He had allowed O'Grady to steer the conversation away from the bodies that had been found, but Preacher wanted to know more about them. "What about those dead fellas you came across?"

O'Grady sighed. "I don't like to think

about that."

Mutters of agreement came from several of the other men.

"This wasn't all at once, you understand. Each man was found one at a time, over a space of several weeks. But they were all the same. Scavengers had been at them some, but they were freshly killed that you could tell what had been done to them." The Irishman paused again.

Impatient, Preacher said, "Well, spit it out."

O'Grady took a deep breath. "Their chests had been hacked open. With a knife or a hatchet, looked like. And their hearts were gone. Somebody had ripped them right out."

The air of hilarity that had gripped the group earlier had evaporated completely. Some of the men looked angry, some scared, some just a little sick.

Preacher could understand all those reactions. "Where was this?" He looked toward the west, where he knew a long ridge lay even though he couldn't see it in the darkness. "Over in Shadow Valley, you said?"

O'Grady nodded. "You know the place?"

"I ran some trap lines there, four or five years ago, I reckon it was. Didn't have any trouble as I recollect. It was sort of gloomy for some reason, like there were clouds even when there weren't, but nobody bothered me."

"No, I don't remember any trouble there, either, until this year. But the men who disappeared . . . they were all either already over there or headed in that direction the last time anybody saw them."

One of the trappers said, "Got to be a bunch of bloodthirsty Injuns moved in. That's the only explanation that makes any sense."

"If that were true and Indians were to blame, I'd almost welcome it," O'Grady said.

"Well, then, what do you think it is?" the man demanded.

O'Grady hesitated, then said, "There are creatures . . . creatures that live in the bowels of the earth like . . . worms."

A couple men made rude noises.

O'Grady glared at them and went on. " 'Tis true, I tell ye! Once they were men, but in their evil they were banished underground, and there they've lived ever since, growing more twisted and depraved. They come up from their holes in the ground, fall on poor, unsuspecting souls, and devour their hearts!"

"You're crazy, O'Grady," a man said.

"Things like that don't exist."

"If they don't," O'Grady said, "then why is every man born afraid of the dark?"

None of the other trappers had an answer for that.

Preacher rubbed his beard-stubbled jaw. "Miles, I ain't sayin' I believe you're right about those critters, but if you are and they're supposed to be stuck underground, how'd they get out?"

"Earlier this year, the earth shook. It was a big quake, and I think it opened a path from the underground world to here. Or rather, to Shadow Valley. I think the mouth of hell waits over there."

Most of the men still looked skeptical, but a few appeared even more worried, including Boone Halliday. The youngster said, "How do you fight something like that?"

"I never saw anything yet that hot lead or cold steel couldn't kill," Preacher said.

"If any of us ever encounters those devils, I pray you're right, Preacher," O'Grady said. "I just hope Audie and Nighthawk haven't run afoul of them."

Preacher stiffened. "What was that?"

"Audie and Nighthawk. You know, the little fella and the Crow —"

"I know 'em well," Preacher cut in. "Shared many a campfire with 'em and fought many a good fight with them at my side. You mean to tell me they're among the missin'?"

O'Grady nodded solemnly. "I'm afraid so. It hasn't been long, though. I saw them less than a week ago, and Audie told me in his long-winded way that they'd found the body of Jacob Rawley. Did ye know him?"

"Met him a time or two," Preacher said.

"Well, Rawley went over into Shadow Valley to look for a friend of his who'd disappeared, and Nighthawk thought he heard shots and screamin'. They went to look and found Rawley's body. His heart had been torn out just like the others. They buried him, then came back over the ridge."

"Then why'd they go back?" Even as he asked the question, Preacher knew the answer. "Audie was just too blasted curious to leave it alone, wasn't he?"

"The little fellow has an inquiring mind, no doubt about that. And where Audie goes . . . Nighthawk goes."

"This was a few days ago?"

The Irishman nodded. "That's right. Four days. Maybe five, come to think of it."

"And you haven't seen them since?"

"Nary a sign."

Preacher looked around at the other men. They shook their heads to indicate that they hadn't seen Audie and Nighthawk, either.

Preacher clenched his jaw. He didn't have any better friends anywhere on the frontier than the former professor and the taciturn Crow warrior. If they were in trouble, he wanted to help them, and if anything had happened to them, he had to know. "I reckon that settles the question of where I'll be headed in the mornin'."

O'Grady frowned. "You mean —"

"Monsters in the earth or not, I'll be goin' over that ridge into Shadow Valley."

CHAPTER 5

Miles O'Grady tried to talk Preacher out of the idea, but he wouldn't be budged.

"Besides," Preacher said, "if I recollect right, I did pretty fair over yonder the last time I trapped that valley. Probably a good number of pelts to be had."

"I wouldn't go into Shadow Valley for all the pelts in the Louisiana Purchase," one of the trappers declared.

Another man nodded. "I don't mind riskin' my life all the usual ways us fellas do, but what's been goin' on around here just flat-out gives me the fantods."

Several other men chimed in to express their agreement with that position.

None of them volunteered to accompany Preacher on his search.

After most of the men had turned in for the night, he went to check on Horse and his pack animal. Mostly, though, that was just an excuse to get up and move around a little. Dog went with him. A couple men were standing guard and the trappers would take turn doing so all night, but Preacher trusted Dog and Horse more than anything or anybody. If anything threatening was in the vicinity, they would sense it and let him know.

When a growl sounded from deep in Dog's throat and Horse's ears pricked up while Preacher was scratching his nose, he paid attention. Moving without undue haste, he lowered his hand and closed it around the butt of one of his pistols. The weapon was double-shotted and packed an extra-potent powder charge. At close range, it would blow a considerable hole in a man.

As he turned around, a man behind him let out a little surprised noise and stepped back hurriedly. "It's just me, Mr. Preacher. Boone Halliday."

"You can forget about that mister business. It's just Preacher. And it ain't wise sneakin' up behind a man, kid."

"I'm sorry, Mister — I mean, Preacher. I didn't mean to sneak up on you. I guess I just naturally move sort of quiet-like."

Preacher scowled. He should have heard Boone's approach. He shouldn't have had to be alerted to the young man's presence by Dog and Horse. That meant one of two things. Either the youngster was as good as he said or Preacher was slipping.

He hoped Boone was that good, although it seemed unlikely given how green the young man was.

"What do you want?" Preacher asked.

"I was thinking about what you said . . . about how you're going over into Shadow Valley to look for your friends . . ."

"Yeah?"

"I think I want to go with you."

"Why would you want to do that?"

"Well, I've heard the men talking about you. Not just tonight, since you came into camp, but other times, too. They say that nobody's ever been better at being a mountain man. Not even John Colter or Jim Bridger."

Preacher grunted. "Folks like to talk. That don't mean what they say is actually true."

"Maybe not, but when it comes to surviving in these mountains, I can't think of anybody it would be better to watch and learn from than you."

"I ain't in the business of teachin' greenhorns," Preacher said curtly.

If Boone was offended by that description, he gave no sign of it. "I could give you a hand with your search, although I'm sure you don't really need any help."

"That's right, I don't." Preacher turned back to Horse and started scratching the stallion's nose again. "These two critters are generally the only partners I've got travelin' with me." He smiled faintly in the darkness. "Besides, didn't you hear Miles? You go over into Shadow Valley and some monster that lives in the ground is liable to crawl up out of its hole and get you."

"No offense to Mr. O'Grady — I know the two of you are friends — but I think that's just a story. I don't believe there are monsters who used to be men living in the earth."

"Well, we agree on that, anyway. It's more likely Injuns causin' the trouble, like the other fellas said."

"So how about it?" Boone persisted. "I learn quick and I won't give you any trouble —"

"No," Preacher said, his voice flat and final. "I don't know what I'm gonna run into over there, but even if it ain't monsters, it's liable to be somethin' pretty bad, else all those fellas wouldn't have turned up dead or disappeared. I don't need to be havin' to watch out for somebody who's wet behind the ears."

For the first time, Boone showed a spark of anger. "I'm not —" He stopped and paused for a moment before he went on. "I suppose there's no point in arguing with you."

"Not a one in the world," Preacher said.

Boone shrugged. "All right. Maybe some other time."

"Yeah." Preacher knew better than to count on that, however. Too many things could happen.

"If you change your mind . . ."

"I won't."

Boone nodded and started to turn away, then paused again and turned back toward Preacher. "What are you going to do if you find out that something's happened to your friends?"

"I'll track down whoever's to blame for it, and then I'll make the varmint wish that he'd never been born."

CHAPTER 6

The night passed quietly, and the men in the group were rather subdued when morning came. Breakfast was a quiet affair, punctuated by an occasional sigh or muttered curse. Preacher suspected that was mostly because they had put away such copious amounts of whiskey the night before. At least half the trappers had hangovers.

"What are you fellas gonna do now?" he asked Miles O'Grady.

"We're planning to stick together until this area is trapped out for the season. 'Tis true that some of the men will take less pelts that way than they would have otherwise, but there's safety in numbers."

"I reckon," Preacher said with a shrug.

"I suppose there's no point in asking if you'd care to throw in with us. As I recall, you never joined large groups even under other circumstances."

Preacher shook his head. "I'll go my own way."

"Good luck to you, then," O'Grady said as he stuck his hand out. "We'll all be hoping that you don't vanish in Shadow Valley, too."

One of the other men laughed. "Any critter crazy enough to try to get hold of ol' Preacher 'll soon wish it had steered clear of him."

Preacher loaded his supplies on the pack animal and said his farewells. He noticed that Boone Halliday didn't have much to say, and he supposed the young man was still a little upset about being told he couldn't come along.

That was just too bad. Where he was going, Preacher wouldn't need the extra distraction.

He swung up into the saddle and left the trappers' camp behind, heading for the ridge beyond which lay Shadow Valley.

The sun was almost directly overhead when he reached the crest. He reined in and gazed out over the valley, which was thickly covered in pine trees. Despite the sunshine, the valley had an aura of gloom about it. Recalling that from his previous visit, it was clear it hadn't changed.

The Sawtooth Cliffs reared up on the far side of the valley, miles away. They were particularly ugly, adding to the valley's sinister aspect. Not for a second did he believe O'Grady's story about foul creatures living in the earth, but if there were such things, it would be a good home for them.

The hair on the back of Preacher's neck suddenly stood up, and the skin prickled. Horse shifted slightly. The stallion wasn't given to skittishness at all; he had stood still in the middle of furious battles with guns going off all around him. But something seemed to have spooked him a little.

Dog growled, too, and when Preacher glanced down he saw that the big cur's ruff was stiff with anger and agitation.

"Yeah, I know. You two would just as soon turn around and go back. Well, I ain't gonna lie to you. Part of me feels the same way. But Audie and Nighthawk been through a hell of a lot with me, and I got to find out if they're all right. Sure does seem like somebody's watchin' us, though, and it ain't a good feelin'."

Despite that, Preacher heeled the stallion into motion. He rode slowly down the far side of the ridge into the valley, his eyes constantly in motion as his gaze roved over the landscape. It wasn't long before the trees closed in around him and he couldn't see very far in any direction. The thick growth blocked most of the sun.

Preacher seemed to be riding in a world of neverending twilight. He listened for birds and the sounds of small animals in the brush but didn't hear any. He and his trail companions might as well have been the only living beings within miles, although he didn't believe that was true.

Somebody was out there. Or some*thing.*

"Dang it, you're startin' to think like that loco Irishman," he muttered to himself. He rode with the flintlock rifle held ready across the saddle in front of him.

He came to a little creek, one of several that meandered through the valley, and as Horse splashed through the water, Preacher looked along the stream and spotted a beaver dam about a hundred yards away. A couple of its architects sat on top of it, watching him.

"Don't you two look fat and sassy," Preacher said to the beaver. They were the first animals he had seen since entering the valley. From the looks of them, the trapping would be good, if a man could take some pelts without losing his own hide.

The beaver suddenly disappeared, and he heard their tails slapping the water in warning. A frown creased the mountain man's face. They hadn't reacted like that to the sight of him. He was far enough away that they hadn't seemed bothered by him.

Something else had spooked them.

Even as that thought crossed Preacher's mind, he reacted instantly, leaning forward in the saddle and jabbing his heels into Horse's flanks to make the stallion leap ahead. At the same time, he heard a faint fluttering sound and glanced around in time to see a spear slice through the air a couple feet behind him. Its sharp point would have driven into his body if he hadn't moved so quickly.

The threat wasn't over. Another spear flew out of the trees to his left. He ducked and let it go over his head. Then a whole flurry of spears came from both directions. Horse's speed was the only thing that saved him from getting skewered. Dog was running low to the ground, so all the deadly missiles went well above him.

A figure in buckskin ran out in front of the stallion, yelling and brandishing a war club studded with sharp stones. Before he could swing the weapon, Horse's shoulder rammed into him and sent him flying.

More shrill cries sounded as several other warriors swarmed out of the trees and joined the attack. Preacher saw the buckskins and the red-hued skin and knew they were Indians, although first glance at their clothes and markings he couldn't tell which tribe. In fact, they wore some sort of leather necklaces the likes of which he had never seen before.

One-handed, he thrust the rifle at a howling face and pulled the trigger. The explosion caved in the man's forehead and blew him backwards.

Preacher swung the rifle and smashed another man's skull. He shoved it back in its sling and jerked out both pistols as he twisted in the saddle to avoid a spear thrust. The roar of the pistols was deafening under the trees. The double-shotted loads scythed down three more Indians.

Dog dashed among them, neatly avoiding the spears, and hamstrung a couple warriors. Normally, he would have paused to rip out their throats as well, but he kept moving. He was close behind Preacher and Horse as they broke out of the ambush.

Preacher had to leave the pack horse behind. It had gone down screaming as warriors drove their spears into it, and he had no choice but to let go of the rope and abandon the animal. He hated to lose the supplies, but he still had plenty of powder and shot loaded on Horse. As long as that was true, he would never go hungry in the woods. For that matter, as long as he had his wits, he wouldn't starve, since he could rig snares for small animals and eat berries and roots.

Of course, starvation wasn't his biggest worry at the moment. . . .

A few more spears flew after him, but Horse easily outdistanced them. They had come through the fight in good shape, but Preacher knew that wasn't the end of it. He had killed several warriors, and the others likely wouldn't rest until they had avenged those deaths.

At least he could forget all about those spooky stories Miles O'Grady had been spinning. Preacher might not know which tribe his enemies belonged to, but he was certain they were flesh and blood, just as he had suspected all along.

By midafternoon, Preacher was nearing the western edge of the valley. The Sawtooth Cliffs rose sheer above him. From a distance, they'd appeared smooth and unbroken, but now that he was closer, he could see just how rough and rugged they were. Deep fissures cut into the stone. The mind boggled at the tremendous forces which had lifted the towering ridge in ages past.

Stopping at a spring, he and Dog and Horse drank their fill, and then Preacher ate some pemmican. It had been a long time since breakfast at the trappers' camp that morning, and the Indian delicacy tasted good.

As he hunkered next to the little pool formed by the spring, he looked around. Something moving in the brush on the other side of the pool caught his eye. Frowning, he straightened and walked around to see what it was.

The atmosphere was stifling without much breeze under the trees, but the air was moving just enough to flutter the thing Preacher had seen. He reached down and pulled it loose. It was a page torn from a book that had gotten caught on a branch. It had the title written on it — *Paul Clifford* — but no author's name, just a note that it was by the same fella who had written a couple other books.

Preacher could read and cipher fairly well, but he had never been much of one to read books. He knew somebody who was, though. *Audie.*

In fact, as his heart began to pound harder, he remembered Audie reading that very book and telling him about it — a piece of popular fiction about some highwayman in England. According to the former professor, no great shakes as literature, but he had found it highly entertaining and had mentioned it to Preacher several times. That had been a few years earlier, and it wouldn't have surprised him that Audie had carried it with him ever since. The little man usually had a pack full of books with him.

Preacher poked around in the brush and came up with several more pages, all of them ragged on the side where they had been ripped loose from their binding. Clearly, somebody had destroyed the book on purpose, tearing it apart violently. That was something that Audie would never do. He had too much respect for the written word.

Audie wouldn't just stand by and allow somebody to rip up a book, either. He hadn't been able to prevent it, and neither had Nighthawk, who would have intervened. He knew such destruction would bother his friend.

Preacher stood there looking grimly at the torn pages in his hand and drew an inescapable conclusion. Something had happened to Audie and Nighthawk, and whoever was responsible had gone through Audie's gear and destroyed the book in some sort of frenzy. Somebody would have to be crazy or filled with hate to do that.

Preacher could only hope that his friends were prisoners — and that they hadn't been ripped apart, too.

CHAPTER 7

Since finding the pages of the book indicated that Audie and Nighthawk had run into trouble, Preacher intensified his search along the base of the cliffs. He didn't find any bodies, so he took that to mean his friends were alive and looked for a clue to which way their captors had taken them.

The ground was rocky and didn't take many tracks, but he found a few marks that looked like something had been dragged along through the trees. That wasn't much, but it was all he had to go by, so he followed the faint trail and started north along the cliffs.

The sun dropped behind the rugged, sawtoothed rimrock and threw the area where Preacher was into shadow even though the rays still shone brightly out in the rest of the valley. That shadow crept inexorably across the valley and the light dimmed more and more, until he was forced to admit that he wasn't going to find anything else that day.

He made a cold camp. With those strange, murderous Indians on the loose, he couldn't risk a fire. He had jerky and pemmican, and although it was a meager supper, it would have to do. There was enough grass for Horse to graze, and Dog disappeared into the woods to hunt for his supper. He came back a short time later licking his chops, so Preacher assumed he had found something.

Even though it was early summer, nights at that elevation were chilly. He rolled up in a blanket and dozed off, knowing Dog and Horse would alert him if anything was wrong.

He had no idea how long he had been asleep when he heard the big cur growl. He came awake instantly, and his hand reached out unerringly in the darkness to close around the butt of the pistol he had placed beside him.

A cry shrill enough to wake the dead ripped out of the night. Preacher's eyes were fully adjusted to the darkness, so he had no trouble spotting the shape hurtling toward him with a war club poised to smash his brains out. The mountain man brought the pistol up and pressed the trigger. With a flash and a boom, the gun went off and drove its pair of lead balls into the attacker's chest. The flash gave him a glimpse of the warrior's stunned, hate-twisted face.

The man's momentum carried him forward, causing Preacher to roll aside quickly to avoid having the corpse land on him and pin him to the ground. As he came up on his knees, he used his left hand to grab the war club the Indian had dropped and swung it around at another figure he spotted from the corner of his eye. Bone snapped under the impact of the powerful swing as he batted the second man aside.

He tried to stand up, but somebody landed on his back and knocked him forward and down onto his knees again. Preacher dropped the club and the empty pistol and reached back with both hands to the man's long, greasy hair. He heaved as he bent forward and used the attacker's own weight against him. The man howled in surprise and pain as he flew through the air and bowled over two of his companions who were charging into the fight.

Preacher scrambled upright, grabbing the war club in both hands and flailing it around him. The warriors who didn't jerk back felt it batter them and went sprawling.

Somewhere close by, Dog growled ferociously as a man screamed. The scream was cut short by a hideous gurgle, and Preacher knew the big cur had just ripped out an enemy's throat.

Horse whinnied angrily. Steel-shod hooves lashed out as the big stallion reared. Between those deadly hooves and Horse's teeth, Preacher knew none of the Indians would be able to get near him.

Since he didn't have to worry about his trail partners, he concentrated on his own attackers. He wasn't surprised that the war party had found him. He hadn't gone to a lot of trouble to conceal his tracks, and they probably knew the valley better than he did. It had never been his nature to run away from trouble. Besides, his attackers were connected to the ones who had taken Audie and Nighthawk. Preacher had no doubt of that. If he could capture one of them, he might be able to force the man to tell him where his friends were.

Of course, in order to do that he had to avoid being captured or killed himself. . . .

Yelling in a language the likes of which he had never heard before, the men pulled back.

Preacher shouted, "Come on, you varmints! You've got us outnumbered, don't you? You don't like it when a fella fights back!"

Enough light from the moon filtered through the trees that he could see the warriors forming a ring around him, Horse, and Dog.

The ring parted to allow a man to step through it. He was one of the biggest Indians Preacher had ever seen, every bit as tall and muscular as the mountain man himself. He wore a headdress and had some sort of wings attached to his back. Lifting the club he held, he shook it, shouting at Preacher in the same unknown gibberish.

"Don't know what you're sayin', mister, but I don't like it," Preacher told him. "If it's a fight you want, then quit flappin' your jaws and get to it." He didn't figure the warrior could understand him any better.

The man must have heard the defiance in the mountain man's tone. He let out a shout and sprang forward, swinging the war club with blinding speed.

Preacher was fast, too. His club came up and blocked the blow. As the lengths of sturdy wood came together, he felt the impact shiver all the way up his arms to his shoulders. He struck at his opponent on the backswing, but the man parried that blow just as neatly as Preacher had a second earlier. For a long moment, they stood there, clubs flashing as they hammered away at each other without landing any devastating blows.

Preacher had been working his way closer during the exchange, and his right foot lashed out in a kick that landed in the warrior's belly. The man doubled over and his club sagged, giving Preacher an opening. His club shot at the warrior's head and would have shattered the man's skull if he hadn't twisted out of the way at the last instant. Still bent over and gasping for breath, he struck low and landed a glancing blow to Preacher's thigh. Had it been full strength, it would have broken the bone. As it was, it merely knocked Preacher's leg out from under him.

As the mountain man toppled to the rocky ground, the warrior recovered, swung his club up, and brought it whistling down at Preacher's head. Preacher rolled aside, avoiding disaster just as narrowly as his opponent had a few seconds earlier. He hooked his right foot behind the man's left ankle and jerked. The warrior went down.

Preacher landed on top of him and rammed the war club crosswise against the man's throat. He bore down and knew that in a matter of heartbeats, he would crush the warrior's windpipe. If the man was the leader of the war party — and it seemed clear that he was, considering the way the others had drawn back and let him battle with Preacher man to man — maybe his death would take the heart out of them.

Preacher didn't get a chance to find out. Something crashed against his head and knocked him to the side. Whatever the weapon, it was enough to make red rockets explode behind his eyes as he collapsed.

That crimson glare was swallowed rapidly by a blackness even darker than what usually gripped Shadow Valley. The last thing Preacher was aware of was hoarse, angry shouting. The warrior he had been fighting must not have liked it that his friends had intervened to save his life. His pride was wounded.

The blackness engulfed Preacher, too, and he knew nothing more.

CHAPTER 8

The sun was in Preacher's eyes when he woke up, which told him he had been out for quite a while. But since he hadn't expected to wake up, the glare didn't bother him much. It told him he was still alive.

But not well. He couldn't move his hands and feet and figured he was trussed up like a pig. He was moving, despite that. Some of his captors were carrying him.

He closed his eyes for a couple reasons. He didn't think he would gain anything by letting the warriors know that he was awake, his head ached abominably, and the sun shining directly into his eyes was liable to make it hurt worse. He stayed limp and let them think he was still unconscious.

After a while, someone spoke. Preacher recognized the harsh voice of the man with the wings on his back, the one he had been fighting when he was knocked out. The man still sounded a little hoarse, but his throat had recovered some from Preacher nearly crushing it.

The men set him down. The ground was rough and rocky and not very comfortable. Something blocked the sun.

Probably one of the warriors, Preacher thought just before a foot slammed into his side in a brutal kick. He couldn't stop a pained gasp from escaping his lips.

The head man said something else.

Preacher decided he must be the one standing over him, kicking him, and he might keep that up as long as Preacher didn't respond. He didn't want that, so he blinked his eyes open and said haltingly, "Hold on there, damn it."

It took a few seconds for his eyes to adjust to the light. He couldn't see the man as anything except a dark, oddly-shaped silhouette then some details started to resolve in his vision.

The tall headdress and the outspread wings gave the man the unusual shape. He glared down at the mountain man and spoke in that strange tongue.

"All right, all right. I'm awake," Preacher said. "I don't savvy a word you're sayin', though. I don't reckon there's any chance you speak English, is there?"

The man leaned over and spat. "Damn it."

Preacher couldn't help but chuckle. "Well, that's progress, anyway. There's a good chance you don't know what you're sayin', though. You just repeated it after I said it. How about 'I'm a big ol', ugly fool'?"

The man said, "Damn it," and kicked Preacher in the side again.

The mountain man grimaced. He could tell that he didn't have any broken ribs yet, but that condition might not last if the varmint kept kicking him. He lifted his head as much as he could and looked around. He saw seven men in addition to the war chief or whatever he was. Their buckskin leggings and tunics were similar but didn't have the gaudy decorations other than those broad leather necklaces. They were shorter and squattier than the chief, too, although still slightly taller than most of the Indians Preacher had run into.

He didn't see Horse or Dog. The animals had either gotten away — or had been killed in the fighting. Until he knew otherwise, he was going to believe that his old friends were still alive, the same way he felt about Audie and Nighthawk. He knew Horse and Dog would remain in the vicinity, foraging for themselves until he was able to be reunited with them.

The chief gestured with the war club he held and jabbered at his companions. A couple started gathering wood. Preacher realized they were going to build a fire and possibly even make camp. Was it late enough in the day for that? He couldn't be sure.

They were still close to the cliffs, which loomed to Preacher's left as he lay on the ground. Had they been going north along those sawtoothed heights all day? Where in the world were they headed?

He didn't have any answers to those questions, but he knew they would be revealed in time. For the moment, he contented himself with testing his bonds. His arms had been pulled behind his back and his wrists lashed together with what felt like rawhide strips. The same sort of bonds secured his ankles. Whoever had tied him up had done a good job of it. He couldn't feel any play in the rawhide.

If he could get it wet, it might stretch a little. He would have to keep his eyes open for an opportunity to do that.

Some of the men opened buckskin pouches and brought out what looked like the same sort of tortillas the Mexicans down south ate. They wrapped the tortillas around dried peppers that also came from the pouches and hunkered on their heels to eat.

Preacher's belly growled from hunger — another indication that he had been unconscious for quite a while. He would have eaten some of the tortillas and peppers if they had offered him any, but it didn't look like they were going to do that.

The head man didn't eat. He stood with his brawny bare arms crossed over his chest and glared at Preacher for a while, then lifted his gaze and stared off all haughty-like, almost as if he were posing for a portrait.

The varmint thought pretty highly of himself, Preacher mused. That was obvious.

From the corner of his eye, Preacher noticed the brush off to one side moved a little. He turned his head slightly to look in that direction without calling attention to himself. He hadn't heard anything moving in the brush, so it probably wasn't a small animal that had caused that branch to move.

What Preacher saw was about the last thing he expected. Peering at him through a small gap in the brush was the face of the young trapper, Boone Halliday.

CHAPTER 9

It took a lot of self-control to keep from reacting to the surprising sight, but Preacher had iron will to spare. His face remained expressionless as Boone lifted a finger to his lips in a totally unnecessary gesture.

Preacher turned his head again and looked at the war chief, who still stood as if basking in the adulation of his admirers. The others were all eating, but he couldn't be bothered with that.

Hunger, Preacher supposed, was for mere mortals, and judging by the man's attitude, he considered himself more than that.

After a while, the light began to fade from the sky as true dusk settled down. Preacher still didn't know where they were going, but obviously it was quite a distance from where he had been captured. The valley was a big one, running for at least twenty miles, and the strange Indians might range all over it.

Preacher glanced toward the brush again.

Boone was gone. Preacher hadn't heard any sound as the young trapper withdrew. Boone seemed to have a knack for being stealthy, just as he had said.

Preacher decided that Boone had ignored his decision and followed him from the trappers' camp where they had met a couple nights earlier. Normally, such blatant disregard for his wishes would have annoyed him, but under the circumstances he was glad Boone had been muleheaded about it. The youngster might be able to help him turn the tables on his captors.

Or Boone might just get himself killed, which would be a damn shame.

Since Preacher wasn't gagged, he figured it was time for him to speak up again. "Hey, you blasted varmints, I could use somethin' to eat and drink. I'm mighty dry, and I'm about to waste away to nothin' over here."

The chief stopped posing and glared at him, then snapped something.

"Well, at least you didn't swear at me," Preacher drawled. "How about some food?" He pretended he was chewing. "You know, somethin' to eat?"

The chief motioned curtly to one of his men. From a pouch, the Indian took a couple dried peppers and rolled them in a tortilla. He took it to Preacher and held it so the mountain man could take a bite.

He swallowed the fiery stuff. The pepper was so hot it brought tears to his eyes. "Whoo-eee! I need somethin' to drink now."

His captors ignored that. The man hunkering next to him just shoved the tortilla toward his mouth again. Even though his lips and tongue felt a little blistered, Preacher didn't know when he'd get a chance to eat again, so he took another bite, chewed, and swallowed. The peppers burned all the way down.

"Good Lord, that's hotter 'n the vittles I ate the last time I was down at Santa Fe. Any of you fellas ever been to Santa Fe? Come to think of it, some of you look a mite Mexican."

Actually, that was true, he realized. Some of the Indians could have passed for Mexicans. That wasn't completely unheard of, he thought. Indian and Spanish blood had intermixed freely in those more tropical climes. Such a blend was rare to see that far north, though.

The Indians ignored his question about Santa Fe.

Preacher ate the rest of the tortilla and peppers. "I could still use somethin' to drink, boys. *Agua?* You hombres savvy Mex talk?"

His voice was loud for a reason. He didn't think yelling would make them understand him any better, but it would help cover up any small noises Boone Halliday might make moving around in the brush.

Of course, he didn't know if Boone was still anywhere nearby. The youngster could have seen what the odds were and decided that the smart thing to do was light a shuck out of there as fast as he could.

Somehow, though, Preacher didn't believe that. His gut told him that Boone was still around and planning something.

The man who had fed Preacher still hunkered beside him. He reached out and poked a finger against Preacher's chest, once and then again.

"Hey, keep your hands to yourself, mister." Preacher's eyes were on a flint knife stuck behind a strip of rawhide tied around the man's waist. If he could get his hands on that knife he could cut his bonds and make a fight of it.

The chief snapped a few words. The man who'd been poking Preacher stood up and moved back over to join the others around the small fire they had made. Clearly, they weren't worried about attracting attention or they wouldn't have kindled that blaze. They considered themselves the masters of the valley — and so far, Preacher hadn't seen any evidence they were wrong about that.

The burning in his mouth gradually subsided as he lay there. He kept working at his bonds but didn't have any real hope of loosening them. He watched as the chief finally stopped posturing long enough to eat a couple tortillas.

So the fella is human after all.

As the fire began to burn down, several warriors stretched out to sleep. They didn't have blankets or bedrolls of any sort. They were accustomed to hardship.

One man went over and sat down on a rock close to Preacher.

My own personal guard, the mountain man thought.

Two more sat up near the fire. They would probably take turns standing watch during the night.

The head man was one who lay down to sleep. He removed his headdress and the ornamental wings, which left him looking more like the others, although slightly bigger and more clean-cut.

Preacher closed his eyes and pretended to doze off, but actually he was still awake. After a few minutes, he opened his eyes to narrow slits so he could keep an eye on his surroundings. He hadn't forgotten about seeing Boone Halliday earlier. If the young trapper was going to try something, it would probably happen during the night while some of the Indians were asleep.

Preacher watched his guard without seeming to. As the night wore on, the man's eyelids began to droop. It had been a long day, and he was getting tired. The deep, regular breathing of the sleeping men made it harder for the guard to stay awake. The two guards by the fire had talked quietly starting out, but they had fallen silent and seemed to be having trouble staying awake, too.

Preacher started to wonder if he could kick his guard off the rock, roll on top of him, and grab the flint knife stuck behind the sash around his waist, just like the one the Indian who'd fed him had had. He didn't know how long it would take him to saw through the bonds around his wrists since he would be working in an awkward position, but it might be worth a try.

While he was thinking that, a loop of some sort suddenly dropped over the guard's neck and jerked tight, cutting off any outcry he might make. He was hauled backward off the rock as he started to struggle. The loop — a length of rawhide, more than likely —

was pulled so tight around his neck that it disappeared into the bronze flesh. The man's eyes widened in panic as it strangled him.

The commotion alerted the guards by the fire. They sprang up and shouted a warning to the others. Instantly, the whole bunch woke up, grabbed their spears and war clubs, and leaped to their feet.

Whoever had attacked Preacher's guard had dragged the man out of sight into the brush. Preacher heard a lot of thrashing around. As the chief yelled orders and led the way, the rest of the men dashed out there. They made a lot of racket as they pursued the attacker.

CHAPTER 10

One man lagged behind the others. Preacher knew he wasn't going to get a better chance. He lifted his bound legs and swung them around, sweeping the warrior's legs out from under him as he ran past. He went down hard, slammed his head against a rock, and then lay still, knocked out cold.

Preacher used great strength to pull himself up to his knees. He jackknifed forward and landed beside the unconscious warrior. Working by feel, Preacher got hold of the man's knife and twisted it around so he could start sawing on the rawhide strips around his wrists. The sharp flint sliced into his flesh now and then, but he ignored the stinging pain and kept trying to free himself.

In the brush, the Indians were yelling and stampeding around. Preacher hoped Boone was leading them on a merry chase that would keep them away from the camp for a while longer.

The rawhide parted, falling away from his bloody wrists. As he sat up, the warrior who had fallen and stunned himself moaned and began to stir. Preacher reached over and rammed the knife into his side, sliding the point between ribs so that it pierced the man's heart. The Indian shuddered and died as Preacher withdrew the blade. He sat up and cut his feet loose, too.

Steps pounded nearby as he stood up. He swung around, gripping the knife tightly. The feeling was coming back quickly into his extremities, but he was a little clumsy. He would have preferred to be a little steadier before he had to fight again.

Boone Halliday burst out of the brush carrying a spear and came to a sudden stop as he saw Preacher in the glow from the fire's embers. A grin broke across his face. "I was hoping I'd have time to cut you loose before they circled back around here. Should've known you'd already have taken care of that."

"Are those varmints right behind you?" Preacher growled.

"They're not far back."

"Let's give 'em a warm welcome." Preacher looked around for weapons. He would have liked to fill his hands with his pistols, but it seemed he would have to be satisfied with the war club that had been dropped by the man he'd just killed, along with the flint knife.

With two men dead, that left six in the war party. Three to one odds weren't very good, but Preacher knew he and Boone would have even less chance if they fled with those howling savages in close pursuit. Better to make a stand among the rocks at the base of the cliff. He motioned for Boone to get behind one of the boulders, then withdrew into cover himself.

With the same sort of reckless arrogance they had displayed so far, the Indians charged back into the camp a moment later, led by the chief. Boone stood up and heaved the spear at the head man as hard as he could.

The throw was a good one and would have found its target, but the man saw the spear coming and twisted aside just in time to let it go past him. The deadly missile buried its sharp point in the chest of the man directly behind the chief. The warrior's momentum kept him running for a couple steps before he collapsed.

In avoiding the spear, the head man brought himself within reach of Preacher, who put a foot on the rock where he had been hidden and bounded over it as he swung the war club. The blow clipped the chief on the side of the head and dropped him. Preacher leaped over him and on the backswing smashed the skull of another man.

Boone's pistol roared and dropped a man with a lead ball in his chest. That left just two of the Indians on their feet. Preacher ducked a spear thrust from one and brought the war club up to catch the man on the jaw. Bone splintered under the impact and the man turned a backward somersault. Moving too fast for the eye to follow in the shadows, Preacher batted aside the last man's spear and brought the war club crashing down on his forehead. The man's skull was so misshapen it didn't even look human anymore as he collapsed.

All the Indians were down. Preacher slashed the throat of the man whose jaw he had shattered, putting him out of his misery and removing him as a threat. He checked the others, found they were all dead except for the chief, who was out cold from the glancing blow Preacher had struck.

"Aren't you going to kill him, too?" Boone asked.

"Nope," Preacher replied. "Got something else in mind for him. Give me a hand tyin' him up. We'd best make sure he's bound good and tight, too. He's a big, strong cuss, and we don't want him gettin' loose."

Boone wondered what Preacher intended to do, but he didn't argue. Within a few minutes, they had the chief tied securely. With that done, Preacher set Boone to gathering up all the spears and war clubs while he had a look around the camp.

He found his pistols, knife, tomahawk, powder horn, and shot pouch in a bag made of animal hide. It appeared that his captors hadn't brought his rifle with him. He hated to lose the weapon, but there wasn't anything he could do about it. Maybe later, he could go back to the place where they had jumped him and find it, he thought.

Having the pistols and his other weapons made him feel better. Although he had no way of knowing for sure, he had a strong hunch the members of the war party weren't the only hostiles in the vicinity. Such a small group probably wouldn't have been responsible for all the deaths and disappearances in Shadow Valley in recent weeks.

He and Boone dragged the dead men into the brush for scavengers to dispose of, then came back to the fire. Preacher put more wood on it and waited until the flames were leaping a little higher. "All right, Boone, tell me what you're doin' here. It ain't that I'm ungrateful for your help, but I told you to stay with O'Grady and those other fellas."

"Well, I'm a little sorry about that, but I've always been pretty bad about doing what I was told to do. I admit it. Just about drove my pa to distraction, it did."

Preacher had to chuckle. "This is one time your stubbornness came in handy, I reckon. I'd have gotten loose one way or another if you hadn't come along, but what you did made it easier. What if that bunch had caught up to you while you were decoyin' 'em away from here, though?"

"I reckon I'd be dead now," Boone said. "Or wishing I was, anyway. You reckon these fellas are the ones who've been going around ripping out hearts?"

"I don't see how it could be anybody else. What I want to know is where they came from and how many more of 'em we're gonna have to deal with."

"Deal with?" Boone repeated with a frown. "Aren't we going to head back over the ridge and get out of Shadow Valley?"

Preacher shook his head. "Not hardly. Or at least I'm not. I think those varmints are holding a couple friends of mine prisoner, and I don't intend to go off and abandon them." He reminded Boone about how Audie and Nighthawk had disappeared, then told him about the pages he had found from the novel Audie had with him.

"Until I know they're dead, I'm gonna believe they're still alive," Preacher concluded, "and some of those other fellas who have vanished may be, too. I'm gonna find them and find out what the hell's goin' on in these parts, too. These Injuns aren't like any I've ever run across before, so there's no tellin' what sort of mischief they may be up to."

"You don't recognize what tribe they're from?"

Preacher shook his head again. "No, and I never heard the sort of lingo they talk, neither. It's got me plumb puzzled . . . and I don't like the feelin'." He paused. "But that don't mean you have to throw in with me, Boone. I appreciate what you've already done, but you can light a shuck out of here and I sure won't hold it against you."

Boone grinned. "No, sir. I came west because life back on the farm was too tame for me. I want to get to the bottom of this with you, Preacher. But how do you figure on doing that?"

Preacher looked over at the unconscious figure of the chief. "That's where keeping that big one alive comes in."

CHAPTER 11

Preacher didn't think it was very likely there were any other war parties roaming Shadow Valley, but since he didn't know that for sure, he put out the campfire. He and Boone took turns standing guard during the night, which passed without any further trouble except when the chief came to and started yelling. Preacher gagged him to keep him quiet, just in case any fellow warriors were around.

In the morning, Preacher and Boone breakfasted on tortillas from the war party's supplies, but they skipped the peppers. After they had eaten, Preacher went over to the chief and knelt beside him.

The man started to yell as soon as Preacher removed the gag, but he fell silent when the mountain man pressed the blade of a flint knife to his throat.

"That's right," Preacher said with a grin as the chief glared up at him. "You may be a doggone polecat, but you ain't totally stupid." He pressed a little harder, just enough to draw some blood. "It wouldn't take much proddin' for me to go ahead and cut your throat, old son, so you best listen to me. Do you speak English?"

The man didn't respond, but Preacher thought he saw a flicker of understanding in his eyes.

"Habla español?" That didn't result in anything except a seemingly genuine blank stare, so Preacher stuck with English. "I'm lookin' for two friends of mine. One of 'em's a big ol' Crow Indian" — he stood up and held out a hand to indicate Nighthawk's height — "and the other fella's really short-growed." He lowered his hand to Audie's height.

Once again he thought he saw a flash of recognition in the chief's eyes. The man knew who he was talking about.

"Where do you come from? Where's your home?"

The man's eyes flicked toward the cliffs before he could stop them.

That didn't make any sense to Preacher. The Sawtooth Cliffs ran in an unbroken line for miles and miles. Honestly, he didn't know how far north and south they extended. He had never explored their farthest reaches. There were no passes he was aware of, and the cliffs were too steep and rugged to climb.

Convinced the chief had at least a general idea of what he was talking about, Preacher increased the pressure on the knife again. "If you won't tell me what I want to know, I don't have any reason to keep you alive, you varmint."

The man responded in just about the way Preacher expected him to. He pursed his lips and tried to spit in the mountain man's face. He missed.

Preacher was looking for it and had moved his head back.

The chief's movement made the knife dig into his neck even more. A drop of blood welled from the cut and rolled down his skin. He started talking, but the words were loud, angry ones that made no sense to Preacher. He choked them off by shoving the wadded-up piece of buckskin that served as a gag back into the man's mouth.

As Preacher stood up, Boone Halliday shook his head. "I don't think he's ever going to cooperate, Preacher."

"Don't look like it," Preacher agreed. "We'll give him some time to think it over, though." He glared down at the man. "Then if he still won't talk, we won't have any choice but to kill him."

He inclined his head in a signal for Boone to follow him. They drifted over out of easy earshot of the prisoner. Quietly, Preacher went on. "I think he can speak a little English. Probably picked it up from those trappers he and his friends have captured. I want to know where they took those fellas."

"How are you going to find out if he won't talk?"

"He's gonna lead us there."

A smile spread slowly over Boone's face. "You have some sort of trick in mind, don't you?"

Preacher scratched at his beard. "Yeah, but it'll be a mite dangerous. We've got to turn him loose without him knowin' we've done it."

A frown replaced Boone's smile. "Won't he just try to kill us again?"

"Maybe, but I'm bettin' he'll take off for the tall and uncut. He's an arrogant cuss, but he ain't a fool. He'll want to fetch some more warriors and then come after us."

"What if he puts up a fight?"

"Then we kill him," Preacher said with a shrug, "and try to find where he came from by ourselves. But I reckon it'll be a lot easier if he shows us the way. We'll let him stew a while longer."

He and Boone talked over the plan, then Preacher made a show of scouting around the camp, knowing the chief's eyes were on him the whole time. Finally he went back over and removed the gag. "Are you ready to talk?"

The man just glowered at him.

"All right. I reckon it's fair to treat you the same way you done for the folks you captured." He took the flint knife and began cutting the chief's tunic open.

The man's eyes widened. Clearly, he understood why Preacher was doing that. When he had made a slash in the buckskin, Preacher ripped the tunic apart, baring the bronzed, heavily muscled chest, and laid the blade's edge against the chief's skin.

Not even the man's stern self-control could stop him from reacting. He began to squirm as much as he could against his bonds, and a torrent of incomprehensible words poured from his mouth. He was furious, but he was also scared.

"Preacher!" Boone called suddenly. "I hear something!"

Preacher stood up. He set the knife on a rock and grabbed one of the war clubs. "What is it?" he asked in a tense voice.

Boone pointed. "Somebody's sneaking around out there in the brush."

"Probably some of this hombre's friends. Let's get 'em!"

Brandishing the war club, Preacher stalked away from the camp and into the thick brush. Boone was right behind him, holding one of the pistols ready to fire.

When they were out of sight of the camp, Preacher looked over his shoulder at Boone, grinned, and nodded. They kept moving, stomping through the brush so the chief could hear them.

"I put that knife down well out of his reach," Preacher said, "but I reckon he can get to it if he works hard enough. We'll give him time to do just that."

"If he takes off like you think he will, how will we know where he went?" Boone wanted to know.

"I'll have to trust to my trackin' ability. It's pretty good most of the time. He'll be in a hurry, and maybe won't be as careful as he might've been otherwise. It's a gamble, sure . . . but most of life is, ain't it?" Preacher shrugged.

"I'm learning that more and more, the longer I'm out here on the frontier," Boone said.

"You didn't happen to see my dog and horse anywhere hereabouts, did you?"

Boone shook his head. "No, I'm afraid not."

Preacher nodded, concerned but not really worried. He knew Dog and Horse could take care of themselves, and they wouldn't stray too far from the place they had last seen him.

He and Boone kept up the pretense of moving around in the brush for a while, then returned cautiously to the camp. There was always a possibility that the chief might be lurking somewhere close by, waiting to ambush them.

When they got there, the area appeared to be deserted. The strips of rawhide they had used to bind the prisoner lay on the ground, obviously sawn apart by the flint knife, which was gone. Preacher looked around and found a few faint tracks indicating that the man had fled northward along the base of the cliffs, the same way the group had been going the night before when they'd stopped and made camp.

"Now we follow him?" Boone asked.

"Now we follow him."

Chapter 12

They followed the trail throughout the morning. Preacher spotted an occasional drop of dried blood and figured it came from the chief's wrists, which had probably gotten sliced up some while he was cutting himself loose. Preacher's own wrists had several scratches on them for the same reason. Such work required a delicate touch, or else a man might wind up opening a vein and bleeding to death before he could get loose.

As he had pointed out to Boone and the young trapper had agreed, life was a gamble.

Preacher didn't get in too much of a hurry. As long as he could follow the trail, he didn't want to catch up to the chief. That wouldn't accomplish his goal of finding out where those strange Indians lived.

Several times during the day it appeared that they had lost the trail, but diligent searching turned it up again. Around the middle of the afternoon, the tracks turned west and led directly toward the cliffs, which were about half a mile away. The chief had been forced to move out into the valley to avoid an area of massive boulders that had fallen from the top of the cliffs during the earthquake Miles O'Grady had mentioned.

"Where's he going?" Boone asked. "I don't see any way through those cliffs."

Preacher squinted at the cliffs. "Neither do I, but maybe their village is right there at the base or even carved into the cliffs. I've seen things like that, down south of here a good ways. Some of the old tribes live in what they call cliff dwellings. I saw some at a place called Mesa Verde. Been there for hundreds of years."

"Yeah, maybe. I never heard of such a thing, myself."

"No offense, youngster, but I reckon there are probably a lot of things you ain't heard of yet."

Boone had to laugh at that. "I expect you're right, Preacher."

As they approached the cliffs, Preacher looked for the sort of dwelling he had told Boone about, but he didn't see any. The cliffs looked as unbroken as ever. The chief's trail led straight toward them, however, and Preacher figured the man had to have a good reason for that.

His puzzlement deepened as they came to an open stretch of rocky ground several hundred yards wide, with the cliffs rising on the far side. He put out a hand to stop Boone while they were still in the trees and brush. A partially broken branch told him that someone had passed that way not long before.

"Where'd he go?" Preacher muttered as he stared at the open ground.

"Shouldn't we be able to see him?" Boone asked. "Even if he's moving along the base of the cliffs, he should be out in the open where we can spot him."

"That's what I thought, but I don't see hide nor hair of the varmint."

It was true. It appeared that the man had vanished into thin air.

Preacher knew better than to believe that, but he couldn't come up with any other explanation. After a moment, he nodded. "All right. I'm going out there to have a look. You stay here."

"Why?" Boone asked.

"I ain't in the habit of explainin' how come I say something . . . but since you're as young as you are, I reckon I'll make an exception. You're stayin' here so if anything happens to me, you'll have a chance to get away."

"I'm not going to run out on you!" Boone protested. "I wouldn't do that, Preacher."

"Well, then, look at it this way. If I get in trouble, you'll be where you can come give me a hand."

"Well, if you want to put it like that . . ."

"Just stay here." Preacher drew both of his pistols from behind his belt and stalked out into the open.

Nothing happened. Spears and arrows didn't rain down from the top of the cliffs, which Preacher had considered a distinct possibility. He continued toward the cliffs, checking the ground as he went.

It was too hard to take tracks, but every so often he spotted a recently overturned rock. He was still on the right trail.

When he was within fifty yards of the cliffs, he stopped and studied them. His eyes narrowed as he spotted a dark line running vertically from the ground to the top of the cliffs. The mark, if that's what it was, was so thin it wouldn't have been visible from much farther away.

Preacher moved forward, veering to his left. The dark line got thicker. When he was twenty yards away, he realized it was a crack in the apparently solid rock wall. The way it angled into the cliff, it would be completely invisible from a distance.

It was impossible to tell how far the fissure extended into the cliffs. Preacher asked himself if it might go all the way through to whatever was on the other side. He had never heard of such a thing and didn't know if it was even possible.

Then he remembered again what Miles O'Grady had said about an earthquake earlier in the year. Preacher hadn't been in those parts when it happened, but he had heard people talk about other earthquakes and knew how massively powerful they could be. Folks in Missouri still talked about the quake more than twenty years earlier that had made the Mississippi River run backwards. Preacher had heard tales of how the ground sometimes cracked and opened up when it began to shake. It seemed to him that such an incredible disturbance in the earth might be able to crack a cliff as well.

He walked all the way to the opening and peered into it. The fissure angled back to the right for fifty yards, then bent to the left so he couldn't see any farther than that. It was about ten feet wide, and even though it ran all the way to the top of the cliff, the bottom was so deep that the sky was only a thin blue line from where he stood. The shadows were so thick that the passage was cloaked in perpetual gloom.

As soon as Preacher got a good look at it, his instincts told him it was where the chief of that strange war party had gone. This had been the Indian's destination all along.

If Audie and Nighthawk were still alive, they were at the other end of wherever the sinister passage led.

The mountain man turned and waved for Boone Halliday to join him. The young man loped out of the trees and hurried toward him. From where he was, Boone couldn't see what Preacher could, but as he approached, the fissure in the cliffs would become visible to him.

Boone wore a look of astonishment as he trotted up to Preacher a few moments later. "This must be where that fella went!" he exclaimed.

"Yep," Preacher agreed. "The trail's well hidden until you're right up on it."

"You think it actually leads somewhere?"

"I reckon it has to. That varmint's tracks brought us here, and he wouldn't have gone in there if he didn't think he could get out at the other end."

"No, I suppose he wouldn't. Are we going through there, too?"

"I'm gonna see where it leads," Preacher said. "Whether you do is up to you."

"I'm sticking with you, Preacher. You ought to know that by now."

"Figured as much," Preacher said with a smile. "But it's a plumb spooky-lookin' place, and I wanted to give you one more chance to back out if you were of a mind to."

"I'm in this to the end," Boone declared.

"Then come on. Let's see where this giant snake track leads."

Chapter 13

The passage zigzagged into the cliff, and it didn't take long for Preacher to lose track of how many twists and turns it had made as he and Boone followed it. The air was stagnant and dusty and had a chill to it. Down where the sun shone so little, only a few minutes a day when it was directly overhead, it probably never warmed up much.

The rock walls on either side rose so high that even though they were perpendicular, they seemed to lean inward as if threatening to close up and crush Preacher and Boone between countless tons of stone, but that wasn't likely to happen unless there was another earthquake. If such a thing ever happened while a man was in there, he would be plumb out of luck.

The passage seemed to run for miles through the cliffs, although Preacher knew it wasn't really that far. He didn't know how long they had been in it, how far they had come, or how much farther they had to go before they reached the end when he and Boone went around another sharp bend and suddenly found themselves confronted by half a dozen of the strange warriors.

They all carried spears, yelled, and charged at the two intruders. Preacher hadn't wanted to fire any shots in there, but outnumbered as he and Boone were, they had no choice. He yanked out both pistols, thumbed back the hammers, and pulled the triggers.

The roar of exploding powder was so loud it pounded the ears like the biggest clap of thunder ever. A split second after Preacher's pistols went off, so did Boone's. Powder smoke clogged the narrow passage. As it began to clear, two of the Indians charged out of the gray cloud. The other four had been knocked off their feet by the heavy lead balls. In the narrow confines, it had been almost impossible for the shots to miss.

Preacher used his left-hand pistol to bat aside a spear that one of the howling savages thrust at him. At the same time, he lashed out with the right-hand gun and smashed the brass ball at the end of its grip against the man's forehead. The warrior's knees folded up. He dropped to the ground, either unconscious or dead.

Boone had dropped his guns, grabbed the last man's spear, and was wrestling over it. The warrior's wiry strength was too much. He wrenched the spear free and slashed its point toward Boone's throat.

The young trapper flung himself backwards and avoided the thrust, but his feet tangled together and he sat down hard. The warrior cried out in triumph and was about to spring forward and jab his spear into Boone's body when Preacher's tomahawk crunched into the back of his skull, shattering bone and pulping brain matter. The Indian dropped the spear and pitched forward.

With blood dripping off the tomahawk in his right hand, Preacher stepped forward and extended his left to Boone. The young man clasped it and let Preacher help him up.

"You saved my life," Boone said breathlessly.

"And you probably saved mine when you helped me get away from those varmints yesterday," Preacher said. "I reckon we're even, although out here it don't pay to keep up too much with such things. Folks just do what they have to and help each other out when they can."

Boone nodded. "I'm much obliged to you, anyway."

Preacher turned to check on the warriors they had shot. All four were dead. At close range those flintlock pistols were devastating weapons.

He reloaded the pistols. "Whoever's at the other end of this trail probably heard those shots. Of course, they probably had a pretty idea we were comin', anyway. That chief must've told somebody we might be trailin' him. That's why these fellas were waitin' for us."

"So we're walking into a trap," Boone said.

Preacher shrugged. "Could be, but whether we are or not, I plan on findin' Audie and Nighthawk . . . or findin' out what happened to 'em, anyway. I ain't lettin' no trap stop me. There's still time for you to turn back, though."

Boone shook his head. "I'm not going to do that. I'll stick, Preacher."

"Figured you would," the mountain man said with a smile. He tucked the reloaded pistols behind his belt. "Let's go."

They each picked up a couple spears. Having extra weapons wouldn't hurt anything.

They hadn't gone very far when they heard a faint rumble, like thunder or the sound of distant drums. He paused and looked up.

"What's that?" Boone asked.

The noise began to get louder.

Preacher had thought earlier that another earthquake might cause trouble, but anything loud enough — like gunshots in a tightly enclosed area — could sometimes cause an avalanche. "Run!" he snapped.

Both men lunged forward as the rumble turned into a mighty roar. Rocks crashed down behind them, small at first but then larger and larger chunks that had sheared off above them, and a cloud of dust billowed and rolled over them, so that they were almost running blind.

The crashing and roaring began to subside, and after a couple hundred yards, Preacher slowed and then stopped. Boone followed suit. They coughed at the choking dust as they looked back the way they had come. As the dust began to clear, they saw the wall of stone blocking the narrow passage. Those six warriors he and Boone had killed were buried permanently under tons of rock.

More important as far as Preacher was concerned, the passage was closed. He and Boone couldn't turn back even if they wanted to.

Neither could those strange Indians continue their depredations in Shadow Valley, not unless they had some other way out, or else they would have been killing and mutilating trappers all along, instead of just in recent months following the earthquake.

"Lord!" Boone exclaimed. "That was too close."

"Yeah. We're alive, and that's all that counts. Let's see if we can get out of here before somethin' else happens."

They were alert for more trouble as they hurried along the passage. It became brighter and light from around a bend up ahead relieved the gloom somewhat.

Preacher knew they had almost reached the end. Soon they would know what was waiting for them. He held out a hand to stop Boone. "We'd better make sure there ain't another ambush waitin' for us right around the corner. I'll take a look."

He pressed his back against the stone wall and edged forward until he could lean out and gaze around the bend. Sure enough, after another fifty yards, the passage came to an end, opening into what appeared to be another valley, judging by what Preacher could see from where he was.

The fissure in front of him was empty, but of course there was no telling who or what might be waiting just outside.

Only one way to find out.

He waved a hand to Boone. "Come on. Be ready for trouble, though."

"I reckon that would be good advice for anybody who plans on spending much time around you, Preacher."

The mountain man let out a grim chuckle. Boone was right.

The afternoon sunlight seemed really bright after spending so much time in the shadows, but their eyes adjusted to it by the time they reached the mouth of the fissure. Preacher motioned for Boone to stay back, then stepped out first. His eyes darted back and forth as he intently studied the landscape spread out before him.

Chapter 14

Just as he had thought, a valley lay below the ridge, just as it did on the other side. It was considerably smaller than Shadow Valley, however. Only a few miles wide, it extended perhaps ten miles from its southern end to its northern. The passage Preacher and Boone had followed opened into the valley approximately in its center.

Mountains that appeared to be impassable rose on three sides of the valley. On the eastern side where Preacher and Boone were, cliffs blocked the way. They were as tall and steep and sheer as the ones on the other side of the ridge, although they lacked the peculiar sawtooth formations along the rimrock. Even without that, they were as much of a geographic barrier as the mountains.

Anyone who lived there would have to spend their entire life there . . . or at least that had been the case until the earthquake opened the fissure through the cliffs. Preacher was more convinced than ever that was what had happened.

"See anybody?" Boone asked from behind him.

"Nope," Preacher replied. "Come on out and have a look."

The valley was something to see, all right. A little pocket of perfection covered with stands of tall, straight pine and fir trees broken up by grassy meadows bright with wildflowers. Sunlight sparkled on a stream that meandered roughly through the center of the valley.

The most amazing thing about it, however, was the city that sat beside that river. It was no Indian village of hogans or tipis or wickiups. It was made up of dozens of stone buildings. Quarrying and stacking those big blocks of rock must have been an incredible undertaking. Some of the streets between the buildings even appeared to be paved with cobblestones, such as Preacher had seen back east.

A more impressive structure stood at the head of the broad main avenue. It rose in receding tiers until it towered over the other buildings in the city, tapering at its highest point to one square stone platform. Preacher had never seen anything like it.

Evidently neither had Boone. The young trapper said in a low, astonished voice, "Good Lord! What's that? What is this place, Preacher?"

"Damned if I know," the mountain man replied. "From the size of that settlement, though, there's a whole heap of people livin' here, not just the ones we've run into." He stiffened. "And it looks to me like some of 'em are on their way up here to find out what all the commotion was about a little while ago."

Several trails led down into the valley from the opening in the cliffs. Preacher had spotted a group of men hurrying along what appeared to be the main trail from the city. They were still about half a mile way, so he and Boone had time to get out of there . . . only there was nowhere to go except into the valley.

With the fissure blocked by the avalanche, the two of them were trapped just as effectively as the people who had built that amazing city.

We'll figure that out later, Preacher told himself.

They needed to concentrate on escaping capture.

"Come on." He broke into a trot along one of the narrower trails leading down into the valley.

The trees closed in around them. Anything could be lurking in that cover, but Preacher didn't think about that. He just kept moving. All his instincts were on high alert. If anything threatened them, he would be ready to act.

The trail led toward the river. Preacher thought he had caught a glimpse of some cultivated fields along the stream, which came as no surprise. He had seen — and eaten — the tortillas the Indians used as food. They had to be growing corn somewhere, although so far north wasn't a very good climate for it.

On the other hand, the way the mountains towered around the valley, maybe they shielded the place from the worst of the winter storms. The air felt warmer than it had on the other side of the cliffs, Preacher realized. Hot springs were scattered throughout that part of the country. If some of them bubbled up in the valley, they might make the climate temperate enough to allow the inhabitants to grow corn, peppers, and other vegetables.

Every so often, Preacher and Boone paused to listen. During one of those stops, they suddenly heard voices not far off. Neither could make out what was being said, but Preacher knew they didn't want to be discovered just yet, so he jerked his head at Boone to indicate that they should get off the trail.

They disappeared into the trees and kept going. There wasn't much underbrush, but the trees were dense enough to provide some cover.

The voices got louder. Evidently they were headed straight toward whoever was talking, instead of away from them.

A woman laughed.

Preacher frowned. He slowed and motioned for Boone to do likewise. He heard water running and knew they weren't far from the river. The smart thing to do would be to move off in a different direction, but Preacher was curious. He wanted to learn as much as he could about the people who lived in that land-locked valley. Cautiously, he edged forward.

Suddenly spotting movement up ahead, he pressed himself to the trunk of a pine. Boone did the same a few yards away. Preacher leaned over to look through the trees. What he saw shocked him.

Boone was pretty surprised, too. The young trapper muttered, "Good Lord!"

The flashes of reddish-gold skin Preacher saw resolved themselves into the bodies of young women moving around the banks of the river as they washed clothes in the stream. As far as he could tell, every one of them was as naked as the day she was born.

CHAPTER 15

Preacher glanced over at Boone and saw that the youngster's face was almost as red as a beet. Having seen his share of unclothed female flesh over the years, Preacher wasn't embarrassed by the sight before them, but neither was he particularly interested . . . when there might well be a search party armed with spears and war clubs looking for him and Boone.

"Come on," he whispered to the young trapper. "We'll see if we can circle around 'em without bein' noticed."

Boone nodded, but he had some obvious difficulty taking his eyes off the women and pulling back away from the river.

Just as a practical matter, during the brief moment he had looked at the women, Preacher had noted that most of them were on the short and stocky side, but a few were taller and more gracefully formed. Their skin had a more golden hue to it, as well.

Those differences were an indication that two tribes had intermarried and merged somewhere along the way. Preacher suspected that one group had originated much farther south, perhaps even in Mexico. The taller women looked more Spanish than Indian.

He and Boone left the women behind and moved south along the river until they were well out of sight of the group washing clothes.

When they stopped, Preacher said, "We need to get across this stream and head back north, toward the city we just saw. If my friends and all those other fellas who've disappeared are in this valley, chances are that's where they're bein' held."

"Preacher" — Boone swallowed hard — "you saw that city. What kind of a place is this? I never saw anything like that in all my born days!"

Preacher rubbed his chin and frowned. "I've been thinkin' about that. Seems like I heard tell of some fellas who used to have cities like that down in Mexico a long time back. Can't recollect what they were called, and I might be makin' the whole thing up. You never know. But some of those gals we saw looked a mite Mexican to me."

"I don't recall ever seeing any Mexican

women back home. And I never saw any women like . . . well . . . without any, uh, clothes on like that . . ." Boone's face turned red again.

Preacher clapped a hand on his shoulder. "Don't worry about that. You're young yet. Plenty of time left for you to see nekkid women."

"If we ever get out of here," Boone muttered. "I don't see how we're going to do that, with that trail through the cliffs blocked like it is."

"We'll find some other way," Preacher said confidently. He wasn't just putting up a brave front. That was just his way. He always believed in himself. So far that had pulled him through plenty of dangerous scrapes.

The river looked like it was deep enough they would have to swim across. Preacher made sure Boone could swim, then they took off their powder horns and held them above their heads along with their pistols as they slipped into the stream and began kicking toward the other side.

The water was surprisingly warm, which made Preacher think again about the possibility of hot springs in the valley. It had a fairly strong current to it, but neither man had to struggle much to get across. When they reached the far side, they stepped out with water dripping from their buckskins. The sun wouldn't take long to dry them.

"You plan to go all the way into that city?" Boone asked as they started north.

"I don't reckon we've got any choice," Preacher said. "We'll just try to stay out of sight as much as possible until we figure out what we're dealin' with."

There could be hundreds of warriors living there. Overwhelming odds, he thought, but he didn't see any point in saying that to Boone and worrying the young trapper even more.

As long as they could remain undiscovered and keep the element of surprise on their side, Preacher thought they had a chance. And if they could find Audie and Nighthawk and the other trappers who had been captured and free them, the odds against them wouldn't be quite so bad.

They came to another trail that led north toward the city. Preacher didn't trust being out in the open, so they stayed in the woods near the trail and paralleled its course, stopping when they reached one of those cultivated fields he had spotted earlier.

Still in the cover of the trees, he studied the field and recognized corn. Several men were working among the plants, picking ears of corn and depositing them in woven baskets. As far as he could tell, they were unarmed but too many to risk jumping them. Preacher motioned to his young companion that they would go around.

They had to make several such detours as they worked their way north through the valley.

During a brief pause to rest, Boone said, "I didn't know Indians grew plants like that. I thought they just hunted buffalo and other game."

"That's just one more way it goes to show you these ain't normal Injuns," Preacher said. "The Cherokee and some of the other tribes back east are farmers, but I never heard of any like that in these mountains."

"But they're warriors, too."

Preacher nodded. "Some of 'em are. I reckon we'd best watch out for all of 'em, though. Leastways until we find what we're lookin' for."

As they approached the city, they could see the tall structure that dominated the settlement. Something about it seemed ominous to Preacher, although he could admire the tremendous effort it must have taken to build such an edifice.

They stopped on a wooded knoll overlooking the city.

Preacher said, "Reckon we'd better wait

here until it gets dark. Quite a few people are movin' around, and if we get any closer, somebody's liable to spot us."

Boone took some jerky out of a pouch and handed a piece to Preacher. In gloomy silence, they stood there gnawing on the stuff. Preacher had forced the fact that they seemed to be trapped in the valley to the back of his mind so he could concentrate on the task at hand, but that threat was never completely out of his thoughts. He was sure it was the same way with Boone.

While they were waiting for night to fall, Preacher studied what he could see of the city. A couple of hundred yards off to their right was a large, natural depression in the ground. People had arranged several concentric rings of low stone slabs around it.

Preacher frowned as he realized that people could sit on those slabs. They had made an amphitheater out of the place. At the bottom of the depression was a single, larger slab. Preacher's frown deepened as he looked at it, not sure what its purpose was. Something about it bothered him.

When the sun wasn't far above the mountains to the west of the valley, people began to come out of the buildings and move toward the natural amphitheater. Men, women, and children were all dressed in buckskin but wearing colorful necklaces, bracelets, and other decorations fashioned unlike any Preacher had seen on other Indian tribes.

They were laughing and talking and seemed to be excited about something. Despite the festive atmosphere — or maybe because of it — the skin on the back of Preacher's neck prickled.

As they filed into the amphitheater and took places on the stone slabs, Boone muttered, "What in the world are they doing?"

"Don't know, but I reckon if we keep watchin', we'll find out."

CHAPTER 16

A group of men carrying spears and war clubs appeared, stalking along one of the cobblestone streets toward a square, windowless building. The stone blocks of which the building was constructed were covered with elaborate carvings. Preacher couldn't make out the details from so far away, but he could tell that a lot of work had gone into them.

A heavy door of polished wood was set into the front of the building and barred with a thick log. The warriors came to a stop and two of them lifted the log from the brackets that held it and swung the door open.

With their spears leveled and threatening, the rest of the party marched inside.

Under the circumstances, Preacher wasn't surprised when the warriors emerged a few minutes later dragging a prisoner with them. Two of them held the man's arms and forced him to walk while another warrior came along behind, prodding the struggling prisoner with a spear point. He howled and cursed with each jab, and Preacher and Boone could hear him well enough to realize the words were in English.

"My God," Boone whispered. "That has to be one of the trappers who disappeared."

"Yeah, I reckon so," Preacher said grimly. He didn't recognize the man, who was scrawny and had a long black beard as if he had been a captive for quite a while. His buckskins hung in tatters around his gaunt form.

The warriors hauled the prisoner toward the amphitheater. As they started down the slope toward the big slab in the center of the depression, Preacher couldn't see them anymore. The crowd that had gathered blocked his view of them. He looked up, then began climbing into one of the trees so he could see better. Boone followed suit.

The prisoner began screaming in terror as his captors forced him closer and closer to the big stone slab. When they reached it, more men took hold of him and lifted him. He tried to kick his legs and flail his arms, but their grips were too strong. They stretched him out on the slab, slipped rawhide thongs around his wrists and ankles, and secured them to iron rings set into the stone.

Boone sounded sick as he asked from the other tree, "What are they going to do to him, Preacher?"

"Nothin' good." The mountain man's rugged face was set in bleak lines as he watched.

Another party of warriors appeared, marching toward the depression. Preacher instantly recognized the man leading the group, even though he was dressed differently. He was the varmint they had followed to the hidden valley, wearing some sort of girdle around his waist that left his legs and chest bare. A long cloak made of eagle feathers was draped over his shoulders, and the eagle wings he had sported earlier were attached to the harness he wore on his back. He wore a helmet shaped to look like an eagle's beak. To Preacher, it appeared that the helmet was made out of gold that had been hammered into the distinctive shape.

In that getup, the chief was a mighty impressive figure. A much smaller man, old and gnarled, hurried alongside him, struggling to keep up. A dozen warriors came along the street behind them.

"I sure don't like the looks of this," Boone said from the tree next to the one where Preacher was perched.

"Neither do I, but there ain't a damned thing we can do about it." Preacher's calm words belied the storm raging inside him. He had a pretty good idea what was about to happen to the prisoner, and a big part of him wanted to charge in there with his guns blazing.

With a couple hundred people in the amphitheater, though, that wouldn't save the prisoner. It wouldn't accomplish anything, in fact, except to get himself killed.

If he'd had a rifle, he might have considered trying a long shot that would put the man out of his misery quickly, but from the range in the tree there was nothing he could do with his pistols. He was helpless to do anything except watch, and he didn't like that feeling.

Didn't like it one bit.

The chief and his group of warriors, along with the old shaman or whatever he was, descended into the amphitheater. The sun was almost touching the western mountains, and the light took on a garish red quality that was appropriate for what was about to happen.

The chief went to the stone slab where the prisoner was tied and threw back the feathered cloak on his shoulders. He raised his bare, muscular arms to the sky, tipped back his head, and began chanting in a loud, powerful voice as everyone else in the amphitheater fell silent.

The words meant nothing to Preacher and Boone. They were just gibberish and seemed to go on forever. Preacher wondered what the chief was waiting for.

A moment later, he understood. The sun began to dip behind the mountains, but its rays still shone through a notch in the peaks, creating a beam of light that slanted down into the valley and hit that big slab perfectly, flooding the stone and the prisoner with crimson light.

The chief turned to the shaman and held out his hand. The wizened old-timer placed a flint knife in the chief's palm.

The chief turned to the prisoner and got to work. The man's screams blended with a huge cheer that went up from the spectators.

Preacher heard Boone's harsh breathing from the other tree.

The young trapper let out a horrified groan. "I can't watch this."

"Then don't. But don't let what you're feelin' get away from you, neither. We can't do a blasted thing for that fella. We've got to remember there may be a dozen other prisoners in that buildin', maybe more."

"Including your friends. I know. We're going to try to help them, aren't we?"

The shouting from the amphitheater grew louder. Preacher looked and saw the chief strutting back and forth beside the slab, his arm held up straight over his head. He had something in his hand. Preacher couldn't make it out, but he didn't have to be able to see the thing to know what it was.

The man stretched out on the slab was quiet, the silence of death. His chest had a dark, gaping hole in it where the heart had been carved out. The heart that the arrogant chief proudly displayed to his followers. . . .

"We've got to help 'em," Preacher said. "No matter what the odds, I reckon you and me are the only chance those poor fellas have of not windin' up like that sooner or later."

CHAPTER 17

The sun didn't take much longer to finish sinking behind the mountains, plunging the valley into gathering shadow as the assemblage at the amphitheater began to break up. People filed out and returned to their homes.

The bonds fastening the dead trapper's body to the slab were untied, and warriors carried the corpse away. Preacher watched as they took it to a dark, circular opening in the ground ringed by paving stones. Casually, the men tossed the corpse into the hole as if it were so much garbage.

Rage burned brightly inside Preacher, but once again he tamped it down, hoping he would get a chance to avenge the man's death, and the deaths of any other prisoners who had been sacrificed in the past. But rescuing those who were still alive had to come first.

He didn't see the chief and the shaman

anymore. The two murderers had slipped off somewhere. The amphitheater was almost empty. Preacher turned his attention to the building from which the warriors had taken the prisoner.

He didn't see any guards posted around, but he would have been willing to bet that somebody was keeping an eye on the place. On the other hand, arrogance seemed to be a natural trait among the valley's inhabitants. Maybe they were so convinced that no one could escape from their jail that they didn't have anyone guarding it.

Some careful scouting once it was good and dark ought to answer that question one way or the other, Preacher thought as he and Boone climbed down out of the trees.

As the shadows thickened, Boone asked, "Are we going to sneak into the city?"

"Yep, that's the idea. We'll wait a while, though, and let everything settle down for the night."

"These people are crazy, Preacher. They're . . . they're barbarians!"

"That ain't necessarily a bad thing. I remember Audie tellin' me once that bein' barbarians is the natural state of mankind, 'cause sooner or later that's the way things always end up. Every so-called civilization goes back to the old, bloody ways if it lasts long enough."

"Maybe so, but I don't see anything to admire here."

"Didn't say I admire 'em. Maybe I understand 'em a mite, though. Doesn't mean I won't kill as many of 'em as I can if I get the chance, especially that big fella." Preacher touched the head of his tomahawk. "I'd sure like to get another crack at him."

Once the sun was down it didn't take long for night to fall completely over the valley. Darkness covered everything even while a faint rosy tinge remained in the western sky above the mountains. Preacher and Boone checked their pistols, then started down the slope toward the city.

Torches had sprung to life here and there, including in the plaza in front of the huge edifice at the far end of the main avenue. Stygian darkness cloaked most of the end of the city where Preacher and Boone were, and that was just the way Preacher liked it. His night vision was keen enough that he had no trouble leading Boone to a spot about a block away from the building where he believed the prisoners were housed.

Preacher signaled a halt with a light touch on his young companion's arm. He leaned closer and whispered, "Stay here while I do some scoutin'."

“What if somebody comes along?”

“Keep out of sight if you can. If you can’t, give a holler and I’ll come give you a hand. Be best, though, if they don’t know we’re here.”

“They’re bound to know we’re somewhere in the valley. After all, we followed the chief through that crack in the cliffs.”

“Yeah, and he set those other fellas on us,” Preacher reminded him. “For all anybody knows, we died in that avalanche along with them.”

Boone nodded in understanding, then whispered, “Be careful, Preacher.”

“I intend to . . . for now.”

The time would come, though, when he would unleash hell on the bloodthirsty savages. It would be better if he could set the prisoners free first, however.

He gave Boone’s shoulder a squeeze and then slipped away into the shadows, vanishing instantly from the young trapper’s gaze. With all the stealth that he had learned over the years, Preacher circled the jail building as much a phantom as any of the times he had slipped into Blackfoot camps to slit the throats of his enemies.

His suspicion that the place was discreetly guarded was confirmed when he heard a man breathing in the thick shadows next to one of the walls. Preacher edged closer and began to make out a patch of deeper darkness shaped like a man holding a spear. In utter silence, Preacher moved up behind him. His heavy-bladed hunting knife didn't make a sound as it slid from its leather sheath.

His left hand suddenly shot around the man's head and clamped over his mouth at the same time he drove the knife into the man's back, burying it to the hilt. The man jerked and arched in Preacher's grip.

Preacher let go of the knife and grabbed the guard's spear to keep it from falling to the ground and clattering on the cobblestones. He leaned it against the wall, took hold of the knife again, and twisted it to finish the job, even though he figured the guard was already dead. He pulled the blade out and lowered the body quietly to the ground, one more strange Indian who would never again stand and cheer while some bloodthirsty varmint hacked out a helpless victim's heart.

Preacher continued reconnoitering. He located another guard on the far side of the building and disposed of him the same way. The two sentries were the only ones he found. Satisfied that the way into the jail was undefended, he returned to the spot where he had left Boone.

The youngster jumped a little and gasped when Preacher put a hand on his shoulder, but he managed not to make any more sound than that.

"See anybody while I was gone?" Preacher asked in a whisper.

"Not a soul. How about you?"

"There are two less strange men now. Let's go see if we can get those fellas out of there." He led the way to the jail's entrance, where he took one end of the beam and Boone took hold of the other. They lifted it from its brackets and set it aside, then Preacher turned the latch and swung the door open. Inside was as black as it could be. Stepping into it was like stepping into nothingness.

He paused long enough to tell Boone, "Stay here and keep an eye out," then he moved deeper into the darkness.

After a moment, he realized there *was* some illumination in there after all. It came from starlight filtering down through small, rectangular openings cut in the roof, no doubt for ventilation. The openings didn't do a very good job of providing that, however. The air was thick and unpleasant with the smell of unwashed flesh and human waste. Preacher caught a lingering scent of decay, too. Somebody had died in there, and it had been a while before they had carried him out.

Preacher couldn't see much of anything, but his gut told him somebody was there. He listened intently and heard the faint rasp of breathing. He was about to say something when a man's voice quavered, "W-who's there? Have you come to k-kill some more of us?"

Something made a noise like feet scuffing frantically against the floor. "Please don't take me! I'll do anything —"

"Stop it, Talbot," another man said sharply. "Don't give these devils the satisfaction of hearing you beg. It'll just be futile anyway."

Preacher's heart leaped. He knew that second voice. He had heard it around many campfires. "Audie, it's me, Preacher. I've come to get you boys outta here."

CHAPTER 18

Stunned gasps greeted those words spoken in English.

Audie said, "Preacher? That can't be! Is it really you?"

Preacher chuckled. "I reckon that's as close to bein' struck speechless as I've ever heard you, old friend. Where are you?"

"Over here. Follow the sound of my voice."

As Preacher started in that direction, he asked, "Is Nighthawk with you?"

"Umm," came the reply from the big Crow warrior.

Preacher bumped into something, reached out in the darkness, and rested a hand on what he realized was Audie's shoulder, which was only waist-high to him.

"Thank God," the little man said. "I don't know how you found us, Preacher, but I'm glad you did."

"It wasn't easy. How many of you are in here?"

"There are eleven of us. One prisoner was taken out earlier." Audie's voice showed the strain he was under. "Do you happen to know what they did with him?"

"I'm sorry," Preacher said honestly. "I'm afraid that hombre's crossed the divide."

"Damnation. That bloodthirsty scoundrel Tenoch ripped his heart from his chest while it was still beating, didn't he?"

"I don't know who Tenoch is, but the poor fella had his heart ripped out, that's for sure."

"Tenoch is their war chief and high priest," Audie explained. "A tall, muscular man. Rather handsome in an arrogant way, I suppose you could say. Usually has a harness with eagle feathers attached to it strapped to his back."

"That's him," Preacher agreed. "I've met him. Fought him a couple times, actually. Don't like him one little bit."

"I don't blame you. He's a monster. He and Toltecatl, the medicine man who's always scurrying along after him. A repulsive little toad."

"Can't argue with you there." Preacher reached up and brushed his fingers against some thick strands of rope. "They've really got you strung up, don't they?"

"Yes, the ropes are tied to iron rings set into the wall. I'm just glad they don't seem to have any chains. That would make freeing us more difficult."

"It sure would," Preacher said as he drew his knife. "I'll have you cut loose in just a minute. All of you. Then we'll fight our way outta here if we have to."

"I'm afraid not all of us will be able to mount much of a struggle. Some of the prisoners have been here for quite some time, and they don't feed us a great deal." Audie's voice took on a wry tone as he added, "No point in fattening us up just to carve our hearts out, I suppose."

Preacher took hold of the ropes binding his friend's wrists and began sawing on them. Made of braided plant fibers, they were stubbornly tough, but the knife's keen edge gradually parted all of them.

Audie's arms dropped. He moaned a little, probably from relief as muscles cramped from being stuck in that awkward position finally eased.

As Preacher moved over to locate Nighthawk and cut him loose, he heard a hiss from the doorway.

"Preacher!" Boone Halliday called quietly. "Somebody's coming!"

Preacher could see the door's outline, since it was little lighter outside than it was in the prison. He hurried over to it and told Boone, "Come in here and we'll pull the door up. Maybe whoever it is won't notice the bar ain't on it. If they do and they start to bar the thing, we'll have bust out and fight. If they bar that door, we'll be trapped in here same as these other fellas."

Audie came up behind him. "Give me your knife, Preacher. I'll see if I can cut some of the other prisoners loose."

Preacher handed over the knife, then he and Boone took hold of the door and pulled it inward, leaving just a small gap. Since it was dark outside, someone passing by in the street might not notice that it wasn't completely closed. The danger lay in them seeing the bar sitting to one side and realizing that something was amiss.

They heard men talking in loud, boisterous voices.

They sounded drunk, Preacher thought, and he wondered if they had some sort of home-brewed firewater they imbibed in. He hoped so. If they had been drinking they would be less likely to notice anything different about the jail entrance.

The men were right outside in the street. Preacher thought they were about to pass on by, when one of the prisoners bawled, "Hey! Help! Hey, out there! Intruders!"

"Talbot, you idiot!" Audie exclaimed.

Talbot was the prisoner who had begged for his life earlier, promising to do anything if his captors would let him live, Preacher recalled. He must have hoped he could curry favor with them by shouting a warning.

The men outside yelled in alarm. One of them grabbed the door and started to open it. Preacher lowered his shoulder, grated, "Come on!" at Boone, and rammed the door open.

The heavy portal crashed against the man just outside and knocked him backwards. Still hopeful of dealing with the threat without rousing the whole city, Preacher left his pistols where they were and yanked out his tomahawk as he bounded into the group of warriors. In the dark, it was impossible to tell how many there were, but he had no trouble finding targets as he slashed back and forth with the tomahawk. Bone crunched under the blows and men toppled backwards.

The sounds of struggle intensified as Boone plunged into the melee, and then a huge figure swept out of the prison, grabbed up one of the warriors, and slung him into the others. Audie had freed Nighthawk, and the big Crow was taking a hand.

Unfortunately, more and more warriors were swarming around the three battlers. The fight swayed back and forth across the cobblestones. Preacher wreaked havoc with his tomahawk, but he realized that he and Boone were going to have to blast their way out with pistols, no matter how much of an uproar it caused. He shifted his 'hawk to his left hand and yanked one of the pistols from behind his belt with his right hand. Before he could bring it to bear, something smashed into the back of his head.

The blow knocked him forward. He tried to keep his balance, but another war club struck him in the small of the back, and he fell to his knees. His movements were more awkward because his head was spinning, but he managed to bring the pistol up, cock it, and fire just as one of the warriors was about to plunge a spear into him. The ball caught the man in the throat and drove him backwards as blood fountained darkly from the wound.

Boone crashed to the street beside Preacher, who couldn't tell if the young trapper was alive or dead. A few yards away, Nighthawk was still struggling, but several men had hold of him and were trying to force him off his feet. More warriors piled on until Preacher couldn't see the Crow anymore.

Preacher tried to get to his feet, but there were too many men around him. He lashed out with the tomahawk and the empty pistol. A war club caught him on the right forearm and made him drop the pistol. Two more men grabbed his left arm and trapped it against his side so he couldn't swing the 'hawk anymore. Someone hooked his legs and yanked them out from under him. Clubs and feet pounded against him as he fell.

He felt the rough cobblestones underneath him as his attackers continued to batter him, but those brutal blows stopped as a high, clear voice shouted orders in that unknown tongue.

Strong hands still pinned him to the ground, but he was able to lift his head and look up. His eyes narrowed against the glare as someone ran up carrying a torch. A figure unlike anything he had ever seen — or expected to see — strode into view.

The woman was tall, lithe, golden-skinned in the torchlight. Her fine-boned features were undeniably beautiful. Her long, straight hair was the color of midnight and hung over her shoulders and down her back.

She wore a large, fanlike headdress made of green feathers and a long necklace of what appeared to be round plates of beaten gold. The necklace hung down far enough to cover her breasts, for the most part. Her only other garments were a green sash tied around her waist from which a long loincloth was draped. It reached to her ankles but was narrow enough to leave her thighs and calves bare, especially as she strode forward. A flint knife hung from a strap attached to the sash and bumped against her skin as she walked.

She was one of the loveliest women Preacher had ever seen, but as she stopped and looked down at him, he saw no warmth in her gray eyes. They were cold as a field of ice. There was no mercy in her.

She proved that a moment later by snapping a command, and a war club in the hands of a warrior lashed out and crashed against Preacher's head. He went spinning down into a well of darkness and knew nothing more.

Chapter 19

Preacher had been knocked out many times over the years. His skull was thick and solid and when he woke up he was usually clear-headed, although his head usually ached from being clouted. He never worried that such blows would scramble his brain.

But as consciousness returned to him and memories of what had happened began to seep into his thoughts, he had to wonder if he had finally gone loco.

He remembered fighting strange Indians with war clubs and spears, warriors unlike any tribe he had ever encountered. The battle had taken place in a hidden, isolated valley, in a city the likes of which he had never seen, either.

And there was the woman . . . a stunning, breathtaking beauty in a scandalously skimpy outfit. Surely he had imagined her. She couldn't have been real. . . .

Preacher became aware that his arms were

pulled above his head and held in place by ropes bound around his wrists. His feet barely reached the stone floor, so the strain on his arms and shoulders was quite painful. His body was lean and wolf-like, but it wasn't exactly lightweight. Strung up like he was, it felt like his arms were about to pop right out of their sockets.

Darkness surrounded him, but when he tipped his head back, he saw stars glittering here and there above him and he realized he was in the prison where Audie, Nighthawk, and the others were being kept. He was seeing the stars through those little ventilation openings.

All of which meant he was a prisoner, too.

He heard harsh breathing, so he knew he wasn't alone. He said quietly, "Audie? Boone?"

"Thank God!" Boone Halliday exclaimed from somewhere nearby, although Preacher couldn't see him at all. "You're still alive, Preacher."

"Yeah, I reckon," the mountain man said dryly.

"We were afraid they had killed you, after that lady told them to start whaling away on you again."

Audie spoke up, somewhere on Preacher's other side. "That was no lady, my young friend. That was Eztli, the high priestess of these people."

Preacher said, "You seem to know quite a bit about these folks, Audie. I thought for a second when I woke up that I must've dreamed the whole thing, but this crazy shootin' match is real, ain't it?"

"All too real," Audie said. "An entire civilization, if you can call it that, centered around blood and death. As difficult as it may be to believe, Preacher, these people are Aztecs."

"Aztecs!" Preacher repeated. "That's it. I've been tryin' to remember the name of the folks you told me about once, a good while ago. How come they ain't down in Mexico, where they belong? That's where they come from, ain't it?"

"That's right. Are you sure you want to go into all this right now?"

Preacher let out a grim chuckle. "Ain't got much else to do at the moment. I reckon you fellas are all strung up like I am?"

"Yes, they recaptured all of us before anyone was able to get away."

"Nighthawk's all right? Last I saw him, a bunch of those varmints were pilin' up on him."

Somewhere in the darkness, the big Crow said, "Umm."

"I'm glad to hear it," Preacher told him. "It figures it'd take a dozen of 'em to bring you down, old son. Audie, you can go on with your story. How come you know all this?"

"One of the priests who comes here from time to time speaks some English, and he likes to practice it with me. I suspect he learned the language from the trappers who have been brought here over the months since the Great Shaking."

"You're talkin' about the earthquake they had in these parts a while back," Preacher guessed.

"That's correct. It was another earthquake sometime in the dim past, at least two hundred years ago, I'd estimate, that sealed this valley away from the rest of the world in the first place, and it took a second earthquake to open a path again."

"Two hundred years ago?" Boone put in. "How long have these savages been here, anyway?"

"The Aztec empire was at its height four hundred years ago," Audie answered. "From what I gather, that's when the ancestors of these people were banished."

"Banished?" Preacher repeated.

"Yes. They were, ah, too bloodthirsty even for that red-handed empire. Hard to believe, isn't it?"

Everything about this mess was hard for Preacher to believe, but he trusted Audie. The little man knew more about more things than anybody Preacher had ever met. He told the former professor, "Go on."

"After they'd been driven out because of their cruel practices, they came north out of what is now Mexico and traveled through the mountains until they reached this region. How long that journey took them, I have no idea. They may have attempted to settle in other places but been forced to continue their pilgrimage for some reason."

"Seems likely other folks wouldn't want 'em around."

"Yes, doesn't it? At any rate, they finally found themselves in this valley, where they began to build their city and intermarry with the Indians who lived here. That was a slow process, too, and some of the familial lines kept themselves what they considered pure as much as possible. Of course, that inbreeding resulted from time to time in some less than perfect specimens. Gradually the population came to consist of two groups, those who are of predominantly Aztec lineage and those who are mostly Indian blood. The Aztecs are in charge, though, make no mistake about that.

They're the soldiers, the priests, the leaders of this society. In fact, many of the warriors are also priests, like Tenoch."

"The fella I tussled with," Preacher said.

"Yes, he's the one. Then there's Eztli."

"The high priestess you mentioned."

Audie sighed. "Yes. She and Tenoch are lovers, and she is, I suspect, even more insane than he is. After the earthquake, she's the one who prodded him to revive the old custom of . . . human sacrifice."

"They hadn't been doing that all along?" Preacher asked.

"No, they prefer to slaughter outsiders. I suppose that's a wise course when you have a limited population," Audie added.

Preacher could understand that. "The whole business of cuttin' out hearts . . . is part of their religion?"

"Most definitely. In the Aztec empire, many of the people who were sacrificed *volunteered* to be killed in order to honor one of their gods. It was considered a privilege. But Eztli and Tenoch follow Huitzilopochtli, the god of war, and to appease him, the blood of enemies must be shed. They offer up the hearts of those enemies so that he may feast on them."

It all sounded crazy to Preacher, but having seen the high priest and priestess close up and witnessed the madness in their eyes, he could believe what Audie was saying. "So once that earthquake cracked the cliffs and they could get out of the valley again, they started capturin' trappers to use as their sacrifices. Some of 'em they brought back here, to keep as prisoners for later, and some of 'em they killed on the spot."

"That's correct."

"Well, they're not gonna be able to do that anymore. There was an avalanche, and that trail through the cliffs is blocked now."

Audie was silent for a long moment, then he said, "Preacher, my old friend, I wish you were right. Knowing that their insanity was bottled up again for all time might be worth the fate they have in mind for us, but I'm afraid that's not the case. I'm sure you saw the pyramid at the other end of the city."

"That's what you call that big ol' buildin'?"

"Yes. The ancient Egyptians built pyramids, too, although they're somewhat different from the ones constructed by the Aztecs. What they have in common is that they're tremendous feats of engineering, especially considering the primitive tools and equipment they were forced to use. They know how to work with huge chunks of stone."

"You're sayin' they'll be able to clear away the debris from that avalanche?" Preacher asked.

"I'm confident that they will. You see, the most valuable tool is something the Aztecs and the Egyptians also had in common. Humanity. The sweat and blood of slaves. I'm afraid that Eztli and Tenoch will work as many of the Indians to death as they have to in order to get what they want."

Preacher's voice was tense as he said, "And what's that, exactly?"

"They want to take over everything west of the Mississippi and establish a new Aztec empire."

Chapter 20

For a long moment, Preacher didn't say anything. He couldn't think of any response that would do justice to the statement Audie had just made. It was so outrageous, so unbelievable.

Finally he just said, "That's the craziest thing I've heard so far, Audie."

"Perhaps, but the priest I've spoken to assures me that it's a fact."

"It'll never happen. The frontier's too big, and to set up any sort of empire, they'd have to unite all the tribes. They're too busy fightin' amongst themselves to ever work together."

"But what if they did?" Audie persisted. "Right now, the old tribal hatreds that have gone on for hundreds of years are still strong. But white men have been out here for a much shorter time, and already many of the tribes hate us worse than they hate each other. Eztli claims that the sacrifices and rituals will cause Huitzilopochtli, their war god, to grant them so much power they'll be able to wipe out all the whites between here and the Father of Waters. If anything might cause the other tribes to set their differences aside and align themselves with the Aztecs, that would do it."

Preacher hated to admit it, but Audie could be right. The more warlike tribes, say, the Blackfeet, had always hated the white trappers, regarding them as unwelcome invaders. Many of the other tribes felt the same way, if not quite so vehemently as the Blackfeet. He could imagine his old enemies throwing in with the Aztecs. Combined, they would be a powerful force. Some of the other tribes would join forces with them, just to avoid being wiped out.

Like a rock rolling downhill, such a movement could pick up momentum until it became an avalanche, destroying anything and anybody unlucky enough to be in its path.

"That's why Eztli and Tenoch will do whatever is necessary to open up that passage through the cliffs again," Audie went on. "They need victims for their bloody rituals. I think they believe in what they're doing, but even if they didn't, they're canny enough to know that they have to continue with the sacrifices in order to keep their followers worked up. That blood lust makes the people obedient and pliable."

A brooding silence settled over the dark prison.

Finally, Preacher said, "You've learned a whole heap since you've been here, Audie."

"The old priest I've been talking to is eager to practice his English, as I said," Audie explained. "And I've picked up some of his language, as well, so we've been able to communicate quite a bit. Also, there's really nothing to do in here except think about the implications of everything I've learned."

Preacher nodded, even though in the thick gloom, none of the others could see him.

Boone said, "So you mean they're going to continue" — he had to pause and swallow hard — "sacrificing prisoners, Mr. Audie?"

"That's right. In the time that Nighthawk and I have been here, they've taken half a dozen out of here, and those men never came back. The conclusion as to their fate is inescapable."

"How often do they do that?" Preacher asked.

"Well, it's difficult to keep track of time in here . . . but I'd estimate they conduct a sacrifice approximately every two weeks." Audie added, "By the way, son, you don't have to call me mister. Out here we tend to be rather informal. In circumstances such as these, there's even less need for it."

Preacher said, "All right. Even workin' folks to death like you say they'll do, it's gonna take a couple weeks to clean out that crack in the cliffs. Maybe longer than that. So maybe they'll hold off on killin' anybody for a while so as to make sure they have victims for a while longer."

"Possibly," Audie agreed, "but we can't count on that."

"I ain't countin' on nothin' except we need to get loose and rattle our hocks outta here as soon as we can."

"Don't say too much," Audie warned. "You never know who you can trust."

That comment was enough to tell Preacher that the man called Talbot was still a prisoner. He had betrayed their earlier escape effort, and Preacher didn't doubt that he would do it again if he thought it would gain him any favors from their captors.

It was enough to know what they were facing. A sacrifice had taken place earlier, so with any luck they would have some time before another prisoner was dragged off to a grisly death. That would give him and Audie the chance to work on an escape plan.

One thing he could do in the dark was check to see how good a job his captors had done of binding his hands. He twisted his wrists against the braided ropes, trying to get some play in them.

After several minutes he was forced to conclude that the Aztecs knew what they were doing. The bonds were secure enough that he would have to work at them for a long time to have any chance of loosening them.

He was doing that when he heard a loud scraping noise from outside. Somebody was taking the bar off the door. A moment later, it swung open. Torchlight spilled into the stone cell, and the glare was blinding to eyes that had become accustomed to the thick darkness.

Preacher squinted, and as his vision began to adjust he saw two Aztec warriors stride into the prison carrying burning brands. The flickering light filled the large room, and for the first time the mountain man got a good look at his fellow captives.

Four of them were strung up along the left-hand wall — Preacher, with Boone Halliday to his right and Audie and then Nighthawk to his left. All of them bore fresh marks of battle, and Audie and Nighthawk sported a number of old bruises and scrapes from when they had been captured. They hadn't been in the prison as long as some of the others so they looked reasonably healthy.

The same couldn't be said of the other prisoners, all of whom were in varying stages of emaciation. Five were tied to iron rings set into the rear wall, and four were strung up on the wall facing Preacher, Boone, Audie, and the big Crow. With each man, the bonds had been shortened so that their arms were pulled up painfully.

Preacher wasn't sure which of the other prisoners was Talbot, but he suspected it was a weaselly-looking gent with a long dark beard shot through with gray whose eyes darted away guiltily as Preacher looked at him.

Four men carrying spears entered behind the torchbearers. They spread out so a tall, regal figure followed by more warriors could step between them. The beautiful priestess Audie had called Eztli stepped up and stood in front of Preacher, staring at him.

If anything, she was more beautiful than ever close up. He wasn't sure if he had ever seen skin quite so smooth. She looked almost like she was made out of molten gold. He couldn't help but be aware that she was almost naked, covered only by the long loincloth and the necklace of hammered gold plates. Even under the dire circumstances, her savage beauty was compelling.

She still carried the knife slung from her sash, and she had added another touch. From her left hand dangled a length of rawhide strung through the empty eye sockets of three human skulls.

He figured it was a talisman of some sort, since she was a priestess. A chill rippled though him at the casual way she held those souvenirs of previous victims.

She spoke, her voice liquid, musical, and utterly incomprehensible to the mountain man. One of the warriors carrying a spear stepped forward and brandished the weapon toward Preacher. Torchlight glittered on the blade.

CHAPTER 21

Preacher glared at the man with the spear. If he was about to die, he would do it with defiance on his face.

The warrior lifted the spear and used its keen edge to cut the ropes between Preacher's wrists, then stepped back.

The mountain man's arms dropped. Pain shot through his muscles, but there was relief, too, as his weight came down more solidly on his feet. He was a little unsteady, but he forced himself to stiffen. He didn't want his captors to see that unsteadiness.

He kept the glare on his face. He was damned if he was going to look grateful to them for not killing him.

Eztli spoke again, never taking her eyes off Preacher. She was still close to him, but several of the warriors had their spears ready to skewer him if he moved so much as an inch in her direction.

When Eztli paused, Preacher asked, "Do

you know what she's sayin', Audie?"

"I . . . I think she's saying that she's taking you with her," the little man replied.

"She can't!" Boone cried. "They already sacrificed somebody just a little while ago."

Audie shook his head. "I don't think that's what she has in mind. I can't tell for sure, mind you, but I get the sense that they're not going to sacrifice you, Preacher."

"Well, I reckon that's a relief," the mountain man said dryly. "Or maybe it ain't. There's no tellin' what somebody as loco as this gal might do."

Anger flashed in Eztli's eyes, and Preacher realized that while she might not actually speak English, she had picked up a few words of the language . . . such as *loco.*

She snapped a command. A pair of warriors reached out, took hold of Preacher's arms, and forced him toward the door.

"Preacher!" Boone called after him. "What are we supposed to do?"

"Don't reckon there's anything you *can* do," Preacher said over his shoulder. "Just stay alive, son, and wait for a chance."

A chance to do what, he didn't say. He supposed that depended on the Aztecs.

The warriors forced him outside, and even though he had no idea what his captors had in store for him, after being cooped up in that stone cell it felt good to draw in a deep breath of clean mountain air. He noticed that it wasn't quite as cool as he would have expected, which lent credence to his theory that the valley might be warmed somewhat by hot springs.

Once they were out of the prison the warriors stopped, but only for a moment so that Eztli could stride imperiously past them and take the lead again, along with the men who carried the torches. Then the procession began again.

They wound through the streets. Preacher thought he could probably find his way back to the prison, but after so many twists and turns he wasn't sure. The instincts that could lead him unerringly through a trackless wilderness weren't as much good in a crowded city.

Finally they came to a stop in front of a building that resembled the giant pyramid at the end of the avenue, although it was much shorter and didn't taper to a single block of stone on top. The walls were covered with elaborate carvings similar to those on the prison. It must have taken an incredible amount of work to chip those decorations into the stone. Some were just meaningless shapes, while others were meant to represent animals. Preacher saw some that reminded him of mountain lions, although the big cats appeared to be covered with spots of some sort. There were eagles and other birds, but some of them were so bizarrely formed they were like nothing he had ever seen before. He could barely identify them as birds.

A short flight of wide, shallow stone steps led up to the building's entrance, which was flanked by stone pillars. Torchlight shone on the polished wood of the door, which one of the warriors opened for Eztli. As she stalked in, Preacher realized she reminded him of one of those big cats in the carvings.

She was probably every bit as dangerous as one of those predators, too.

The warriors forced Preacher up the steps and into the building, although to tell the truth they didn't have to try very hard. He wanted to find out what she had in mind for him. If he got the chance, he planned to grab her and use her as a hostage. If she was as important to the Aztecs — and to Tenoch — as Audie made her sound, they might be willing to release the other prisoners in order to keep her safe.

Of course, with the path through the cliffs blocked, Preacher and the others wouldn't be able to escape from the valley, but they would deal with that when the time came.

The stones that formed the floor tiles inside the building were polished to a high sheen, like the door. Eztli glided over them on bare feet as she led the way into a large chamber. The only furniture, if you could call it that, consisted of blocks of stone placed here and there around the room. Some of them were covered with animal skins, and more skins were piled on the floor.

They were primarily bear skins, but he saw hides from mountain lions, deer, and antelope, as well. They reminded him of the buffalo robes many of the Indian tribes used in their lodges.

Torches were already burning and set in niches carved into the walls. Most of the warriors left. Only two remained just inside the entrance, holding their spears and standing at attention like soldiers as they gazed straight ahead, not seeming to see anything.

Preacher was willing to bet the rest of the guards were right outside. If he made a move toward the high priestess, a shout would summon them in an instant.

Eztli turned toward Preacher and spoke. He had no idea what she was saying, but her tone wasn't as strident and commanding as before. She set aside the skull talisman and moved to an alcove where a clay pitcher and a pair of cups waited on a shelf. She poured liquid from the pitcher into one of the cups, picked it up, and carried it toward Preacher.

She was offering him a drink, he realized. When she held out the cup to him, he took it but didn't lift it to his lips. The liquid inside was almost clear. It might have been mistaken for water, but he felt confident that it wasn't.

When he didn't drink, Eztli let out a laugh. The sound was every bit as pleasant and musical as her voice when she spoke. She returned to the shelf and filled the other cup, then carried it over to him as well. She held it out to him and gestured. He could tell that she was offering him his choice.

"I reckon this'll do me." He lifted his cup slightly as if toasting her.

She laughed again, raised her cup to her lips, and drank deeply. Preacher followed suit, and as the stuff bit fiercely into his mouth and throat, he knew his guess had been right. It wasn't water. It reminded him of the tequila he'd had in the cantinas of Santa Fe, but if so, it was the strongest tequila he'd ever tasted.

If Eztli was planning to get him drunk, she was going to be disappointed. He had put away so much tanglefoot in his life that his capacity for liquor was enormous. He licked his lips as the drink warmed his belly.

The high priestess smiled at him. "Eztli." She touched the fingertips of one hand to the valley between her breasts as she spoke.

Preacher already knew her name from Audie, but he nodded as if he were just learning it. He tapped his own chest. "Preacher."

"Pree-char," Eztli repeated.

"Close enough."

"Eztli."

She seemed to be expecting him to say it, so he did.

"Eztli. Mighty pretty name." Flattery never hurt anything where a gal was concerned, he thought — even a bloodthirsty Aztec Indian gal. She couldn't understand the words, but he thought she might savvy that he was complimenting her.

She must have, because she seemed pleased. She took his empty cup and cocked her head to the side. He knew she was asking if he wanted another drink.

"Reckon I'd better not," he said as he shook his head. "Liquor don't muddle me none, even on an empty stomach, but I've had enough."

She took the cups and placed them on the

shelf in the alcove. He couldn't help but admire her graceful movements. If she hadn't been an insane killer, he would have been attracted to her. It was impossible to forget all the bloody deaths she'd had a hand in, though.

She was just living according to her own lights, he reminded himself. To her way of thinking, she and her people weren't doing anything wrong. The white trappers were the enemy. To those who worshipped that war god Audie had mentioned, the one with the long, crazy name, enemies existed only to be sacrificed.

Preacher had run into many grim, bloody customs among the tribes he had encountered over the years. Just because he might understand a little of *why* the Aztecs felt like they did, didn't mean he was going to forgive them for what they had done. He would battle all he could to put a stop to their plans and free his friends, no matter who got in his way.

Eztli spoke again. The words sounded good in her voice, but to Preacher they were all nonsense. He shook his head to indicate that he didn't understand.

She moved closer, put a hand on his chest, spoke earnestly for a moment. Then she turned and swayed over to one of the piles of bearskins. She stretched out on them, extended a bare arm toward him, and said, "Pree-char."

He took a deep breath. The invitation was pretty damn plain, he thought. He glanced over at the two spear-carrying guards by the door. Their gazes were still focused straight ahead, which must have taken a heap of determination. Most men wouldn't have been able to stop themselves from staring at such an abundance of beautiful female flesh sprawled out on a bearskin robe.

As for Eztli, she didn't seem to care that the guards were there. Either she was confident that they wouldn't watch whatever mischief she got up to — or she just didn't care if they did.

As for Preacher, he had never been burdened by an overabundance of shame or modesty — spending a winter or two among the Indians would take care of that in a hurry for most men — but what Eztli was suggesting seemed a mite raw even for him.

He knew it was liable to make her mad, but he shook his head.

He was right. Anger flared in her eyes for a moment. Her tone was more curt and commanding when she spoke again.

He said, "Sorry. I just don't reckon it'd be a good idea."

She rolled onto her side and came up on her knees, as lithe and sinuous as ever. The impatience she felt was obvious in her demeanor and her voice as she ordered him to join her.

Preacher just stood there, unmoving.

Maybe she would get mad enough to sic the two guards on him. Preacher would welcome the chance to take their spears away, kill them both, and make Eztli his prisoner and hostage . . . if he could do it without alerting the warriors who waited outside.

She came to her feet and stalked toward him. Angry words spilled from her mouth. Preacher heard the two guards start forward, but Eztli motioned them back and took him by surprise. Her open hand flashed toward his face.

He wasn't going to just stand there and let her slap him. His own hand was a blur of speed as he reached up and caught her wrist before the blow could land. His fingers closed tightly around her flesh. She trembled a little as she stared intently at him from only a few inches away. A furious scowl darkened her face. She was no match for his strength as he held her hand away from him easily.

She lifted her other hand slower and

moved it to the back of his neck. Only a few inches shorter than him, she didn't have to come up on her toes much to press her lips to his. Preacher could have turned his head away from the kiss, but he didn't.

Despite everything, she tasted good. Not good enough to make him forget about all the dead men for whom she was partially responsible, but the sensation itself was undeniably pleasant. He wondered if she made a habit of playing a little game of slap-and-tickle with some of the other prisoners before they had gone to their deaths.

He wondered, too, what ol' Tenoch would have thought about it if he'd walked in. According to Audie, Tenoch and Eztli were lovers, so Preacher figured the big varmint wouldn't have been too happy.

Like an actor in some play who had been waiting offstage for his cue, Tenoch chose that moment to stride into Eztli's chamber. A brief commotion at the door and a couple words snapped in a harsh voice were the only warnings Eztli had.

Preacher let go of her wrist and she took a hurried step away from him, but not fast enough to keep Tenoch from realizing what was going on.

He bellowed something as Preacher swung around. The big warrior priest was still dressed in the extravagant getup he had worn earlier during the sacrifice, with one addition. A machete was slung from the girdle around his waist. His lips pulled back from his teeth in a grimace as he reached for the long, heavy-bladed weapon. He barked an order at the two guards, and since they stayed right where they were, Preacher guessed that Tenoch had told them to stay out of what was about to happen.

As Eztli continued to back away, Preacher glanced at her and saw that she looked worried, but excitement shone in her eyes, as well. Eager anticipation for what she was about to see gripped a part of her.

With a roar, Tenoch brandished the machete and charged.

Chapter 22

Preacher wanted another chance at Tenoch, but the conditions weren't the best in which to fight a battle. The high priest might intend to settle things man-to-man, but if it looked like their leader was about to be killed, the guards would probably rush in and take a hand, even though they had been ordered not to.

A little too close in Eztli's private chamber, Preacher would have preferred the fight take place outside where he would have plenty of room to move around.

Tenoch wasn't giving him a choice, though. The machete swept toward him in a blindingly fast stroke that would lop his head right off his shoulders if it landed.

He dropped under the deadly blade and lunged forward to meet Tenoch's attack with a charge of his own. He tackled the warrior around the knees and heaved. With a startled yell, Tenoch went over backwards, landing hard on the stone floor, but the impact didn't knock the machete out of his hand as Preacher had hoped.

Tenoch lashed out with a sandaled foot in a vicious kick aimed at Preacher's head.

The mountain man shifted aside in time to take the blow on his left shoulder, but it was powerful enough to deaden his arm momentarily and send him rolling across the room. Along the way, he got tangled in one of the bearskins scattered on the floor. Turning that to his advantage, he came up on one knee, tore loose from the bearskin, and flung it toward Tenoch just as the man leaped toward him again with the machete held high.

The bearskin enveloped Tenoch's head, blinding him and catching the machete in it, too. Preacher surged to his feet and launched an uppercut aimed at where Tenoch's jaw ought to be located under the bearskin. The powerful blow landed with a solid smash that shivered satisfyingly up Preacher's right arm all the way to his shoulder.

Tenoch didn't go down, but he staggered back a step. Preacher bored in with his left hand, recovered from the kick, and slammed a hard left and then a right into the warrior's slab-muscled midsection.

Tenoch was shaky but stubbornly refused to collapse. He finally succeeded in ripping the bearskin away from his head, just in time for Preacher's left fist to crash against his nose. Blood spurted hotly over Preacher's knuckles as Tenoch's head rocked back from the blow.

Moving fast, Preacher grabbed the wrist of the hand that held the machete. He pivoted, trapping Tenoch's arm as he wrapped his leg around the priest's leg. The mountain man twisted, putting so much pressure on Tenoch's elbow that he had to turn with Preacher to keep the joint from snapping. The machete slipped from Tenoch's fingers and clattered on the stone floor at the mountain man's feet.

Instantly, Preacher released the arm and bent to grab Tenoch's leg. A powerful heave toppled the warrior again, and before he even hit the floor, Preacher had scooped up the fallen machete.

He dropped to one knee beside his opponent, pressed the blade to Tenoch's throat, and shouted to the anxious guards as they started forward. "You boys better stay back or I'll chop your boss's head clean off!"

They might not know the words, but they understood the threat and pulled back as

Preacher bore down on Tenoch's throat with the blade.

"Drop those spears and kick 'em over here —" Preacher stopped as he heard a whisper of sound behind him. He hadn't forgotten about Eztli, but he didn't have eyes in the back of his head. He hoped she would be so afraid for Tenoch's life that she would stay back.

He sensed as much as heard something coming at his head and glanced back just in time to see the clay pitcher Eztli was swinging at him with both arms. She was strong, and the pitcher shattered as she crashed it against his skull.

Preacher didn't lose consciousness, but the blow stunned him and sent him slumping forward over Tenoch. The warrior batted Preacher's arm aside, knocking the machete away from his throat, which bled from the small cut the blade left. Tenoch grabbed Preacher's throat with his other hand and rolled the mountain man over to smash his head against the floor.

For the second time that evening, oblivion swallowed Preacher whole. The last thing he was aware of was Eztli's voice angrily spitting out a word.

"Pree-char!"

Chapter 23

If Preacher had been able to think about it, he would have figured that if he ever woke up again, it would only be for a last moment of terrible agony while Tenoch carved his heart out of his chest. But when consciousness stole back into his brain after an unknowable time, he slowly realized that he was not only alive but intact. His heart still resided safely in his chest. He could hear his pulse pounding inside his skull like a crazed drumbeat.

Heat completely surrounded him. Not in waves such as what would come from a fire, but an overall, almost liquid heat as if he were immersed in it. The crimson glare against his closed eyelids told him the heat came from the sun.

He tried to move around but was powerless. Staked out, his wrists and ankles were tightly tied so that his arms were stretched above his head and his legs were splayed out to each side. Rough stone underneath him pressed hotly against his bare skin.

It had to be the day after his latest battle with Tenoch, he told himself. His captors had stripped him and staked him out in the sun. There was no telling how long he had been pinioned . . . wherever he was. Since he felt at least half cooked already, likely it had been a while.

There was no point in opening his eyes, either. He wouldn't be able to see anything except the huge, hot ball of the sun floating in the sky overhead as it baked him. The terrible glare might blind him permanently if he stared into it for very long. He wasn't going to risk that, even if he didn't know how much longer he had to live.

Time had no meaning in that hell. Preacher lay there for what seemed like an eternity with his blood boiling in his veins. After a while he grew numb. Eventually, he was no longer even aware of the heat.

It took him a while to realize that the sun had set. Blessed darkness rolled over him, bringing with it cool relief.

Inside, though, he still burned.

He must have slept at some point, because when he became aware of his surroundings again, the sun was back, shining down on him. After a few moments, he was able to tell that it wasn't directly overhead, but rather off to the side, the rays slanting across his tortured body.

He turned his head away from the light as much as he could and risked opening his eyes.

The world started spinning crazily around him as he realized he could see half the valley rolling away from him. He seemed to be floating on his back, hundreds of feet in the air. He felt like he was falling, and the sensation made him sick. He retched, but there was nothing inside him to come up. Everything had been leeched out of him by the awful heat.

Eventually he became aware of something rough against his cheek. Trembling, he forced his eyes open again. The vertigo wasn't as bad . . . and he understood why.

He was staked out, all right — on that big stone slab at the top of the huge pyramid overlooking the Aztec city.

No wonder he was hot. He was closer to the sun than anything else in the valley.

Eventually he dozed again . . . or passed out. Either would have been right as far as he was concerned. He was gone. . . .

And then he was there again.

Something sharp jabbed him in the side. A familiar voice barked a sharp command.

Preacher felt the stretched-out muscles in his arms and legs go slack as his wrists and ankles were freed from their bonds. Strong hands gripped him and lifted him from the stone. He hung limply from those hands as they carried him away. The swaying movement lulled him back into a stupor.

He came out of it when water splashed into his face. The cold liquid hit him like a fist. He gasped and tried to jerk upright, but he was too weak. All he could do was lie there with water dripping off him.

"My God, Preacher! They've roasted you!"

That was Boone Halliday's voice.

Even in his misery, Preacher was glad the young trapper was still alive. He'd been worried that Tenoch might have slaughtered all the other prisoners in a fit of rage after the scene in Eztli's chambers.

"I must say the young fellow is right, Preacher." That was Audie, of course. "Once when I was in Maine, I saw a lobster that had been boiled alive, and you bear a distinct resemblance to the poor creature."

"Umm," Nighthawk said in agreement.

Preacher instinctively sought darkness after the terrible light to which he'd been subjected, so his eyes were squeezed tightly shut. He forced them to open, and when he looked around he saw that he was back in the stone prison with the others.

Enough sunshine filtered through the ventilation holes for him to make out his fellow prisoners in the gloom. They were still strung up on the walls like they had been before, but he was loose, lying on the floor.

He managed to raise himself on an elbow. "How come . . . they didn't tie me up again . . . like you fellas?"

"I suppose they don't consider you a real threat at the moment," Audie said. "You're too blistered and too weak from thirst and hunger to put up a fight."

"That's what . . . they think," Preacher rasped. "Just lemme . . . get my hands on a gun . . . or a tomahawk . . ." He groaned and slumped down again as what little strength he had deserted him.

When he could talk again, he asked, "How long . . . was I gone from here?"

"A day and a half," Boone told him. "Where were you, Preacher?"

"They had me staked out . . . on top o' that damn . . . big pyramid."

"Good Lord," Audie muttered. "No wonder you look like you've been baked. Were you up there the whole time?"

"As far as . . . I know."

"They took you there when Eztli came

and got you two nights ago?" Audie asked.

Preacher thought back. His lips cracked painfully as a faint smile pulled at them. "Not . . . the whole time . . . She took me from here . . . to where she lives. I reckon she . . . wanted me to spend the night with her."

"You mean —" Boone choked off the words and sounded embarrassed again.

"I do believe that's what he means," Audie said. "For all of her considerable flaws, Eztli is a very beautiful woman. It's none of my business, Preacher —"

"That's right . . . it ain't, but it don't really matter. Tenoch showed up . . . and tried to split me from gullet to gizzard . . . with a big ol' machete . . . like the Mexicans use in the fields down south."

"A remnant of their Aztec culture, no doubt. Clearly he didn't succeed."

"Naw . . . We had . . . a pretty good tussle, though. I just about . . . had the best of him . . . when Eztli cracked a clay pitcher . . . over my head."

"I'm surprised Tenoch didn't have you killed."

"You and me both. I guess he figured . . . that'd be makin' things too easy for me." Now that he had recovered some of his strength, Preacher was able to sit up. He looked down at himself. He was still naked. His hands and face were browned to a deep, permanent tan by his life spent outdoors, but the parts of his body normally covered by his buckskins were not. Most of the time they were pale, but they were burned a painful-looking red. Blisters had popped up in places, burst, and were oozing clear liquid. He discovered that moving even the least little bit was miserable.

Slowly, he forced himself to climb to his feet and began to totter around. Since he was loose, he had to take advantage of the opportunity to look for anything he could use as a weapon.

He didn't have a chance to search much. With the usual scraping sound, men lifted the bar from the door. Preacher turned in that direction and instinctively clenched his hands into fists.

Audie said quietly, "Preacher, no. You can't fight them now. Not in the shape you're in. If you anger them too much, they might just damage you even more."

"I may not be at my full fightin' strength —"

"You're weak as a kitten and probably half-dead from thirst."

Now that Audie mentioned it, he really was spitting cotton, Preacher realized. He felt like there wasn't a drop of moisture left in him.

The door swung open. Several warriors came in, grabbed Preacher, pushed him over against the wall, and strung him up like the others, using those tough, braided ropes to bind his wrists. The fact that he wasn't able to put up a fight gnawed at his guts even worse than hunger did, but Audie was right. It wasn't the time.

When Preacher was secured, the warriors at the doorway stepped back so that four women could enter the cell. They wore buckskin dresses and appeared to be from the part of the tribe with more Indian blood. Of course, the Aztecs were Indians, too, he reminded himself, but it wasn't exactly the same thing.

Two of the women carried jugs and took them to the prisoners so the men could drink from them.

When Preacher felt that cool water sliding into his mouth and down his throat, he thought it was the best thing he had ever tasted in his life. He would have guzzled down every drop in both jugs if they had let him, but he didn't get that chance.

The other two women took tortillas from baskets they carried and held the food so the prisoners could eat. Now that he wasn't quite so desperately thirsty, Preacher realized his belly thought his throat had been cut.

He could have gobbled down a tortilla in one bite, but he forced himself to take it slow and easy. He knew that if he ate too much, it would make him sick, just as it would if he drank too much. A man couldn't get over an ordeal like the one he had endured all at once.

As he slowly chewed a bite of tortilla, he realized that one of the women was lingering in front of Boone Halliday. She had already given him a drink but gave him another one.

Boone swallowed, licked his lips, and nodded. "I'm sure much obliged to you, ma'am."

The woman smiled at him, the expression wreathing her round face. She might have offered him yet another drink, but one of the guards snapped at her. She ducked her head and moved away from Boone, but Preacher saw the glance she darted back at the young trapper.

That was interesting, Preacher thought. Mighty interesting. It might not mean anything in the long run, but obviously, it would be easier to escape from the prison if they had some help. The smile that the young Indian woman had directed at Boone was something to keep in mind.

Preacher's body might be weak and blistered at the moment, but the wheels of his brain were starting to turn once more. He was dangerous again . . . as Tenoch, Eztli, and the rest of his Aztec captors would find out sooner or later, he vowed.

Chapter 24

Imprisoned, it was difficult for Preacher to keep track of the days. He could tell when night fell, because absolute darkness filled the cell at those times. The prisoners were fed and given water twice a day, so he could have tried to count those times . . . but then he would be out of his head for a while and couldn't figure out how long he'd been that way or how much he had missed.

Eventually he gave up and concentrated on recovering from the torture Tenoch had put him through. Before he did anything else, he needed to regain his strength.

That proved to be more difficult than keeping up with the days. A couple tortillas and a few swallows of water every day were enough to keep the prisoners alive, but not much beyond that. Preacher could feel himself wasting away.

The weeping blisters on his burned skin eventually dried up and the damaged skin peeled off. It didn't hurt as much to move . . . not that he *could* move very much, strung up like he was. Despite everything, Preacher knew he was getting better. The key would be whether or not he got an opportunity to make a move before the near-starvation weakened him too much.

If there was one thing that gave him some hope, it was the way one of the young Indian women had taken a shine to Boone Halliday. She always managed to be the one who gave him a drink or fed him a tortilla. Preacher noticed that sometimes she even slipped a pepper or a chunk of meat into the tortilla without the guards being aware of it.

Even though it didn't amount to much extra food, Preacher didn't resent Boone for getting fed better than the rest of them. Maybe the young trapper wouldn't be as weak when the time came to make a break for it as he might have been otherwise.

One day while most of the other prisoners were dozing in the perpetual gloom of their cell, Preacher suggested quietly to Boone, "See if you can find out the name of that little gal who's sweet on you."

"I already have," Boone whispered back. "We've managed to learn enough of each other's language to talk a little. She's called

Zyanya."

"Zyanya," Preacher repeated. "Pretty name. She's sure got her eyes set on you."

"She's going to be disappointed," Boone said with a touch of bitterness in his voice. "Sooner or later they'll take me out and sacrifice me."

"Don't go givin' up just yet. I figure as long as a man's still drawin' breath, he's got a fightin' chance."

"A fighting chance? Preacher, we're strung up like sides of meat, and we're half-starved! Even if we got loose, we couldn't fight our way out of here."

"You'd be surprised what a man can do. Even a hungry one. Hell, maybe even *especially* a hungry one." And the thing Preacher hungered for most was vengeance on their murderous captors.

The other things that he found of interest and that helped break up the dreadful monotony of their imprisonment, were the visits of Nazar, the priest who had sort of befriended Audie. The man was short, stocky, and bald except for a couple of tufts of gray hair that stuck out from his head behind and above his ears. His scalp was wrinkled, his face sharp-featured with a beak of a nose. He reminded Preacher of a snapping turtle.

Nazar talked for hours with the former professor, both men using a mixture of English and the Aztec language and speaking so fast that Preacher couldn't really follow most of the conversations. His interest perked up one day when he heard Nazar say something about the cliffs.

The rest of the talk didn't mean anything to him, but he saw a worried frown appear on Audie's face. Audie and Nazar talked for a while longer, then the priest took his leave.

"What was that about, Audie?" Preacher asked when Nazar was gone. "You look a mite worried about somethin'."

"I am," Audie said. "According to Nazar, Tenoch has had dozens of slaves out at the cliffs every day, clearing away that avalanche. It won't be much longer until the trail to the outside world is passable again."

Preacher bit back a curse. That was both good news and bad news. If the trail was open again, he and his friends would be able to get out of the hidden valley — if they could escape from their prison.

But it also meant that Tenoch and his followers could resume their bloodthirsty ways and venture out to kill more trappers in adjoining Shadow Valley, as well as lay their hands on captives to bring back to meet an equally grisly fate in the Aztec city.

Preacher's eyes narrowed as he glanced toward Talbot. The man appeared to be asleep, but Preacher didn't trust him. If they made any plans, Talbot might betray them to their captors. It could be that he still hoped sooner or later they would let him go without killing him, if he made himself useful enough.

Preacher knew that Audie spoke several languages, including Latin, French, and Spanish. If Preacher had been able to understand those tongues, he and the little man could have conversed without Talbot knowing what they were saying. The only other languages Preacher knew, however, were a smattering of Indian tongues. Audie would know those, too, but since Talbot was a trapper and spent time among the tribes, there was a chance he would understand them, as well.

They would just have to risk it, Preacher decided. Keeping an eye on Talbot so he'd see it if the man betrayed himself by any reaction, Preacher leaned his head closer to Audie. "We got to figure out a way to get out of here. We're runnin' out of time."

"Indeed we are," Audie agreed. "It's almost time for another sacrifice, and given the grudge that Tenoch bears against you, you're liable to be the choice when he and

Toltecatl come for one of us."

"Hey, it wasn't my fault that gal Eztli took a shine to me," Preacher protested.

"No, I suppose not, but that won't make Tenoch any more kindly disposed toward you." Audie paused. "Speaking of young women taking a shine to someone . . ." He leaned forward and looked past Preacher at Boone Halliday.

"You've noticed that, too, huh?" the mountain man said.

"It would be difficult not to notice. The question remains is there any chance the girl would help us?"

"Maybe, if she's fallen for Boone as much as it seems like she has."

Boone heard Preacher whisper his name and turned his head toward them. "What?"

On the ropes holding him up, Preacher swayed over toward the young trapper. He whispered, "Keep your voice down," and nodded meaningfully toward Talbot, who still seemed to be in a stupor.

A look of understanding came over Boone's haggard, bearded face. He used what little play was in his ropes to move closer to Preacher and whispered back, "What are you talking about?"

"How to get out of here," Preacher told

him. "I reckon it's gonna depend mostly on you."

Boone's eyebrows rose in surprise. "Me? How do you figure that?"

"That gal Zyanya's in love with you. You got to convince her to help us escape."

Boone shook his head. "I can't do that. She'll get in bad trouble if she tries anything like that. They might even kill her."

"They'll kill *you* . . . they'll kill all of us, sooner or later . . . if we don't escape."

Boone couldn't dispute the grim truth of Preacher's words. They were all doomed if the situation went on like it was.

"What do you want me to do?" he asked.

CHAPTER 25

Not surprisingly, Zyanya was among the women who brought supper to the prisoners that day.

She wasn't going to miss a chance to see Boone, thought Preacher. He watched as she gave the young trapper a drink from the jug she carried, then hesitated before moving on to the other captives.

Boone leaned his head forward and spoke to her with an earnest look on his face. His voice was low enough that Preacher couldn't make out what he was saying in the mixture of languages Boone and Zyanya used to communicate.

Obviously, she understood him just fine. A look of fear suddenly appeared on her face. She controlled the reaction, but not quickly enough to keep Preacher from seeing it. He knew Boone had just suggested to her that she might find a way to help them escape.

Zyanya lowered her eyes and shook her head, the movement small enough that none of the guards would notice it. She was telling Boone she couldn't help. He spoke to her again, more urgently.

She turned away without giving him a second drink the way she usually did.

Preacher felt a flash of discouragement, but he wasn't about to give up hope. That wasn't his way. Besides, he had known from the start that it might not be easy to persuade Zyanya to help them. After all, she had lived her whole life under the iron heel of the priests and warriors. She wasn't in the habit of doing things to defy them.

When the women and the guards were gone, Boone caught Preacher's eye, sighed, and shook his head.

"Don't give up, son," Preacher whispered. "We're just gettin' started."

It galled him that he and his friends had to place their fates in the hands of a young woman, but if that was their only chance, they would seize it rather than surrendering to despair.

Over the next couple days, despair seemed to be winning. Zyanya didn't show up with the other women. Her place had been taken by someone else, a woman who glared at all of them as if she resented being pressed into duty. Clearly, she wasn't going to be any help.

Boone was almost beside himself with worry. When it became obvious that Zyanya wasn't coming back, he said to Preacher, "What if she told somebody about what I asked her, and they killed her?"

"They wouldn't have any reason to do that," Preacher assured the young trapper.

In truth it was hard to predict what the Aztecs might do. Savagery seemed to run deep in their blood, at least for some of them.

He went on. "They ain't treatin' us any different than they were before, so chances are she didn't say anything. Maybe she's just thinkin' it over, pretendin' to be sick or somethin', while she figures out what to do." That might be a slender hope, he realized, but he was going to hang on to it anyway.

The next day, the priest Nazar came to the prison. Audie had explained to Preacher that it was Nazar's job to study the signs and portents and suggest to Tenoch which of the prisoners should next be sacrificed to the war god Huitzilopochtli. The final decision was Tenoch's, of course, as the high priest, but he relied on Nazar's counsel.

Since Nazar had befriended Audie, it was likely he would keep the former professor alive as long as possible, and he might even extend that courtesy to Nighthawk, since the big Crow was Audie's partner. So far, however, Nazar hadn't seemed overly friendly to Preacher or Boone.

Nazar planted himself directly in front of Preacher and glared at him. His bald head swayed forward on his scrawny neck, making him look more like a snapping turtle than ever. Nazar said something over his shoulder to the pair of guards who had come into the cell with him. They backed off into the doorway.

Nazar surprised the mountain man by saying to him in English, "You are the one called Preacher."

It didn't sound like a question, but Preacher said, "Yeah, that's right."

"You are the leader of these men."

"I wouldn't say that. Reckon I'm in the same boat they are, if you hadn't noticed, old son. And when did you learn to talk English so good?"

"I've been teaching him more, Preacher," Audie said. "He wanted to be able to talk to you. He knows how to recognize a natural commander when he sees one, I suppose."

They were all whispering, but Nazar inclined his head toward Talbot and said, "Quietly. We do not want that one to hear."

"Fine by me," Preacher said. "What is it you want, Nazar?"

"You are the one who told this boy to ask Zyanya for her help. To ask her to risk her life."

Preacher's jaw tightened. So Zyanya had said something after all. The jig was up.

Or was it? Nazar wasn't yelling for their heads or threatening them. Maybe the priest had something else in mind.

"You're the one spinnin' this yarn," Preacher grated.

Nazar lowered his voice even more as he said, "I have told no one. Zyanya is the daughter of my sister. I would not betray her. But neither will I allow her to throw her life away."

"Nobody's askin' her to do that."

Nazar got a contemplative look on his ugly face. "She truly cares for the young man called Boone. She came to me and asked me what she should do. I told her that she does not dare help you unless two promises are made."

Preacher's spirits leaped. His word was his bond, but at the moment, he would promise just about anything if it meant they had a chance of getting out of that miserable cell. "What does she want?" he asked Nazar.

The priest scowled. "When you leave this place, she wishes to go with you. She would be Boone's woman."

Preacher glanced over at Boone, who looked interested but puzzled. He probably couldn't make out what they were saying.

"I don't reckon that'll be a problem," Preacher said.

"You speak for the young one?"

"I do."

If Boone didn't like it, they could hash that out later. Anyway, he'd acted like he was genuinely fond of Zyanya, and she was a comely young woman, so Preacher didn't figure it would be a problem.

"What's the other thing she wants?" Preacher asked.

"Before you leave this valley . . . you must kill Tenoch. She fears his vengeance if she betrays him and he still lives."

Preacher looked intently at Nazar for a long moment, then said, "It's sort of hard to guarantee somethin' like that, but I can promise you I'll do my dead-level best to kill that miserable varmint."

He wasn't sure at first if that was going to be enough for Nazar, but finally the turtle-like priest nodded.

"Tonight, she will once again be with the women who bring food and water. She will bring drink for the guards as well, special drink that will make them sleep. When they are no longer awake, she and I will come and free you. She will go with your young friend and the others and leave the valley."

Preacher took a deep breath. "The trail through the cliffs . . . ?"

"A passage has been opened. It is narrow, but one man at a time can get through it."

Preacher nodded. "What about you and me? You didn't say what we're gonna do?"

"We will fulfill the second part of the bargain," Nazar said. "We will go to the temple where Tenoch's quarters are, and there you will slay him."

A grim smile played over Preacher's lips as he nodded. "You got yourself a deal, mister."

CHAPTER 26

Once Nazar was gone, Preacher told first Audie and then Boone about the plan he and the priest had hatched.

Boone gulped. "You told him I'd marry Zyanya if we got out of here?"

"Seemed like the thing to do at the time," Preacher said dryly, "what with him makin' that a condition of them helpin' us."

"But Preacher, I hadn't really planned on getting hitched quite so soon . . ."

"You probably didn't plan on gettin' your heart carved out by a bunch of heathen Aztecs, neither," Preacher pointed out. "You and Zyanya can work everything out between you once we've escaped from this hellhole. Until then, we're gonna do whatever we have to."

Boone nodded. "You're right, of course. Anyway, I'm pretty fond of Zyanya." He summoned up a smile. "This might turn out all right after all."

Preacher just grunted. That evening couldn't come too soon to suit him. He was ready to get out of the prison — and more than ready for another showdown with Tenoch.

Of course, because of that eagerness, time seemed to drag more slowly than ever.

Finally, the faint light that came through the ventilation openings began to dim with the approach of dusk. The women would be there soon with their meager food and water.

A few minutes later, Preacher heard the guards removing the bar from the door. The heavy panel scraped open. Spear-carrying guards came in first, followed by the women. He didn't see Zyanya among them. His jaw tightened as he thought that the plan must have fallen through for some reason.

She appeared in the doorway, carrying one of the regular water jugs as well as a small earthen jug that she handed to one of the guards. The man laughed as he took it and said something that meant nothing to Preacher. She smiled shyly in response, and he knew she was playing up to the man. The guard turned to his companion, grinned, and hefted the jug meaningfully.

Neither of them drank from it, but

Preacher told himself it was just a matter of time.

The rest of the meal proceeded as usual. Zyanya seemed nervous when she gave water to the prisoners, but he could tell she was trying to control the feeling. She didn't linger with Boone the way she usually did but rather treated him exactly the same as the others. Clearly, she didn't want to arouse any suspicion in the guards.

After all the prisoners had been fed and given a drink, the women left. The door closed, and the bar fell back into its brackets with an ominous thud.

All they could do was wait.

Time crept by again. The walls of the prison were so thick that even Preacher's keen ears couldn't hear anything that might be going on outside. No one knew about the escape plan except Preacher, Boone, Audie, and Nighthawk, so the other captives dozed off as they usually did. Several of them began to snore loudly.

The sound of the bar being taken off the door roused them from sleep. One man muttered, "It ain't mornin' yet. What the hell . . . ?"

The door swung open. Against the faint light from outside, Preacher saw the silhouettes of two people enter quickly.

"What's going on here?" Talbot asked in a loud, frightened voice. "Are they coming for another sacrifice? They can't do that at night —"

"Hush," Preacher hissed. "Shut your mouth, Talbot, if you want to live."

One of the figures approached Preacher. A stray beam of starlight from one of the openings in the roof reflected off metal. Preacher figured it was a knife.

Question was, would the person use the blade to cut Preacher loose — or slash his throat?

The mountain man got his answer a second later as the figure raised the knife and began sawing on the tough, braided ropes around his wrists.

"Be quiet," Nazar whispered. "We will have you free as quickly as we can."

Preacher heard movement to his right. That would be Zyanya cutting Boone loose, more than likely.

A moment later, the young trapper gasped involuntarily as his arms dropped from their long confinement. "Damn it. I can't even feel my hands anymore."

"You will," Preacher told him. The ropes holding him parted and allowed him to lower his arms, as well. Almost immediately, his fingers began to tingle painfully as blood rushed into them again. He shook his hands to speed up the process while Nazar moved on to cut Audie loose.

"Are the guards out cold?" Preacher asked.

"For now," Nazar replied. "I do not know how long they will remain that way. We have no time to waste."

"Don't intend to. Boone, gimme your shirt."

"My shirt?" Boone asked, sounding surprised.

"Yeah. I reckon you fellas have probably gotten used to me bein' nekkid since they brought me back from bein' staked out on that pyramid, but I haven't. Don't particularly want to run around this city with no clothes on, neither."

"All right. Here."

Preacher reached out, found the buckskin shirt that Boone was extending toward him, and tied the sleeves around his waist so the garment served as a crude loincloth. He figured he looked more than a little ridiculous but didn't really care.

He wished they had a torch so he could see what was going on, but they couldn't afford to show any light. He moved toward the doorway, which was visible as a faint gray rectangle, and paused on the threshold to look outside.

The two guards were slumped a few feet away. Preacher stepped over to the closest guard and picked up a spear that had been dropped when the guards passed out.

For a second, he considered plunging the weapon into the warrior's heart, killing him while he was unconscious — probably the smartest thing to do. A man who left enemies alive behind him sometimes found that moment of mercy coming back to haunt him.

Before he could strike, the former captives began shuffling out of the prison. Audie and Nighthawk were first, followed by Boone and Zyanya, then Nazar and the rest of the trappers. They were all gaunt and weak from hunger and couldn't move very fast.

Nazar faced Preacher. "Now you will come with me to the temple. Zyanya will take these others to the Path of the War God."

"I reckon that's what you folks call that trail through the cliffs."

"Yes. Tenoch and Eztli proclaimed it a gift from Huitzilopochtli given to our people so that they could resume the sacrifices in his honor."

Preacher was prepared to honor the bargain he had struck with the turtle-like priest, although the odds of him being able to invade the temple, kill Tenoch, and get out alive were pretty damn slim. The mountain man had given his word, though.

First, he wanted to see his friends safely on their way. He turned to Audie, Nighthawk, and Boone. "I'll see you fellas on the outside —"

Talbot chose that moment to make a break for it. Preacher knew the man intended to betray them, so he wheeled around to give chase, but Nighthawk beat him to it. The big Crow bounded after the fleeing man, reached out, and grabbed Talbot's shoulder, jerking him to a halt. Talbot opened his mouth to shout an alarm, but he barely got a peep out before Nighthawk's big right hand clamped over his mouth and stifled the yell.

Nighthawk didn't stop there. He slipped his left arm under his right, took hold of Talbot's shoulder in an iron grip, and held the man steady while his right hand pulled back sharply, twisting Talbot's head so far to the side that his neck snapped with a sound like a breaking branch. When Nighthawk let go of him, the man folded up in a limp heap.

"Umm," Nighthawk said quietly.

"You're right," Audie said. "We never

would have been able to trust him. Even if we'd stopped him from alerting anyone now, he would have tried to betray us again at the first opportunity. Fear dissolves some men's resolve."

With that threat taken care of, Preacher quickly said his good-byes. He shook hands with Boone, Audie, and Nighthawk. Zyanya tugged on Boone's arm, urging him to hurry. The group faded away into the darkness, leaving Preacher and Nazar standing in front of the prison.

"Now we must hurry as well, to the temple —" the priest began.

The scuff of a foot on stone warned Preacher. He turned in time to see that one of the guards had regained consciousness. The man had picked up his spear, and he lunged forward with the point streaking toward the mountain man's heart.

CHAPTER 27

Preacher reacted instantly. He still held the other spear, so he used it to parry the deadly thrust. The shafts clashed against each other as he turned the guard's spear aside.

The next second, as the guard's momentum carried him closer, Preacher reversed his motion and buried the head of his spear in the warrior's chest. The man gasped in pain and shock. Preacher drove forward with his feet against the paving stones, forcing the guard backwards until the man hit the wall of the prison.

The spear head ripped all the way through his body and grated against the carved stone wall behind him. The man's head slumped forward and his arms drooped in death. His spear clattered on the ground as he dropped it for the second and final time.

Instead of trying to pull his spear free, Preacher released it and let it fall to the ground with the guard's body. As he stooped to pick up the second spear, he heard a gurgling sound and looked over to see Nazar straightening from being bent over the other guard.

A dark pool was already spreading around the man's head. Nazar had slashed his throat with the same knife he had used to cut the prisoners' bonds.

"I regret taking the life of any of my people," he said quietly, "but they were followers of Tenoch. Their hearts already belong to the War God. Now their spirits do, as well."

"You're a priest. Don't that make you one of 'em?"

Nazar shook his head. "Not all of us are devoted to Huitzilopochtli, nor do we like seeing one group of our people enslave the other."

"Well, however you feel about it, I'm glad you're on our side right now," Preacher assured him. "Lead the way to that temple you were talkin' about. It ain't where Eztli took me that other time, is it?"

"No. It stands before the Great Pyramid."

The two men hurried along the street in silence. The hour was late enough that no one was out and about. The city seemed eerily deserted, although Preacher knew there were hundreds of Aztecs nearby in the buildings they passed, but as long as the city slept and no one raised the alarm, that was the only thing that mattered.

As they approached the Great Pyramid, the huge edifice loomed over them. Preacher didn't like the looks of it. He remembered all too well the time he had spent up there at the top of it, baking in the merciless sun.

Nazar veered to the side before they got there, and led Preacher toward another large building, though the pyramid dwarfed it for sheer size. The impressive building resembled Eztli's domicile, but it was larger and more ornate than the building where the high priestess lived.

It made sense that Tenoch had claimed the fanciest place in town for himself, thought Preacher. A fella as arrogant as the high priest wouldn't be satisfied with anything less.

A couple guards were posted outside the door, visible in the light from a torch stuck in a bracket on the elaborately carved wall. Nazar drew Preacher into an alcove, pointed to the two sentries, and whispered, "I will distract them, but you will have to get close enough to finish them off."

"Keep their eyes on you and I'll do it," Preacher promised. "Just give me your knife."

Nazar hesitated before handing over the blade, but only for a second.

Preacher waited as Nazar strode forward boldly and entered the circle of light cast by the torch. If the wizened little priest was nervous, he gave no sign of it. The guards raised their spears as he approached, then relaxed as they recognized him. They appeared to be puzzled as to what he was doing there at that time of night, however.

He began speaking in a rapid, urgent voice, no doubt spinning some sort of wild tale to keep the guards' attention while Preacher slipped through the shadows at the edge of the street until he was edging along the same wall of the building where the guards stood at the entrance.

He stopped where he was still hidden by the darkness and hefted the spear, judging its weight and balance. He did the same with the knife, which was a regular hunting knife that must have been taken from one of the captive fur trappers, rather than a sharpened flint weapon of the sort the Aztecs used in their bloody rituals.

When he was confident that he was familiar enough with the spear and the knife, he moved forward and struck rapidly. As he reached the edge of the torchlight, he heaved the spear with deadly accuracy. It whipped past Nazar, who didn't seem to be running out of steam, and struck the guard on the left of his chest, the head penetrating so deeply the man died instantly on his feet as his heart was skewered.

Nazar had the sense to throw himself to the ground out of the way, so Preacher had a clear shot at the other guard. He threw the knife with a snap of his wrist, making the knife revolve once in its flight before the blade lodged in the guard's throat. The man dropped his spear and made a choking sound as he pawed at the knife. He succeeded in pulling it free, but that just made his bright red blood spray out with more force. He collapsed, falling forward across Nazar.

With a look of revulsion on his turtle-like face, the little priest scrambled out from under the corpse. His buckskins were stained with the man's blood. He glared at Preacher as the mountain man hurried up to him.

"Sorry," Preacher said with a grim smile. "But as long as it ain't your blood, I reckon you'll live."

"Gather the weapons," Nazar snapped. "There will be more guards inside."

Preacher picked up the knife and wrenched the spear loose from the first guard's body. He didn't give the knife back to Nazar but tucked it into his makeshift loincloth then took hold of the larger of the two men and started dragging him toward the shadows.

"What are you doing?" Nazar asked impatiently.

"This fella's leggin's and moccasins look like they'll fit me close enough. I can move around and fight better if I got some clothes on." Preacher could tell by the way Nazar muttered something in response that the priest wasn't happy about the delay. He ignored that and quickly got dressed in the dead man's leggings and moccasins. The shirt was too soaked with blood to bother with. Preacher tried to put on Boone's shirt, but it was too small for his shoulders. Better to go barechested than to have the garment binding on him, he decided.

With that done, he picked up the spear and rejoined Nazar at the door.

The priest said, "There will be more guards inside. Let me go first."

"Fine by me. You're the one who knows your way around. Just be careful."

Nazar swung the door open, straining to budge its heavy weight. The hallway inside was dimly lit by torches. Preacher didn't see any more guards, but he took Nazar's word for it that they were there somewhere.

Figuring it would be a good idea, he dragged the other dead guard into the shadows, too, so that if anybody happened by, the carcass wouldn't be lying out there in plain sight. He couldn't do anything about the blood splashed darkly on the paving stones, but maybe that wouldn't be quite so noticeable. The stones were already pretty dark in places.

Back at the doorway, he looked along the hall but didn't see Nazar anywhere. A grimace tightened the mountain man's lips. The corridor inside was long and straight, with no doors that he could see. He didn't understand how the priest could have gotten out of sight so quickly.

Standing in the open was just asking for trouble, Preacher told himself. He stepped into the building and eased the door most of the way closed behind him, leaving a small gap between the door and the jamb so he could grab the door and get it open in a hurry if he needed to.

Holding the spear at the ready, he catfooted along the corridor. The soft moccasins on his feet made no sound on the stone floor.

Every few steps, he paused to listen. The place was quiet . . . or almost so. As he stopped for the fourth time, he heard something and realized it was a murmur of voices. He couldn't make out any of the words, but since whoever was talking probably was speaking the Aztec tongue, he wouldn't have understood it anyway.

Suddenly, a man let out a pained yelp.

That was Nazar, Preacher thought, hurrying forward. As he came even with a woven tapestry hanging on the wall, he heard more noises from behind it.

The tapestry covered a doorway. He thrust it aside and stepped into a room where Nazar was struggling with two more guards. One had hold of him, and the other, wearing a big grin, was about to smash the little priest's brains out with a war club.

CHAPTER 28

Preacher leaped forward and rammed the spear into the guard's back with such force that the point went all the way through his body and tore a bloody exit wound in his chest. The war club slipped from the dying man's fingers.

Preacher caught it before it hit the floor.

The other guard was so surprised by his comrade's grisly, unexpected death that Nazar was able to writhe desperately out of his grip. With the priest out of his way, Preacher swung the war club with one hand and crushed the second warrior's skull with brutal efficiency.

As that man's corpse crumpled to the floor, Nazar stared at Preacher and exclaimed, "Never have I seen anyone kill so swiftly, so skillfully! Are you certain you are not the god of war himself in human form?"

"Not hardly," Preacher said. "I've had to get good at killin' because so damn many folks have tried to kill me over the years. Only reason I'm still here is 'cause I was able to beat 'em to it." He hefted the war club, freshly stained with blood, and nodded approvingly. "Reckon I'll take this along with us. It's a handy little thing."

He put his foot on the dead man's body to brace it while he pulled the spear free then Nazar pushed the tapestry aside and they returned to the dimly-lit corridor.

"Any more guards in this place that need killin'?" Preacher asked in a whisper.

"I do not know. Probably not, but there could be."

"How come those two were fixin' to murder you? You're an important fella around here, ain't you?"

"I was," Nazar replied with a bitter edge in his voice. "There was a time when I would have been high priest. But Tenoch rose to power after the Great Shaking by claiming that Huitzilopochtli was responsible for rending the earth and opening a path out of the valley. His followers were warriors, so they have been able to force their will on everyone else in the city."

"Leavin' you out in the cold, eh?"

Nazar shrugged his scrawny shoulders.

It could be that Nazar had decided to help them because he was jealous of Tenoch's power, Preacher reflected. And maybe Nazar wanted the beautiful Eztli for himself, although Preacher couldn't quite imagine those two together. Maybe it was really Nazar who wanted Tenoch dead more than Zyanya did.

None of that was important. No matter what Nazar's motive for helping them might be, he and Zyanya were the only friends Preacher and the other former prisoners had in that lost valley.

The corridor began to turn sharply back and forth.

The Aztecs didn't seem to care much for straight lines in their construction, thought Preacher. Everything was angles and bends with them.

Nazar lifted a hand and motioned for Preacher to stop as they approached another turn. He was glad that the priest seemed to know where they were, because he sure didn't. Nazar tiptoed up to the bend to peek around it, then crooked his fingers to summon Preacher.

Another short corridor lay around the turn. After a few feet, it opened into a large chamber. Broad marble steps led down to a sunken area piled with furs for sleeping.

Tenoch was stretched out facedown on those furs, snoring. His powerfully muscled body was nude.

Beside him, also asleep and equally unclothed, sprawled the sleek reddish-gold form of Eztli.

Nazar pointed at the slumbering forms and whispered, “Kill them. Kill them both!”

So he didn’t want Eztli for himself after all, thought Preacher.

“I promised you I’d kill Tenoch, but I don’t much cotton to the idea of killin’ a woman in her sleep.”

“You fool! She is just as dangerous as he is. No, she is more dangerous! Either of them would torture you to death and smile as they did it.”

Preacher didn’t doubt that, but his mind was working and his thoughts went back to the plan he’d had briefly, a couple weeks earlier. With Eztli as a hostage, his chances of getting out of the valley alive might improve considerably. “I’ll take care of Tenoch then we’re gonna grab Eztli. I’ll keep her quiet while you lead the way outta here.”

Stubbornly, Nazar shook his head. “No one knows that I betrayed them. All the guards who might have seen me are dead, and Zyanya is on her way out of the valley with your friends. Once Tenoch and Eztli are dead and you are gone —”

"You can grab that power you wanted all along, is that it?" Preacher interrupted him.

Nazar glared at him. "You wanted my help, and now you question me!"

"It was that little gal of Boone's who brought you in on this, not me. And I don't care what you do once I'm gone. All I know is I'm not gonna put a spear in that woman's heart or stove her head in while she's sleepin'. That just ain't the sort of thing I can do."

Nazar made a disgusted sound and whispered, "Such worthless argument is the practice of lizards and idiots! Give me back my knife. *I* will kill her."

Preacher shook his head. "I don't intend to do that, neither. You can come with me, and if you need to, grab her and keep her quiet while I'm dealin' with that big varmint."

Nazar looked like he wanted to argue some more, but after a moment, he jerked his head in a nod. "Come. We have already wasted enough time."

Preacher leaned the war club against the wall, figuring a spear thrust would be the quickest, surest way of killing Tenoch. He didn't want the high priest putting up a fight. Preacher had regained some of his strength after the torture he had endured, but he wasn't at his peak. An all-out battle against Tenoch was too risky.

A small flame guttered from a wick in a vessel full of oil, casting a dim, flickering light over the sleepers as Preacher and Nazar approached them. Preacher felt no compunction about killing Tenoch in his sleep. He had done the same thing to dozens of Blackfoot warriors over the years because he knew they would be all too happy to kill him if they got the chance.

Logically, he knew he should feel the same way about Eztli, but he couldn't quite cast aside the way he had been raised. Evil or not, she was a woman.

A beautiful woman, he thought as he ran his gaze over the smooth skin made even more tawny by the candlelight. Her long hair lay over her shoulder like a sweep of pure midnight. Her breathing was soft and regular.

Preacher and Nazar abruptly froze as Eztli made a small murmuring sound and moved. She was just shifting around in her sleep, though, and her breathing smoothed out again in seconds. Preacher stepped closer and raised the spear, preparing to drive it home in Tenoch's back with both hands and all the strength he could muster.

The thrust had not yet fallen when he realized a subtle change in Tenoch's snoring.

Preacher's instincts began to clamor in alarm. The high priest was shamming! He knew an enemy was slipping up on him and was only pretending to be asleep, waiting until the intruder was close enough for him to make his move!

Even as that flashed through Preacher's mind, the mountain man lunged forward and brought the spear down with blinding speed. Tenoch was incredibly fast, too, and rolled aside at the last instant. The spear point went through the sleeping furs and hit the stone floor with such a powerful impact that the shaft snapped, leaving Preacher holding only a length of polished wood. Tenoch kicked out and slammed the sole of a bare foot against the side of Preacher's knee.

Preacher staggered from the kick but managed to stay on his feet. He slashed at Tenoch's head with the broken shaft. The high priest blocked it with a hastily upflung forearm.

From the corner of his eye, Preacher saw Eztli struggling to wake up. A state of confusion obviously gripped her, and before she could figure out what was going on, Nazar threw himself on her and clamped a hand over her mouth to keep her from shouting.

Tenoch rolled again, avoiding another

swipe of the broken spear, using his momentum to surge lithely to his feet. He and Preacher faced each other across several feet of stone floor.

Tenoch grinned. "Pree-char."

Obviously, Eztli had taught him the mountain man's name.

He said something else, but Preacher didn't understand it. However, it seemed almost like Tenoch was glad to see him.

Of course. Tenoch relished the opportunity for another showdown with Preacher . . . especially since the mountain man wasn't in top fighting form. Tenoch figured it would go quickly and be a savage pleasure for him.

Preacher would just have to show him that he was wrong about that.

With a laugh, Tenoch charged him, powerful hands reaching out with the desire to smash and crush.

Chapter 29

The stars and a quarter moon cast enough light for Audie, Nighthawk, Boone, Zyanya, and their companions to see where they were going. Seeing the cliffs looming to the east, Audie and Nighthawk could have led the others in that direction, but Zyanya was more familiar with the Aztec city than any of them, so Audie was perfectly content to let her take the lead. She held Boone's hand and tugged the young trapper along beside her as the group of fugitives hurried through the streets.

Audie gave thought to what he knew about the Aztec empire. It was very old, the settlement one of the final remnants. It had flourished when many European civilizations were just beginning. But it had developed in a different place, under different conditions, with a different culture and traditions. Aztec cities had no walls around them, no stockades with a castle looming in the center as many European fiefdoms did. The outskirts of the city were open, gradually turning into cultivated fields.

This is good for us, Audie mused. *We won't have to make it past any gates or guards.*

If they could leave the city behind them without being discovered, they stood a good chance of getting away.

There was still one possible obstacle. The craggy peaks and the sheer cliffs served as a natural barrier around the valley, protecting it the way stone walls and moats did in those European settlements Audie had been thinking about. If Tenoch was any sort of tactician at all — and since he was the war chief, he had to have at least some cunning — he would have posted guards at the newly reopened passage through the cliffs.

Quietly, Nighthawk said, "Umm."

"I was just thinking the same thing, old friend," Audie said. "You and I are living proof of the old adage about great minds working alike."

Zyanya suddenly stopped and pulled Boone into the dark mouth of an alley with one hand as she waved the other at the rest of the trappers, motioning for them to follow. They all retreated quickly into the shadows. Boone put his mouth next to Zyanya's ear and whispered, "What is it?"

"Warriors," she whispered back, nodding toward the street they had just abandoned.

For the next minute or so, the trappers all held their breath as several buckskin-clad Aztec warriors walked by in the street, carrying spears and war clubs.

Audie couldn't detect any urgency in their attitude. They were talking quietly among themselves, and the few words he could make out sounded innocuous. They were either going somewhere to take up guard duties, or else they were some sort of night watch, patrolling the streets.

In a couple minutes, the warriors were gone, and the desperate men hiding in the shadows were able to heave sighs of relief.

They resumed their flight, with Zyanya leading the way.

A short time later, they left the city behind without encountering any more warriors. Zyanya kept them moving at a fast pace. Audie struggled to keep up.

After a while, Nighthawk picked him up to carry him. Normally, Audie would have protested, but under the circumstances it was imperative that they not waste any time. He knew his pride and dignity were less important than escaping from the Aztec city.

Since it was the middle of the night, the fields were empty. The fugitives used the main trail leading to the cliffs without having to worry about someone seeing them. The farther behind the city fell, the better Audie felt about their chances.

He just wished that he knew how Preacher was doing.

If there was anybody in the world capable of attempting something as daring as invading Tenoch's inner sanctum and slaying the brutal high priest, it was the big mountain man called Preacher. Audie had absolutely no doubt about that.

The closer they came to the cliffs, the taller those dizzying heights soared, blocking out more of the stars. Audie began to hope they would reach the passage to Shadow Valley — the Path of the War God, old Nazar had called it — without incident.

Zyanya suddenly hissed and darted off the trail into the trees, taking Boone Halliday with her. Audie, Nighthawk, and the others followed without wasting any time. Crouched in the shadows under the spreading limbs of the pines, Nighthawk lowered Audie to the ground. The former professor rested a hand on the rough trunk of a tree and peered intently back toward the trail.

He heard footsteps and voices, then saw half a dozen warriors troop past, heading toward the city. Boone leaned down and whispered in Audie's ear, "They must've been out at the cliffs. No other place for them to be around here."

Just as quietly, Audie said, "Ask Zyanya if the passage is guarded."

Boone consulted with the young woman, then returned to Audie's side. "She doesn't know. She worked in the fields or in the city and never had anything to do with that."

"It's the only thing that makes sense. Those men must have been posted there for the first half of the night. Judging by the stars the last time I looked at them, we're about halfway to dawn. Just the right time for guard shifts to be changing. That was probably what was going on with those warriors back in the city."

"And the fellas who just went past us are the ones who got relieved to go back to the city."

"That's the way I figure it," Audie said grimly. "I'm open to any other explanation you care to come up with."

Boone sighed and shook his head. "Nope, that's the only thing that makes any sense. It means when we get there, we're gonna run right into half a dozen warriors who were put there to stop anybody from going through."

The men they had hidden from were gone.

Audie stepped to the edge of the trees and looked back at the city. He didn't see any lights or hear any outcry. They had hoped that their escape wouldn't be discovered until morning, and so far that seemed to be the case.

He returned to the others. "At least we'll have surprise on our side. The guards won't expect anyone to try getting out of the valley tonight. We can't just walk up to them openly, though. Now that we have a strong indication that the path is guarded, we need a plan to deal with them."

"It'd help if we all had pistols and rifles," Boone said.

"Umm," Nighthawk said.

Audie chuckled. "Yes, if wishes were horses, indeed, old friend." He looked around at the other fugitives. The group numbered eleven, counting himself. "At least the odds are on our side, if not the weaponry. I believe that here is what we should do . . ."

A single tall figure approached the head of the trail, where it ended at the passage through the cliffs. In the faint light, the bulkiness of that figure was barely noticeable.

Audie was counting on that as he clung to

Nighthawk's broad back. They had pulled this trick before, but usually it was easier because Nighthawk slung a blanket over his shoulders and let it hang down to conceal Audie. They didn't have a blanket, so Audie had to hang on to Nighthawk's buckskins and press himself as close to his friend's powerful form as he could.

The extra weight was nothing to the big Crow. He walked as tall and straight as ever. His stride was bold as brass as he approached the opening in the cliffs.

Three warriors suddenly appeared, emerging from the shadows to confront Nighthawk with leveled spears. Nighthawk stopped, crossed his arms over his broad chest, and regarded the Aztecs with complete disdain.

One of the guards spewed words at him. Audie understood enough to know that the man was demanding to be told where Nighthawk thought he was going. Nighthawk must have gotten the gist of the question, too, because he leveled an arm at the dark passage and declared, "Umm."

That brought laughter from the guards. One of them spoke over his shoulder, and the other three warriors came out of the passage to join them. That had been one of the goals of the ploy, to draw all six guards out into the open, and that had been accomplished. They just needed to get a little closer . . .

One of the warriors who seemed particularly amused by the confrontation stepped in front of Nighthawk and lowered his spear, jabbing a hand against the big Crow's chest as if to shove him back toward the city.

That was the moment, and Audie and Nighthawk knew it. Nighthawk's hand flashed up, grabbed the guard's outstretched arm, and jerked him closer.

At the same instant, Audie let go of Nighthawk's buckskins and dropped to the ground. Rushing nimbly around his friend's tree-trunk-like legs, he clubbed his hands together and brought them up with crushing force into the groin of the nearest guard, who howled in pain and doubled over as he dropped his spear.

Instantly, the trail was a whirlwind of action.

CHAPTER 30

As soon as Nighthawk had the guard within reach, he grabbed the man's clothes at the waist and lifted him by that grip and the one he had on the man's arm. The guard was too shocked to do anything, and by the time he tried to fight back, it was too late.

In an awesome display of strength, Nighthawk lifted the man over his head and pitched him at the other guards.

They went down like ninepins, except for the man who had already collapsed from Audie's blow.

Audie snatched up that man's spear and thrust it into him — nothing diminutive about the strength in the little man's arms and shoulders. He buried the spear point deep in the guard's chest.

Nighthawk bounded among the fallen guards. He reached down, grabbed two by the neck, and slammed their heads together. The crunch of bone at the impact meant they wouldn't be getting up any time soon — if ever.

In a matter of seconds, three of the guards were out of the fight. The violence had been that swift and brutal.

The remaining three guards shrieked in rage as they scrambled to their feet to put up a fight. One of them thrust a spear at Nighthawk, who twisted out of the way just in time.

Before that guard could strike again, Boone came flying out of the night and tackled him from behind. As they went down, two more trappers joined the fight, swarming over the warrior and wrenching the spear away from him. He made a choking sound as one of the trappers drove the point through his neck.

Several more trappers joined the melee, jumping another guard, dragging him down, and bludgeoning him with rocks they had picked up.

The third guard swung a war club at Audie's head, but Audie dived out of the way. A couple trappers hit the guard from behind. Already off balance from the missed swing, he couldn't stop himself from falling. Once he had, he didn't have a chance. Still holding one of the spears, Audie rolled over and skewered it through the man's guts.

That finished off the last of the guards.

As Audie climbed to his feet, he saw that all of his companions were breathing hard, except for Nighthawk. Audie was pretty winded, himself. All of them were in bad shape from their captivity, except the indomitable Crow. He seemed to be made of iron, as always.

Zyanya ran out of the trees and threw her arms around Boone's neck, hugging him tightly.

He returned the embrace for a second, then asked, "Is everybody all right?"

One of the men said, "Looks like Rankin's hurt pretty bad."

Audie stepped over to the wounded trapper, who was sitting on the ground with his back propped up by a man who knelt behind him. Even in the bad light, Audie could see the dark stain at Rankin's midsection. "What happened?"

"One o' them . . . damn warriors . . . got me with a spear while we were scufflin'," Rankin gasped. "Felt like it . . . went pretty deep."

"I'm sorry, my friend," Audie murmured. "I fear your judgment is accurate."

"I'll be . . . goin' under . . . won't I?"

Gently, Audie probed the injury with one hand. Rankin's breath hissed between his teeth as he took a sharply indrawn breath.

"Your vitals have been pierced," Audie said. "I'm afraid there's nothing we can do." *Nothing except hope that death comes quickly, rather than lingering,* he thought.

"You reckon you could maybe . . . say somethin' purty? I've always . . . plumb admired . . . the way you talk, Audie."

"Of course. I'm sure there are some Scriptures that would be of comfort —"

"Naw, I never was . . . much of a churchgoer. . . . Don't know if . . . the Lord'll have me . . . or not."

"The immortal Bard of Avon, then," Audie said as he gripped Rankin's shoulder. "From *Julius Caesar,* I quote: 'Cowards die many times before their deaths; the valiant never taste of death but once.' You're a valiant man, my friend."

"Yeah . . ." Rankin breathed. "That's more . . . like it."

Audie had to swallow hard before he could go on. " 'We few, we happy few, we band of brothers; for he today that sheds his blood with me . . .' "

Rankin's last breath went out of him with a sigh.

" '. . . shall be my brother,' " Audie finished in a whisper.

A respectful silence followed the words,

but everyone knew they couldn't afford to delay too long.

After a moment Boone said, "We'd better get going."

"Damn it," one of the trappers rasped. "Ain't we even gonna bury him?"

"There's no time —"

"Nighthawk and I will do it," Audie said.

Boone looked at him. "Wait a minute. You're not coming with us?"

"Umm," Nighthawk said.

Audie came to his feet. "Yes, I've been thinking about it a great deal, too. We'll give poor Rankin a proper burial, or at least build a cairn over him, and if Preacher hasn't shown up by then, we're going back to find him."

"Are you . . . ? That's crazy, Audie! We just got out of that city, and now you want to go back?"

"We're not going to abandon our friend. We've been through too much with Preacher, Nighthawk and I have. He would never abandon us, and we can't do that to him."

"He told us all to go on and get out of this damn valley," Boone pointed out.

"I'm aware of that. Still, the duty of friendship remains."

"I consider Preacher a friend, too, you know."

"But you haven't known him as long as we have," Audie said with a smile.

"I can't talk the two of you out of this?"

Audie shook his head. "No."

Zyanya was tugging impatiently on Boone's arm. He glanced down at her, then looked again at Audie and Nighthawk and nodded. "I think I understand. At any rate, all I can do is wish you good luck."

"Umm," the big Crow said.

"Nighthawk speaks for me in wishing you the same," Audie added.

With that, Boone turned toward the passage through the cliffs and put his arm around Zyanya's shoulders as she fell in beside him. Several of the other trappers said so long to Audie and Nighthawk, then they followed the young couple.

Within minutes, all of them had disappeared, swallowed up by the utter darkness inside the crack in the earth that led to Shadow Valley.

Audie picked up one of the spears and told Nighthawk, "I'll see if I can scoop out a shallow grave with this. You find some rocks that we can put on top of it to form a cairn."

Audie knew that with Nighthawk's great

strength, the Crow would find rocks big enough that no scavengers would be able to budge them once they were in place. Rankin's body would not be disturbed.

Audie picked a place well off the trail, and the two of them set to work.

Digging a grave with a spear was a difficult task, especially when the ground was as rocky as it was. Audie kept at it, though, as the stars wheeled through the ebony sky overhead. After a while, having piled some suitable rocks nearby, Nighthawk took over the digging.

When they had a hole a couple feet deep and big enough for Rankin's body, they lowered the man into it gently. They had no blanket or any other sort of shroud to wrap around him, but that couldn't be helped. They scraped the dirt back into the crude grave, then Nighthawk placed the rocks on top of it, building a low mound.

Both men stepped back.

Audie said, "Even though Rankin claimed not to be a churchgoing man, I don't think he would object to us saying a brief prayer for his immortal soul."

Nighthawk nodded solemnly. "Umm."

"As usual, you're more eloquent than I, my friend. Thus we commend his spirit to the Creator of us all."

They left the grave behind and returned to the trail. There had been no sign of Preacher while they were working, and they thought that the mountain man should have shown up already — if he was able to.

Audie peered toward the distant city. "I suppose we should head back to the city. Are you sure this is what you want to do?"

"Umm."

"Yes, I feel the same way. Preacher would do the same for us, no doubt about that." Audie shouldered one of the spears and picked up a war club with his other hand. A reckless smile spread across his face. "Let's go find that big galoot."

Chapter 31

As Tenoch charged at him, Preacher summoned up all the speed he could and darted to the side. He pivoted, grabbed one of Tenoch's outstretched arms, and heaved, using the high priest's weight and momentum against him.

Off balance and unable to stop himself, Tenoch flew forward and crashed into Nazar and Eztli, who had gotten to their feet but were still struggling. The collision sent all three of them sprawling haphazardly on the floor.

Still holding the broken spear shaft, Preacher bounded after Tenoch. The end of it was jagged. He might be able to use it as a weapon. As Tenoch pushed himself onto his knees, Preacher tried to ram the broken shaft into the man's back.

Tenoch twisted and the jagged wood ripped a long gash across his bare back. He bellowed in pain and outrage and swung a muscular arm into Preacher's midsection. The mountain man doubled over from the blow. Tenoch grabbed him around the knees and jerked his legs out from under him.

The animal hide robes spread on the floor absorbed some of the force of his fall, but he still landed with bone-jarring force. He whipped the spear shaft at Tenoch's head. The glancing blow barely slowed down the high priest as he leaped at Preacher.

Grappling fiercely, they were locked together and rolled over and over among the furs. Each man's left hand gripped his opponent's right wrist.

Preacher knew he didn't have the strength for a long fight and needed to end it quickly. He tried to gouge the broken end of the spear shaft into Tenoch's throat, but Tenoch was well-rested and enormously strong. He held it off.

Tenoch rammed his knee in the direction of Preacher's groin. Preacher writhed out of the way and attempted to return the favor, but Tenoch took the blow on his slab-muscled thigh. Inexorably, he brought his right hand closer to the mountain man's face. Tenoch's fingers were hooked like talons, and Preacher knew if his opponent got a chance, Tenoch would pop his eyes out of their sockets like grapes.

With his strength fading, Preacher couldn't hold the man off much longer.

A terrified scream filled the chamber. He glanced over from the corner of his eye and saw that Eztli had Nazar down and was hitting him. He tried to fend her off, but lithe and stronger, she wrapped her hands around his throat and began banging the back of his head against the floor.

Preacher couldn't do a thing to help him. He had his hands full. As Tenoch loomed over him, leering, Preacher raised his head and butted him in the face. Tenoch grunted in surprise and pain, and his grip on Preacher's wrist slipped.

Preacher jammed the broken end of the shaft into the side of Tenoch's neck. The high priest howled and rolled away as blood welled from the wound. He thrashed a couple times and then lay still. Preacher rolled onto his side, came up on his knees and then his feet.

Nazar's face was turning purple from Eztli choking him.

Preacher took a couple steps and hit her from behind, swinging a fist to the back of her head. He might have drawn the line at killing a woman in her sleep, but he was willing to hit one to keep her from strangling the only ally he had left in the city.

Eztli pitched forward, stunned. She landed on top of Nazar, her hands falling away from his neck. He gasped for breath, looking pretty groggy from the lack of air and from having his head pounded against the floor. Still conscious, he was able to sit up as Preacher rolled Eztli's senseless form off him.

Nazar rasped something in his own language, then said, "She . . . was going to kill me!"

"Did you expect her to do anything different?" Preacher glanced at Tenoch, lying a few yards away with a pool of blood slowly spreading around his head. "Come on, we gotta get out of here."

Nazar rubbed his bruised throat. "What about . . . her?"

"We're takin' her with us," Preacher said.

"That is a bad thing to do."

"We're doin' it anyway." He began looking around for something he could use to tie Eztli's hands and feet.

He wound up using the knife to cut strips of hide from one of the robes spread on the floor. He would have rather had something better, but sometimes a man had to make do with what he had on hand. He bound her wrists together behind her back, then lashed her ankles together.

She was starting to come around, and Preacher knew she would yell her head off soon. He crammed a piece of hide in her mouth and tied it in place to serve as a gag. As the last of the fogginess cleared from her eyes, she glared murderously up at him and started making muffled sounds.

She was probably cussin' him out in Aztec, he thought, but as long as she couldn't raise the alarm, he didn't care.

"What do we do now?" Nazar asked hoarsely.

Preacher lifted Eztli and draped her over his shoulder. "Now we light a shuck." When Nazar frowned at him uncomprehendingly, he added, "We get outta here and head for the cliffs."

Nazar nodded. "I will lead the way."

"Good, 'cause I ain't sure I know how to get back out of this maze."

Nazar knew the path and led Preacher through the dim corridors. Eztli tried to squirm off his shoulder, but he had a tight grip on her. Under much different circumstances that might have been a pretty pleasant experience, but he knew good and well all she wanted to do was kill him.

After a few minutes, they reached the long hallway that led back to the building's entrance. It was empty, just like before.

They hurried along. At the door, they realized the torch in the bracket next to it had gone out, since no guards were on duty to replace it.

Their bodies were still lying nearby in the shadows of the alley where he had left them, Preacher supposed.

Nazar went first, opened the door, and stuck his head out on the end of his long neck. He peered up and down the street then motioned for Preacher to follow him.

The thick shadows that cloaked the street were very welcome. In the gloom, even Preacher's keen eyes could barely make out Nazar as he followed the little priest.

"Are you leavin' the valley, too, once we get to the cliffs, or do you figure on turnin' back and tryin' to take over here?"

"I will remain with my people, but you must promise me that you will never allow Eztli to return." Nazar paused, then added in a grumbling tone, "I still think it would be best if we killed her."

"Nope, she's gonna get me outta here with a whole hide if we run into anybody who wants to stop us," Preacher said.

That comment prompted her to kick and make noises behind the gag, but he just tightened his grip on her. He went on. "If you wind up in charge here, you don't plan on keepin' up with those sacrifices, do you? I'd hate to think I was leavin' you here to cut folks' hearts out."

Nazar shook his head. "The practice of human sacrifice had dwindled away to nothing before Tenoch and Eztli revived it. I will let it disappear again."

Preacher grunted. "Glad to hear it."

"There is much to be admired about our Aztec heritage, but such wanton spilling of blood is too much. With Tenoch and Eztli gone, their followers will no longer enslave the rest of us. We will return to our peaceful ways."

Preacher hoped Nazar was right, but he had a hunch the little priest might be too optimistic. One of the other warrior-priests who followed Huitzilopochtli might decide the time was ripe for him to take over. If it came down to a fight, those who followed the ways of war always had an advantage over those who believed in peace.

It all went back to what Audie had said about barbarism being the natural state of mankind. To some folks, blood was only meant to be spilled, and in the end, theirs would be the ultimate triumph.

Preacher put those grim thoughts out of his mind and concentrated on following Nazar. When they were close to getting away, it wouldn't do for him to get lost and wind up wandering around in circles.

He came up closer behind the priest and asked, "Will there be guards out there at the cliffs?" He was worried that Audie, Nighthawk, Boone, and the others might have run into trouble.

"I do not know," Nazar replied. "I would not be surprised. Tenoch is very protective of the Path of the War God. It is, after all, the key to his power —"

A sudden shout behind them made Nazar fall silent. Preacher's heart slugged hard in his chest as he swung around to look back the way they had come. A group of warriors charged into sight around a corner, several of them carrying torches.

And leading the way, a huge war club studded with sharp stones clutched in both hands, was a man he had figured would have already bled to death.

Tenoch.

CHAPTER 32

Damn. Was he *ever* going to be able to kill that sidewinder? Preacher wondered fleetingly. The neck wound he had inflicted on the high priest should have done it. By the time he and Nazar had left the chamber with Eztli, Tenoch had already lost so much blood he *never* should have regained consciousness.

But obviously he had. A bloody bandage was tied around his neck. He had pulled on a leather girdle decorated with shiny stones like the one he had worn during the sacrifice Preacher and Boone had witnessed the day they came to the Aztec city.

Eztli started squirming harder and trying to yell through the gag. Nazar let out a frightened yelp and started to run.

Preacher's every instinct told him to stand and fight. Running away was fine for Nazar, but it went against the grain for him. Unfortunately, outnumbered the way he was and burdened with the captive priestess, he knew that a battle couldn't end well for him.

He turned and fled, too, with Tenoch and the other warriors howling after them like a pack of wild dogs.

Preacher had lost sight of Nazar. The little priest was pretty nimble when he wanted to be. Without him to lead the way, Preacher was running blindly, but maybe he could give the slip in the thick shadows that were almost everywhere. He darted in and out of the darkness, hoping he wouldn't run head-on into some unseen obstacle.

"Preacher!" a familiar voice suddenly croaked. "Over here!"

Preacher angled toward Nazar's voice. The priest appeared at the mouth of an alley, clutched Preacher's arm, and drew him into the darkness. There were no paving stones, only hard-packed dirt that their feet slapped against as they ran.

Nazar pulled Preacher to the side, pausing in some sort of alcove. The priest was breathing so hard Preacher worried the searchers would be able to hear him and follow them to the hiding place.

He put his mouth next to Nazar's ear and whispered, "Be as quiet as you can, old son. Too much huffin' and puffin' is liable to lead those varmints to us."

"I . . . I know." Nazar groaned softly. "I am not meant for such danger as this!"

"Trouble's got a way of findin' folks whether they're meant for it or not. Where are we?"

"I do not know. This is a quarter of the city where I do not go. There are rough people here . . . thieves, concubines, those who play at games of chance and death. . . ."

"I oughtta be right at home, then," Preacher said dryly. "Where do you reckon that bunch went?"

Shouts answered his question before Nazar could. Tenoch and his warriors were close by. Preacher saw torchlight reflected off the wall of a building across the alley.

The light didn't get any brighter, though, and the shouts didn't get louder. The searchers weren't coming down the alley. They'd paused in the main street and seemed to be arguing about something.

Tenoch's voice roared out and put an end to the wrangling.

"What are they sayin'?" Preacher asked.

"Tenoch is dividing his forces to search in more places," Nazar explained. "And he is sending a runner back to the temple to bring more men."

"Sure wish that fella had had the sense to

go ahead and die when he was stabbed in the neck," Preacher muttered. "I thought sure he was dead when we left outta there."

"Tenoch has declared that no mortal man can kill him," Nazar went on. "He claims to be blessed by the god of war, to be the living embodiment of Huitzilopochtli in this realm."

"Every fella who ever drew breath can be killed. Sooner or later, I'll prove it with that varmint, too."

"I begin to fear that day will never arrive." Nazar whispered urgently, "Quiet! They come."

The light grew brighter as one of the warriors carrying a torch started down the alley toward them. Preacher could tell from the voices that at least three men were in the group. The odds weren't as bad as they could have been, but they weren't good. Not only that, but the other men in the search party were pretty close by, too. The commotion of a fight would draw their attention.

Still, it looked like it was going to come down to that.

Before he could slide Eztli's bound form off his shoulder and set her down so he could move around, he heard a scraping sound behind him.

Nazar put a hand on his arm. In barely a whisper, he said, "This way."

The priest had found a door or some other way out of the alcove, Preacher realized. He backed up, following Nazar, and found himself in even deeper darkness. Nazar shoved the portal closed behind them.

"Where are we?" Preacher whispered.

"I know not. But we will wait here until Tenoch and his men are gone."

Eztli kicked her bound feet against Preacher's side and made noises.

He told her, "Hush up. You realize I'm the only reason you're still alive, don't you?"

As far as he knew she didn't understand any English, so she probably didn't know what he was saying. She could figure out what he wanted by his tone of voice, though.

Several minutes dragged by. Preacher thought the search party must have moved on.

Nazar believed the same thing. "I will go look. See if it is safe for us to leave."

"Be careful," Preacher said unnecessarily. He knew Nazar wasn't going to take any more risks than he had to. Courage wasn't what fueled the little priest. His ambition and his hatred of Tenoch were enough to do that.

Preacher couldn't see anything and couldn't hear anything except Eztli's breathing, which sounded angry. After a few moments, his instincts told him that they were alone. Nazar had gone somewhere and hadn't come back.

Had the priest abandoned them? That seemed unlikely, after all the risks he had run to help the prisoners escape. He was probably just double-checking to make sure it was safe for them to leave the place of concealment.

Preacher stiffened as his keen ears picked up a noise from somewhere behind them. Eztli began making more muffled sounds. He shifted his grip on her and closed a hand around her throat so she couldn't make any sound at all. "Best be quiet," he breathed into her ear. "I don't want to, but I'll break your neck if I have to."

She stopped wiggling around.

Preacher held her against his broad chest. She smelled of herbs and spices, and once again he was reminded that he had an armful of warm, firm female flesh.

It really *was* a shame the only thing she wanted to do was cut his heart out, or at least watch Tenoch do it.

Somebody was moving around close by. The possibility that Nazar had circled around and was coming in behind them seemed unlikely, but Preacher couldn't rule it out. He was weighing whether or not he should whisper the priest's name when somebody struck flint and steel, and the resulting sparks were momentarily blinding to eyes spent so long in the dark.

Preacher squinted against the glare as a torch flared to life. He had his right arm around Eztli and held the spear in that hand. He let go of her and allowed her to slip to the floor as he swung the spear up to defend himself.

As his eyes adjusted to the light, he saw a ring of warriors surrounding the two of them. Eight or nine spears were leveled at him. If he so much as twitched, they could make a pin-cushion out of him.

A voice spoke, filling the room with harsh, guttural words, and seldom in his life had Preacher been so surprised.

He was shocked. He knew the words. He had heard the language many times before, usually when he was in trouble.

One of the spear-wielders had just demanded to know who he was . . . and had asked the question in the Blackfoot tongue.

Chapter 33

Preacher's war with the Blackfeet went back a long way. Many years, in fact, to the days of his youth when he had first come to the mountains in the company of a couple veteran fur trappers who had taken him under their wing. It was a Blackfoot band that had captured him and threatened to burn him at the stake, giving rise to the incident that had earned him his name.

In the light of the torch, he looked at the men surrounding him as he tried to gather his wits. For the most part, they appeared to be the same sort of Blackfeet he had encountered many times, although the slightly different cast of their features told him they had some Aztec heritage, as well.

Preacher's mind worked rapidly. He recalled Audie telling him about the Aztecs who had come to the valley after being banished from their home in Mexico, some four hundred years earlier. They had found

Indians already living there, had subjugated them, intermarried with them, and gradually assimilated them into their latter-day Aztec civilization.

Some strains of the Aztec bloodline had remained more pure, and judging by what Preacher saw, so had some of those belonging to the valley's original inhabitants, who must have been Blackfoot. They had kept some of their old ways alive, including the language. It was the only explanation that made any sense.

The man who had spoken repeated his demand to know who Preacher was. Outside the valley, most Blackfeet were aware of his identity, whether they had ever crossed trails with him or not. Warriors spoke of him with respect, despite their hatred for him, and mothers told their little ones stories about him to make them behave.

But the folks who had grown up in the valley, shut off from the rest of the world with no contact between them and their bloodthirsty kin knew nothing about the man called Ghost Killer and White Wolf. . . .

"I am called Preacher," he said in the Blackfoot tongue. "I am a friend to your people." That was an outright lie, of course, but he didn't see any point in telling them the truth.

Their eyes widened, and several murmured in surprise. They probably hadn't expected to hear their ancestral language from the white man who had barged in with a naked high priestess draped over his shoulder.

"You speak our tongue," the spokesman said.

"As I told you, I am a friend."

Another man said, "I know you. You are one of the prisoners brought here to be sacrificed to Huitzilopochtli."

"I was," Preacher admitted. "Now I'm just a fella who wants to get out of this blasted valley with his whole hide."

The first man pointed his spear at Eztli. "What are you doing with *her*?"

It was obvious from the sound of his voice that he didn't have any fondness for the high priestess. In fact, most of the men were glaring at Eztli as if they wanted to use their spears on her. They all hated her.

Preacher didn't see any lust on their faces, despite her beauty, and said, "She is my prisoner. I plan to use her as a hostage if I need to, in order to get out of here."

For the first time, the warriors looked uncertain about how to proceed. At a nod from the spokesman, the others lowered their spears slightly.

The man came closer to Preacher and said, "I am called Elk Horn. In the language of those who enslave us, I have another name. All of us do. But here, between ourselves, we use the words of our people."

Preacher nodded. "It is good to remember the ways of our ancestors, along with their words."

A savage grimace twisted Elk Horn's face. "They try to take it all away!" he spat out. "They force us to live in these buildings of stone, instead of lodges of hide and wood. They make us dig in the dirt instead of hunting and killing our food like men should! Once we were proud warriors. We were Blackfoot! Now we are slaves."

Angry muttering came from several of the other men.

"I know what you're talkin' about, Elk Horn," Preacher said. "I wish I could help you."

"We never saw white men before the Great Shaking. Tenoch and his priests left the valley and came back with white prisoners to be sacrificed. Outside of this valley, do the Blackfeet still roam free? Are they and the white men friends?"

Preacher hesitated before answering. He was honest, even blunt by nature. It went against the grain for him to be cunning and use a lie to gain what he wanted. But it wasn't going to do any good for him to tell Elk Horn and the others that the Blackfeet and the white fur trappers had been at war for several decades, ever since Lewis and Clark had encountered the tribe on their famous expedition.

He nodded. "Good friends. Because of this, I would like to help you if I could. But I am only one man."

"Tenoch searches for you and the woman," Elk Horn said harshly. "We saw them. Tenoch might reward us if we turn you over to him."

"He might, but why would you help a man who forces you to live in stone buildings and dig in the dirt? Why would you help a man who enslaves you?"

Elk Horn scowled but had no answer for that. Nor did any of the other men.

Finally he pointed his spear at the floor. "We will help you, Preacher. You will stay here among us until Tenoch and his men have moved on. But then you must leave. It would be very bad for my people if you and the woman were found here." Elk Horn grunted. "Tenoch would have *our* hearts."

Preacher didn't doubt that for a second. "There was a man with me. A little fella who looks like a turtle —"

"Nazar," Elk Horn said with a note of disdain in his voice. "We saw him. He is not as evil as Tenoch and this one" — he looked down for a second at Eztli, who glared back at him — "but he is a priest and cannot be trusted. His kind made us slaves as well."

"Do you know what happened to him?" Preacher asked. "He went to see if the searchers had gone on, but he never came back."

Elk Horn shook his head. "This we did not see. We can try to find out."

"That'd be a good idea," Preacher replied with a nod. "He could be wanderin' around somewhere in these alleys. I swear, parts of this city are like a rat's nest."

"Stone buildings." Elk Horn grimaced again and shook his head in disgust. He turned and spoke to his men, telling them to search for Nazar but to be careful. Then he said to Preacher, "Come with me. Bring the woman."

Preacher bent, lifted Eztli, and put her over his shoulder again. She didn't fight him. He supposed she was getting tired of her futile struggles.

Elk Horn held the torch and led them along a narrow, stone-walled corridor. As Preacher followed, he was struck by how out of place the Blackfoot looked in the cramped surroundings. He had no love for Elk Horn's tribe, but he respected them as dangerous enemies. Seeing a Blackfoot warrior shut up between stone walls, thinking about such men tilling the soil instead of stalking their prey through the wilderness . . . well, it was just wrong, that's what it was.

It wasn't natural.

His comparison of the city to a rat's nest extended to their quarters. The usual maze of corridors led from small chamber to small chamber. From what he could tell, a lot of people lived in them. He saw women and children peeking from around corners, but none dared come out in the open. Evidently, they were all afraid of the strange white man or of Eztli — or both.

They came to a larger chamber where Elk Horn halted. "We will wait here for the others to return with news of your friend."

Preacher thought about correcting him, telling him that Nazar wasn't exactly his friend, but there didn't seem to be any point to it. He lowered Eztli to a pile of hides and stepped back. Pure murder glittered in her eyes as she watched him.

Elk Horn called out, and one of the women finally came out in plain sight, carrying a pitcher made from some sort of gourd. She brought it over to Preacher and offered it to him. The gourd held what looked like water, but he remembered the drink Eztli had given him in her quarters, a couple weeks earlier. That stuff had been more potent than tequila. He tasted the libation cautiously.

It was water, pure and cool and sweet. Gratefully, he drank it down and felt it invigorate him. He could have done with something to eat, too, but the water was most welcome.

He handed the gourd back to the woman. "Thank you." She smiled shyly, and he wondered if she was Elk Horn's wife. That seemed likely.

Eztli made noises behind her gag.

Preacher looked at her and said, "Yeah, I imagine you're thirsty, too, after havin' that gag in your mouth for a while. But I ain't gonna risk takin' it out just —"

A sudden shout nearby interrupted him.

Elk Horn jerked around and reached for his spear, which he had set aside. Preacher grabbed his spear as a man burst through a doorway leading into the room from a different corridor and yelled something in a bastardized blend of Blackfoot and Aztec that Preacher had trouble following.

He caught one word just fine, though. *Tenoch.*

The newcomer abruptly stumbled. His eyes opened wide, and his mouth seemed to be trying to frame a scream even though no sound came out. He staggered a couple more steps and pitched forward on his face.

The shaft of the spear buried in the man's back swayed slightly as he lay there motionless in death.

Right behind him, yelling stridently, came several of Tenoch's warrior-priests, brandishing spears and war clubs, primed for slaughter.

Chapter 34

One of the attackers hurled a spear at Preacher. The mountain man reacted instantly. Even in his less than top-notch condition, he flung himself to the side. The spear missed him, but, he heard a cry of pain behind him.

Preacher glanced over his shoulder and saw that the spear had struck the woman who had just given him the water. The point was sunk in her chest. She dropped the gourd and tried to grasp the weapon, but she was already too weak. Her fingers slipped off the shaft as she collapsed.

Elk Horn roared in rage and launched himself at the warriors. His spear ripped into the man who had injured the woman. Bullying that man aside, he caught another by the throat with both hands.

Preacher put up a fight, raking the point of his spear across a man's throat and opening a vein that spouted crimson as the man gurgled and staggered. Preacher rammed the point into the chest of another man, but instead of pulling it free, he let go and grabbed the man's war club. Bones snapped and shattered under the impact as he lunged into the middle of the attackers, swinging the club back and forth.

He wasn't the only one similarly armed. A club crashed down across his shoulders and knocked him forward. As he staggered, a warrior thrust the shaft of his spear between Preacher's calves and twisted it. No way could he could keep his balance, but as he fell Preacher dropped the club, grabbed a couple attackers, and dragged them down with him.

The fight continued once he was on the floor as he rolled and thrashed among the enemy. Rock-hard fists lashed out and collided with jaws. The heel of his foot slammed into a man's groin, making the warrior let out a high-pitched scream. Preacher grabbed another man's ankles and jerked his legs out from under him, bringing him crashing down. All the while, Preacher was struggling to get back to his feet.

More and more of Tenoch's men poured into the room. Finally, they stopped trying to fight Preacher and simply piled on, warrior after warrior flinging himself onto the mountain man until their sheer weight pinned him to the floor. Once that happened, the hubbub in the room began to die down.

Preacher lay there with his pulse pounding wildly inside his skull. A fighting fury still filled him, but held down, there was nothing he could do about it.

He was lying on his belly with his head turned to the side and his bearded cheek pressed uncomfortably to the rough stone floor by the weight of the men on top of him. He couldn't see anything except the floor and part of a buckskin-clad body belonging to one of his captors.

But he could hear just fine. As Tenoch strode into the room and started issuing orders in his usual loud, arrogant tone, Preacher was well aware of it. He'd expected the high priest to show up sooner or later.

Little by little, the weight on Preacher grew less and less.

A shrill cry and a sudden torrent of furious, high-pitched words told him that somebody had taken the gag out of Eztli's mouth. She kept yelling, no doubt cussing him up one way and down the other, until Tenoch said something sharply that shut her up.

A moment later, strong hands grasped Preacher and hauled him to his feet.

He wouldn't have been surprised if they killed him out of hand while they had him helpless. If he was going to die in the next few moments, he took some small comfort in the knowledge that he had helped Audie, Nighthawk, Boone Halliday, and the other prisoners escape. He had killed a heap of vicious, blood-thirsty varmints during his various clashes, so that was something else to be pleased about.

Nobody stabbed him with a spear or dashed his brains out with a war club, but he was gripped securely by several men. Tenoch planted himself in front of him and glared.

Eztli stood just behind and to one side of Tenoch, and she looked ready to start hacking Preacher into little pieces. It appeared that she was too angry to care about being nude in the middle of the crowd of men or she didn't care about that to start with.

Tenoch said something, but Preacher couldn't tell anything except that the high priest was pleased with himself. Tenoch looked a little washed-out, which was understandable considering how much blood he had lost from that neck wound. Obviously, he had an iron constitution or he wouldn't have been alive, let alone up and leading the chase after the escaped prisoners.

The stains on the bandage around his neck were more brown than red, indicating that the blood had stopped flowing from the wound and was starting to dry. As long as the injury didn't fester, he ought to recover just fine.

Yeah, he should be dead but would live to carve the hearts out of more victims, Preacher thought grimly.

Tenoch swayed abruptly, proving he was still a little shaky from loss of blood. Eztli caught hold of his arm to steady him, then snapped something at the warriors. A couple helped him over to one of the stone slabs that served as a bench.

While the high priest was sitting down, Eztli took over giving the orders. One of the men handed her a knife, and her lips drew back from her teeth as she stepped closer to Preacher.

Tenoch spoke again. Whatever he said stopped her in her tracks. Eztli trembled slightly as if her desire for bloody revenge on Preacher was warring with whatever command Tenoch had given her. Finally, after a few seconds that seemed much longer, she stepped back.

Preacher had a chance then to look around

the chamber. The woman who had given him the drink lay crumpled and twisted on the floor with the spear still sticking out of her chest. He could tell that she was dead.

Elk Horn was sprawled not far from her, his head bloody from a blow from a war club. His chest still rose and fell, though, so he was unconscious, not dead. The body of the man who had brought the warning was still there, but he was the only other Blackfoot in the room. Evidently, the others had escaped, and Tenoch hadn't sent his men after them.

The mountain man would have bet a coonskin cap that the high priest would make things harder on the slaves who tried to maintain their Blackfoot traditions.

Tenoch spoke again. A couple men hurried out, and a minute later they came back, shoving Nazar along between them. The little priest's face was bloody and bruised as if he had been knocked around some, but he didn't appear to be badly hurt. Based on the wild-eyed look on his wrinkled, turtle-like face, he was plenty scared, though.

Eztli's face contorted at the sight of Nazar. She took a step toward him with the knife gripped in her hand, and he quailed in terror. He would have collapsed if not for the firm grip of the warriors holding him up.

Eztli stopped, curled a lip disdainfully, and then spat at him. He flinched as if afraid that her spittle would burn him. She turned away from him in disgust.

Tenoch spoke.

The warriors dragged Nazar over in front of him. Tenoch had quite a bit to say to Nazar, and as the diatribe went on, the older man paled and sagged in the grip of his captors. Finally, Tenoch lifted a hand and gestured curtly toward Preacher.

The men took Nazar over to him.

Nazar swallowed hard. "Since I . . . speak your language, Tenoch has charged me with telling you what will happen to us. Tomorrow, you and I and this man" — Nazar looked at the senseless form of Elk Horn — "will be taken to the bowl of the gods, and at the moment of the sun's farewell, our hearts will be offered in sacrifice to the great god Huitzilopochtli. This will be our punishment for daring to defy the will of Huitzilopochtli and for laying hands on the emissaries of the god in this world."

"I can't say as I'm surprised," Preacher replied. "Unless it's by the fact that he don't plan to kill us here and now."

"Tenoch would never miss an opportunity to display his power for the entire populace of the city. Also, this slave's death will be a lesson to those of his kind."

"A shame we blundered in on him and his folks." Preacher sighed. "And got his woman killed, to boot. I'm mighty sorry about that."

"We are to be slain, and you think of someone else?"

Preacher didn't dignify that question with a response. "I reckon they grabbed you when you went to see if they'd gone on?"

"Yes. I was captured. And then —" Nazar stopped short.

At least he had the good grace to look a little ashamed, thought Preacher. "Then you told 'em where to find me."

"They were going to kill me!"

"And just what is it they're plannin' to do at sundown tomorrow?" Preacher pointed out.

"I know." Nazar looked at the floor. "I am sorry."

"Don't worry too much about it. Just be grateful you helped some other folks get out of here, so they can go on with their lives."

Nazar made a little face and shrugged.

Tenoch started jabbering again. The men who had hold of Nazar steered him toward the door. Preacher's captors forced him in the same direction. The mountain man glanced over his shoulder and saw a couple warriors pick up the unconscious Elk Horn and join the procession.

Within moments, they were outside under the stars again.

Preacher welcomed the fresh air, after breathing the stale, trapped atmosphere inside the hulking stone structure. He could certainly understand why Elk Horn and the rest of the Blackfeet didn't like their living conditions.

The warriors trooped through the streets.

Tenoch and Eztli hadn't come along, Preacher noted. They had probably returned to Tenoch's quarters so that he could rest and recover from his injury.

After all, he had to be strong enough to hack out the hearts of three helpless victims in less than twenty-four hours, Preacher thought dryly.

Within a short time, they found themselves back at the same prison from which Preacher and his companions had escaped a couple hours earlier. The warriors took them inside and strung them up. Nazar began sobbing as his arms were tied to the wall above his head. Still senseless, Elk Horn hung limply from his bonds.

Preacher stood stoically as the warrior carrying a torch went out, leaving them in the darkness of the cell. A moment later, the heavy door boomed shut, and the bar thudded into its brackets. He was a prisoner again, but he wasn't giving in to despair. He had gotten out once, and some way he'd do it again.

Granted, it was likely to be a mite harder . . . but he had never given up on anything in his life, except the idea of being happy spending the rest of his born days on a farm. That was why he had headed west in the first place, prepared to face whatever dangers the untamed frontier might hold.

Of course, he had never reckoned on anything quite like this . . .

Chapter 35

Boone Halliday was out of his depth and he knew it. He hadn't been on the frontier long enough to be in charge of anything, but the men who had escaped with him seemed to be looking to him for leadership as they started along the passage through the cliffs. He took a deep breath and told himself he would just have to do the best job he could.

"Will there be guards at the other end of this trail?" he asked Zyanya as she walked alongside him with a hand resting on his arm.

"I do not know," she replied. "There might be. Tenoch is . . ." She paused as she searched for the right word in her rudimentary knowledge of English.

A foul animal, or *evil* would work, thought Boone.

Finally Zyanya went on. "Tenoch is a careful man."

"All right." Boone's hands tightened on

the spear he carried. "Then we'll have to be careful, too."

It was almost pitch black inside the passage. The few stars visible in the thin line of open sky far above them didn't cast down much light. They had to feel their way along, and every few minutes Boone bumped face-first into a stone wall as the passage bent sharply one way or the other.

They came to the area that had been blocked by the avalanche. Tenoch's slaves had opened only a narrow path. The fugitives had to go through it single file. In places, the rocks closed in so much that they scraped Boone's shoulders.

His heart pounded hard and his nerves were stretched so tight it felt like they might snap at any second. It was the thought of being closed in by all those tons of rock that made him react like that. He had never liked narrow places.

At last they reached the end of the avalanche area and the passage widened out again. It still wasn't very spacious but Boone felt a lot better when Zyanya could walk beside him again.

When it seemed like they had to be getting close to the trail's eastern end, he stopped the others and whispered, "I'll go take a look ahead and see if I can find out if there are any guards."

He wished Audie and Nighthawk were there to take charge and handle the scouting chore. He *really* wished Preacher had been able to come with them . . . but it was up to him. He was going to live up to that responsibility.

Besides, in one way he was the best man for the job. A couple weeks of captivity in harsh conditions had weakened him, no doubt about that, but the other men had been prisoners for longer and were in worse shape.

For better or worse, *he* was the one who had to get them out safely.

Zyanya put her arms around him in the darkness. Hugging him, she pressed her head against his chest. "Do not be killed."

"I'll try my best not to," Boone promised her as he returned the embrace.

It felt mighty good holding Zyanya. She was solidly built but had plenty of intriguing curves, and she was really warm as she pressed up against him. Maybe Preacher promising old Nazar that he, Boone, would marry her wasn't going to turn out to be such a bad deal after all.

Before he could think much about that, they had to get out of there. Reluctantly, he let go of Zyanya, slipped out of her arms, and stepped away from her. "I'll be back," he whispered.

He left them and started forward with the spear in his right hand and his left held out so that his fingers brushed the wall. That kept him going in the right direction when he couldn't see anything at all. It would have been mighty easy to get turned around in the all-encompassing darkness.

He tried to count how many bends were in the trail after he'd left the others, so he would know how to find them when he came back, but he quickly lost track of the number. It didn't matter, he told himself. If he retraced his route, he couldn't help but run into them.

He came to an abrupt halt when he heard quiet voices somewhere ahead of him.

Although Boone wouldn't have thought it was possible, his heart began pounding even harder in his chest. He stood frozen for a long moment, then forced himself to draw in a deep breath through his nose so it wouldn't make any noise. He felt his pulse slow down slightly. After a moment more, he was able to move again.

He tried to move in utter silence, but he was sure he made a few small noises. It helped that the men ahead of him were talking. That might cover up any sound he made. Also, they wouldn't be expecting trouble from his direction. They didn't have any way of knowing the prisoners had escaped.

Boone listened. They didn't sound worried about anything. He was close enough to make out individual words in the Aztec tongue. He could tell from the tone that the men were making the same sort of bored conversation sentries did after a long shift.

It grew lighter in the passage as he approached the eastern end. He realized he was looking out through the mouth of the great cleft, surprised to see a tinge of gray in the sky. Dawn probably wasn't more than an hour away.

The faint light allowed him to see two guards posted at the end of the trail. They were a few yards inside the passage, standing near the left-hand wall, leaning on their spears. They had their backs to Boone and were watching the slope that led down into Shadow Valley.

He turned to make his way back to the others. Now that he knew where the guards were, he and the other men could jump them.

Before he took a step, he paused. It would take some time to return to where he had left Zyanya and the rest of the former prisoners and then more time to get back to the entrance. The sky would just get lighter, making it more likely they would be spotted as they approached.

It would be better, he decided, if he could dispose of the guards by himself and then fetch the others.

That is insane, a small voice in the back of his mind warned. Weak, inexperienced, and outnumbered two to one? Really, what chance would he have of overpowering the guards?

He watched the guards. As lax as they were in their vigilance, he gained confidence that he could get close enough to drive his spear into the back of one man before they even knew he was there. That would make the odds even.

He heard one of the men yawn, and that helped him make up his mind. They were already sleepy. It would be a good time to jump them.

Preacher would do it if he were there. Preacher would seize the opportunity.

But Boone Halliday was no Preacher, and he knew it.

He drew in another deep breath. He could do this.

He crept forward.

The two sentries fell silent. One of the

men leaned against the stone wall. His head drooped forward.

He was dozing off, thought Boone. He needed to strike at the other man first since the sleepier one might be groggy when the attack roused him from his half-slumber.

It was a plan — of sorts — but it was the only semblance of one Boone had.

He closed to within ten feet of the guards. The one leaning against the wall was actually snoring a little. Boone's hopes rose. He poised the spear in front of him with both hands, then before doubt could creep in, he bounded forward and rammed the weapon at the nearest guard's back.

The sharp point went deep into the man's body and grated on bone. He arched his back and cried out in agony. Boone had put so much force behind the blow, the spear went all the way through and burst out the man's chest. The bloody point protruded a good six inches from the front of his buckskin tunic.

Boone tried to pull the spear free, but the wounded man reached up and grabbed the part sticking out of his chest. His fingers closed around it with spasmodic strength, even though he was dying, and when Boone tried to wrench it out, it wouldn't come.

He hadn't counted on that. Nobody could have.

The wounded man twisted away, tearing the spear out of Boone's hands.

Jolted out of his sleep as the scream filled the passage, the second guard whirled toward Boone with surprising speed. Being sleepy didn't seem to be slowing him down as much as Boone had hoped it would. The man brought up his spear and lunged, driving the weapon straight at Boone's chest.

CHAPTER 36

Boone leaped back frantically. Tripping over the man who had just collapsed was all that saved his life. As he fell backwards, the spear passed within inches just above him. Boone reached up and grabbed the shaft, then hung on for dear life as the guard tried to jerk it back and strike again.

Boone kicked out, aiming toward the man's legs although it was hard to see anything in the bad light. His foot crashed against something, and the Aztec grunted and went down. Both men lost their grip on the spear, which clattered away on the rocky floor of the passage.

They grappled hand-to-hand, rolling and gouging and kicking. Boone was taller than the guard, but the man outweighed him, which was much more of an advantage in a fight.

The warrior was a more experienced brawler, too. It was no surprise that after a minute or so of desperate combat, Boone found himself flat on his back with the guard trying to get his hands around his neck.

Boone couldn't fend him off. The man slammed a punch to Boone's face that stunned him long enough for the guard to clamp his right hand on Boone's throat. A second later, he added the left hand to the grip and bore down hard in an attempt to crush the young trapper's windpipe.

Boone flailed punches at the man's head, but they missed or glanced off. Red explosions began to burst behind his eyes, and the blood pumping through his veins seemed to roar in his ears. He knew it would be only seconds before he passed out — and not long after that before he died.

Vaguely, he heard a loud thud. The guard's hands suddenly loosened and fell away as he slumped toward him. Boone had no time to get out of the way before the guard sprawled on him, covering the young trapper's face and threatening once again to suffocate him.

He got his hands on the man's shoulders, strained to push him up, and rolled him to the side. Something hot and wet dripped on Boone's face. Reflexively, he wiped it away and shuddered as he gasped for air. He figured what had fallen on him was blood.

"Boone Halliday!" a voice said. "Boone Halliday!"

That was Zyanya. The first time he had told her his name, he had used both first and last names, and she had persisted in calling him that ever since. As he struggled to a sitting position and looked around, he spotted her standing beside him with a war club clutched in both hands. He glanced over at the second guard, who was motionless.

From behind Zyanya, one of the trappers said, "Are you all right, boy?"

Boone looked up. The rest of the group stood behind her.

"Yeah, I-I reckon I am." His throat was a little sore from being choked, which made him hoarse, but other than that he was uninjured.

The man chuckled. "Dang, as hard as that little Injun gal walloped that fella, I expected his head to come flyin' plumb off his shoulders. Never saw a gal hit somebody like that, with a club or anything else."

Boone realized that Zyanya had saved his life. She and the rest of the former captives had followed him along the trail.

Well, now that he thought about it, he hadn't exactly *told* them to stay there. He'd assumed that they would. What he had told them was to let him go ahead and scout for the guards, and they had done that.

He certainly couldn't complain about them showing up when they had.

One of the men gave him a hand getting to his feet. When he was upright again, Zyanya dropped the club and threw her arms around him. Boone patted her on the back and murmured assurances that everything would be all right. Even though he knew she might not understand everything he was saying, she would get the gist of it.

"Any more guards on this end of the trail?" a man asked.

Boone looked at the others over Zyanya's shoulder as he continued to embrace her and shook his head. "Not that I saw. Surely if there were, all that commotion would have drawn them by now."

The same trapper said, "Yeah, the girl took off runnin' lickety-split when she heard that caterwaulin'. Reckon she knowed you was in trouble."

"It's a good thing for me she did," Boone said.

The man turned to his weary companions. "This means we're free, boys. We made it through!"

"Unless Tenoch sends men after us,"

Boone cautioned. He felt Zyanya tremble a little in his arms as he mentioned the high priest's name. "They may not have discovered yet that we've escaped, so we need to keep moving and put as much distance between us and these cliffs as we can."

"Maybe a couple of us could climb up to the top, shove some more rocks off, and block the trail again," a man suggested.

Boone put his hands on Zyanya's shoulders and moved back a step from her. He shook his head. "We can't do that," he said emphatically. "Preacher, Audie, and Nighthawk are still behind us somewhere. I won't close off the only escape route they have."

"You don't know they're even still alive," the man protested.

"I don't know that they're *not,* and as long as there's a chance of them getting out, they're going to be able to take it."

The trapper shrugged. "Fine. It was just an idea. Never said it was a good 'un."

Boone smiled as he glanced at the eastern sky, which had paled during the life-or-death struggle with the guards. "Let's go." He left his spear lodged in the body of the man he had killed and picked up the weapon that had belonged to the other guard. With Zyanya beside him, he started down the slope, deeper into Shadow Valley. The rest of the men strung out behind them.

Boone knew all the men were exhausted and wanted to rest. He felt the same way and knew Zyanya did, too, but he'd meant what he said about the need to keep moving. They couldn't afford to waste any time when Tenoch and other Aztecs could be behind them, eager to cut out their hearts.

A while later, the sky had begun to turn rosy with the sun's approach when Boone suddenly stopped. Beside him, Zyanya was breathing hard. She needed to rest for a few minutes, but that wasn't why he had called a halt.

He lifted his head, sniffed the air, and then asked, "Do any of you smell that?"

The other men tested the air, too, then one of them exclaimed, "That's wood smoke! Somebody's got a campfire goin'."

Boone thought the same thing. His mind went back to the time he had spent with Miles O'Grady and the other trappers, before they'd encountered Preacher. He knew that O'Grady and the rest of the men planned to stick together in a group for safety and come into Shadow Valley to take as many pelts as they could. Boone couldn't think of anybody else who would likely to have a campfire going in the area.

The idea of a large group of savvy, well-armed frontiersmen being that close by filled him with a pang of relief. All he had to do was lead his fellow fugitives to the camp, and they would be safe. The responsibility would be off his back.

He explained his reasoning to the others, some of whom knew Miles O'Grady and agreed with Boone's assessment of the situation. His hand tightened on the spear he carried. Zyanya hadn't gotten to rest for very long — none of them had — but maybe their flight wouldn't last much longer. Maybe in another few minutes, they wouldn't have to worry anymore.

"Let's go."

Chapter 37

The smell of wood smoke grew stronger as Boone led the group through the woods. With so many trees around them, he couldn't see the smoke rising against the early morning sky. The scent of it was the only trail he had to follow.

That was enough. He was confident they were going in the right direction.

The aroma of cooking meat began to blend with the pungent tang of the campfire. The men up ahead were cooking their breakfast.

The smell made one of the former prisoners moan softly. "I don't know what kind of critter that is they're roastin', but I want some of it!"

Several men muttered in agreement. They all had been on short rations for so long that they were half-starved.

Boone sniffed the air again in hopes that he might catch a whiff of coffee. He wanted that as much as he wanted a chunk of hot, grease-dripping meat. He didn't smell any coffee, though. He supposed they didn't have it on to boil yet.

The woods began to thin out ahead of them. Seeing a clearing, Boone figured that was where the camp was located. He wanted to rush forward, but his newfound feeling of leadership suddenly stopped him. Charging blindly into *any* situation was a bad idea, he realized. He could almost hear Preacher cautioning him about that. He held up a hand and signaled for the others to halt.

"What's the matter?" a man asked. "Don't you smell what's cookin'?"

"I smell it," Boone said, "but we can't be sure exactly *who* is doing the cooking."

"It's O'Grady's bunch, like you told us. Ain't nobody else it could be, is there?"

"Not that I can think of," Boone admitted. "I still believe we should be careful. I'm going to take a look. This time, I want all of you to stay here until I get back."

He thought a couple men looked like they wanted to challenge his decision, but then one of them shrugged and said, "All right. Just don't take too long about it. The smell o' that meat cookin' is about to drive me plumb loco."

Once again, several of them muttered agreement.

Stealthily, Boone headed off in the direction the smoke was coming from, then was surprised to glance over and see Zyanya beside him. "You're supposed to wait back there with the others," he told her.

She shook her head and held up the war club she was still carrying. "Go with Boone Halliday."

"I know that's what you want to do, but you'll be safer if you stay here."

"Go with Boone Halliday." Her round face wore a stubborn frown.

Well, she *had* saved his life a short time earlier, he thought. There was no denying that. And arguing with her would just waste time — an argument that he would more than likely lose in the end, anyway. "All right," he said with some reluctance. "Come on."

He moved forward through the trees, crouching slightly as he held the spear with both hands in front of him. Zyanya was a step to his right and just behind him, clutching the war club with which she had crushed the skull of the man about to kill Boone a while earlier.

They made a formidable pair, he thought with a wry smile. Formidable enough, he hoped, to deal with any trouble they might run into.

He paused as he heard voices up ahead. Something about them was wrong, he realized. He'd expected to hear the rough, jovial voices of Miles O'Grady and the other trappers, but the words weren't English . . . and they didn't sound like any other European language Boone had ever heard of, either.

The tongue-twisting, guttural nature of the speech was familiar, however. Boone's heart plummeted when he figured out where he had heard it before. The men in the camp just ahead were speaking the same tongue as his Aztec captors.

The shock was almost enough to make him gasp out loud. He had believed that they'd left all the bloodthirsty Aztecs back in the hidden valley on the other side of the Sawtooth Cliffs. The idea that some of their enemies were right in front of them — between them and safety — was almost too much to bear.

He looked over at Zyanya and saw that she appeared equally horror-stricken. She had betrayed her people in order to help save Boone and the others. She could expect no mercy if she ever fell into their hands again.

She motioned urgently that they should go back, making a sweeping gesture to indicate that they needed to circle around the camp. Boone knew she was right, and yet his brain had started to work again after the initial shock. He wanted to know more about the group in front of them. Such knowledge might come in handy in the future.

He put his mouth next to her ear and whispered, "Let's try to get closer."

She drew back and stared at him in wide-eyed amazement and disbelief. She gestured again, more urgently.

Boone shook his head. "I want to find out what they're saying. That's going to be up to you."

It was Zyanya's turn to shake her head emphatically.

"We need to know what they're planning so we can avoid them," Boone explained.

She looked at him like he had completely lost his mind.

Maybe he had, he thought. Maybe he was thinking too much when he should have been acting on instinct and getting the hell away from those savages . . . except he couldn't help but remember that O'Grady and the other trappers could be somewhere around there. The Aztecs camped up ahead might be planning to ambush them. Boone wanted to be able to warn his friends if he needed to.

"Let's just get a little closer," he said to Zyanya.

Finally, and with great reluctance, she nodded.

They crept forward again and then went to hands and knees as they made their way carefully through the undergrowth. Eventually, they dropped all the way to their bellies and crawled to the edge of the clearing. Boone moved a branch aside to create a tiny gap through which he and Zyanya could peer. They were looking down into a slight depression with a campfire in the center and a lot of buckskin-clad men around it. Boone estimated there were between twenty and thirty, many wearing the same sort of decorations the Aztecs in the city had worn.

But to his surprise, half a dozen were dressed differently. They had on buckskin shirts and leggings, like the others, but the garments were fashioned differently and didn't have the same sort of beadwork. Although the men definitely were Indians, they didn't seem to be members of the same tribe as the Aztecs. Even Boone's inexperienced eye could see that.

But who in blazes were they?

The men from the other tribe weren't prisoners — they were all armed and moved around freely — but Boone sensed an air of coolness, almost of suspicion and distrust, between them and Tenoch's men. He had no doubt that the Aztecs were members of the high priest's sect. Tenoch held all the power in the lost city, and the only way they could have gotten out through the cliffs was if he had sent them.

The language in which the two groups were conversing sounded stranger to Boone than the Aztec tongue. He had picked up some words from Zyanya, although to be honest she had been more successful in learning English than he had in learning her language. He heard some words and phrases he recognized, but many others didn't sound right at all. Zyanya looked puzzled by what she was hearing, too.

Finally, Boone figured out it was some sort of pidgin dialect made up of words from two different languages, the Aztec one and whatever Indian tongue the strangers spoke.

They weren't getting in any hurry to break camp. Maybe they were waiting for the sun to come up, he thought. It wouldn't be much longer.

Zyanya squeezed Boone's shoulder and

motioned with her head that they ought to withdraw. When he hesitated, she whispered, "I know who they are."

Boone's curiosity was too strong for him to resist. He nodded and began worming his way backwards through the brush. Zyanya followed suit.

When they were a good hundred yards away from the camp, Boone stopped and asked her, "Who were those other Indians? What in the world is going on here?"

"Those men are Blackfeet," Zyanya explained quietly. "I have heard of them. There are stories among my people about how the Blackfeet lived in the valley when the Aztecs first came here. It is even said that some people in the city cling to the Blackfoot ways. I never knew if those legends were true, but they must be. Tenoch's men speak enough of the language to talk to each other, and they had to learn it from someone in the valley."

"That doesn't explain what they're doing here with Tenoch's men."

"Tenoch sent for them. Weeks ago, before the passage through the cliffs was closed by the falling rocks when you and Preacher came through, he sent some of his followers to find the Blackfeet on the outside and invite their leaders to our city. He wants to . . . be friends with them."

"Form an alliance, you mean. Like Nazar was talking about. Join forces with other tribes to kill all the white men and establish a new Aztec empire in the Rocky Mountains."

Zyanya shook her head. "I do not know about this. Such things are hard for me to understand."

Boone understood, though. It was like countries over in Europe sending emissaries back and forth and establishing treaties. Tenoch wanted to do the same thing with the Indian tribes in the mountains. And it was a pretty safe bet he would declare himself emperor if he succeeded.

"So they're on their way back to the city now."

"Yes. They made camp to wait for morning, since they did not want to go through the cliffs at night."

"Can't blame them for that," Boone muttered. "It's black as sin in there."

"They know nothing about us," Zyanya went on. "If we stay out of their way, they will go on and not harm us."

Boone knew she was right, but he was torn. Getting Zyanya and the others to safety was his first priority, but he hated to think about Tenoch successfully forging an alliance between the Aztecs and the Blackfeet. He didn't believe for a second that Tenoch's dream of a new Aztec empire would ever come true, but he could wreak an incredible amount of bloody havoc in the attempt.

What could Boone do to prevent that? The answer, he had to admit, was absolutely nothing. Fewer than a dozen men, weak from captivity, would stand no chance against more than twice that many seasoned, well-armed fighters. He had seen a few flintlock rifles in the camp and knew they must belong to the Blackfoot visitors, weapons they had taken from white trappers they had killed in the past.

Zyanya was right. They needed to lie low, wait for the Aztecs and Blackfeet to pass them by, and then light a shuck out of those parts as fast as they could.

He had just reached that decision when an outburst of savage yells filled the early morning air, coming from somewhere behind them — where they had left the other former prisoners.

Chapter 38

Boone's first instinct was to bolt upright and run in that direction. Whatever was going on, he wanted to help the other trappers. But he had Zyanya to think about, too. She had already risked her life to help him and had survived an incredible amount of danger. He had to protect her if he could. "Stay here," he said in a low, urgent voice.

"No! Go with Boone Halliday!" She brandished the war club for emphasis.

"Then stay behind me," Boone told her, once again not wanting to waste time arguing. When Zyanya looked like she was going to protest anyway, he added, "I need you to watch my back."

That explanation seemed to mollify her. She nodded and looked fierce.

They weren't the only ones who had heard the commotion, Boone realized as he stood up and started hurrying through the forest. Shouts came from the combined force of

Aztecs and Blackfeet as they crashed through the woods. From the sound of it, he and Zyanya were caught between two deadly dangers. They might need some luck to escape those rapidly closing jaws.

Men still yelled up ahead. Someone let out a scream so full of agony Boone knew that the man had to be mortally wounded. He was convinced of that grim assumption when the cry choked off in the middle.

He looked back, saw Zyanya right behind him with the club. He couldn't see the Aztecs and the Blackfeet through the undergrowth, but he knew they were back there, closing in quickly.

A moment more of wild flight through the woods, and then he came in sight of the desperate battle going on. Instantly, his stunned eyes took in the scene. The men left behind while he and Zyanya scouted ahead had been jumped by half a dozen Aztec warrior-priests. Must have been a scouting party, thought Boone, or perhaps the Aztecs had been out hunting when they came across the fugitives.

Whatever the circumstances, they had attacked the trappers, despite being outnumbered. It didn't really make much difference. The white men were practically dead on their feet, worn out by their long captivity and the hard, all-night journey they had just made. Throw in the element of surprise, and the trappers didn't stand much of a chance despite their superior numbers.

Two were already dead, their skulls bashed in by war clubs. Another man lay on the ground, curled around the spear thrust all the way through his body and either dead or unconscious. If he still clung to life, it wouldn't last much longer.

The others were fighting desperately, trying to fend off the spears and clubs. One man tripped and went down, and his attacker swooped in to finish him off, lifting a war club high.

Boone rammed his spear into the warrior's back before the blow could fall. The man howled, dropped the club, and fell to his knees. Boone kicked him the rest of the way to the ground and wrenched the spear free.

He whirled and used the spear to block a thrust from another warrior. For long seconds they fought back and forth, parrying each other's strokes and darting back and forth as they sought an advantage.

Boone knew he couldn't keep that up for very long. The other man was much more experienced in that sort of fighting. It was only a matter of time until he saw an opening and managed to run Boone through.

Zyanya dashed up behind the man, crushing his skull with one swing of her war club. As he collapsed at Boone's feet, Boone gasped for breath and summoned up a grin for the young woman who had just saved his life yet again.

A look of horror appeared on his face as he saw movement behind her. One of the warriors lunged at Zyanya with his spear leveled.

Boone cried, "Look out!"

Zyanya tried to spin around and get out of the way, but she was too late. The spear point ripped into her side. Boone let out an inarticulate shout of rage and fear as he saw a flash of crimson. Zyanya's knees buckled.

As she fell, Boone leaped forward and threw his spear past her. It thudded into the chest of the man who had just struck down Zyanya. The warrior's eyes widened in shock. He stumbled, pawed at the spear's shaft, and then pitched forward, driving the spear even deeper into his body as he landed on the ground.

At that moment, the area was filled with the combined force of Aztecs and Blackfeet who had come from the camp. The shouts and cries grew louder as the trappers were overrun.

Boone grabbed up a fallen war club and

flailed back and forth around him as he fought his way toward Zyanya's crumpled form. If he was going to die, he wanted it to be at her side. He'd never had a serious sweetheart before he came west. She was the first girl he'd ever had any real feelings for. He realized he wanted to spend the rest of his life with her — even if that life was numbered only in moments.

That wasn't destined to be. One of the warriors grabbed the club and wrestled it out of his hands. At the same time, something struck him across the shoulders and knocked him to his knees. He tried to get up, and to his own surprise he made it.

He looked in front of him and saw one of the Blackfoot warriors holding a rifle. The man pointed the weapon at him, and before Boone could move, the rifle boomed. Flame and smoke spurted from its barrel.

It was the last thing Boone saw. The next instant something crashed against his head and knocked him into what he figured had to be eternal blackness. It felt as if his entire head had exploded. He never knew when he hit the ground.

Nobody could have been more surprised than Boone Halliday was when he regained consciousness and realized that he was still alive. Or maybe he was dead and in hell. It sure felt like all of Satan's imps were beating drums inside his skull.

No, he was alive, he decided. He heard men talking, and they were conversing in that damned Aztec gibberish.

In addition to the pain in his head, Boone's arms and shoulders ached intolerably. His stomach was a roiling mass of sickness, and it got worse every time he swayed back and forth. He could tell that he was moving, but he wasn't quite sure how that was possible.

Eventually, he forced his eyes open to narrow slits. Although it was an effort to think when his brain hurt so bad, he had figured out that he was a prisoner again. The Aztecs had recaptured him, and for some reason they hadn't killed him.

There could only be one reason for that, he thought grimly. They were taking him back to the lost city so Tenoch could carve his heart out.

Because he was a prisoner, it might be best if they didn't realize he was awake again. Squinting, he watched tree branches flow past like a river, moving from his feet toward his head. The sight disoriented him, and he got sicker for a moment. He forced the feeling back down.

He began to understand what was going on when he saw his arms up toward those tree branches. His wrists were crossed over some sort of pole made from a branch. Rawhide thongs lashed them together. That was why his arms and shoulders hurt. He was tied to that pole and hanging from them.

His feet were tied the same way. He dangled under the pole by his arms and legs as men carried it through the forest.

He wanted to lift his head and look around, but that would have required too much effort. He didn't have the strength. Besides, doing so would have tipped off his captors that he had regained consciousness. Better to just hang there like a side of meat.

He really wanted to know if Zyanya was still alive. Had they brought her with them? Boone remembered seeing her collapse with blood welling from the wound in her side.

She had to be dead. Even if she hadn't died from the spear thrust, the Aztecs would have finished her off. Because they had been outside of the hidden valley for a while, they wouldn't be aware that she had helped the white men escape from the city, but she had fought against them and that was all they would need to know.

He couldn't hold out any hope that

Zyanya was still alive. And he was convinced that he would soon be joining her in death.

As that bleak thought was going through his mind, the party came to an abrupt halt. Boone's captors lowered him to the ground. He still feigned unconsciousness, but let his head loll loosely to one side so he could look in that direction. The cliffs loomed above them, seeming to rise to even more dizzying heights than they did in reality.

They had reached the passage to the hidden valley. The sun was up, and it wouldn't be long until they were back in the Aztec city.

Nearby, the Aztecs and Blackfeet were having some sort of conversation. Maybe the Aztecs were explaining to their guests about the winding passage that led through the cliffs to the hidden valley.

Boone saw two more prisoners tied to poles the same way he was. They were bloody and battered, unconscious but alive.

There was no sign of Zyanya. His heart sank. Even though he had known she must be dead, he had clung to a tiny, unreasonable hope that she wasn't.

He was certain that they had left her body behind for the scavengers, along with the other fugitives who had been killed in the brief, futile battle.

Everything they had gone through had been for nothing, Boone thought bitterly. Zyanya had risked her life and ultimately sacrificed it, and they were all going to wind up dead anyway.

Some mountain man he was. Preacher never would have let things get this bad.

That thought reminded Boone that he didn't know what had happened to Preacher. He had set out with Nazar to kill Tenoch. Had he succeeded? It probably wouldn't matter all that much if he had, Boone mused. Somebody else, some other bloodthirsty savage, would just take Tenoch's place. Maybe the beautiful but evil Eztli would take over.

And what about Audie and Nighthawk? They had gone back to the city to see if they could find Preacher and give him a hand. Had they been in time? Had they been able to help the mountain man escape?

Maybe . . . if those three were still on the loose somewhere . . . maybe there was a sliver of hope after all.

But not for Zyanya, Boone reminded himself. She was gone, and nothing else mattered.

The conference between Aztec and Blackfoot seemed to be over. Warriors picked up the poles with the prisoners tied to them and carried them into the passage. As they entered the trail, the cliffs blocked out the sun. Shadows swallowed them up.

Boone felt like he was being carried along a tunnel that led directly into the bowels of hell — and considering the fate that awaited him on the other end, that was just about the size of it.

CHAPTER 39

The night before, after leaving Boone Halliday, Zyanya, and the others at the mouth of the passage through the cliffs, Audie and Nighthawk had retraced their steps toward the Aztec city.

As they came closer to that outpost of the ancient, no-longer-in-existence empire, Nighthawk gestured toward the trees and said quietly, "Umm."

"You're right," Audie said. "We need to get off the trail in case a patrol comes along. It wouldn't do for us to run into such a group. Smart thinking, as always, old friend."

The two men moved into the trees and continued on their way, following a course parallel to the trail that eventually would lead them to the city.

"Preacher and Nazar were going to Tenoch's quarters to kill him," Audie mused. "Unfortunately, we don't know where those quarters are, not having seen any of the city except what we witnessed when we were brought in as prisoners. Since then we've seen nothing except the inside of that wretched prison. It really should have been built underground so that it could be referred to as a dungeon. Honestly, these Aztecs seem to have no appreciation for the conventions of melodramatic literature. Our old friend Bulwer-Lytton could set them straight, eh? Of course, Preacher is much more the sort of character who would be found in the works of Fenimore Cooper. Natty Bumppo has nothing on our friend the mountain man, eh?"

"Umm," Nighthawk said.

"Yes, I know. I talk too much. But I tend to do that when I get nervous, and heading back into the lion's den is a bit of a strain on the nerves. You're quite correct. Stealth is the order of the day."

Although he didn't know exactly where they were going, it seemed to Audie that wherever Preacher went, some sort of ruckus soon followed. Once they reached the city, they would stay out of sight and try to find signs of a commotion. If they could backtrack the disturbance to its source, that was likely where Preacher would be.

Audie explained the plan to Nighthawk,

who nodded in agreement.

Staying out of sight became more difficult when they got to the cultivated fields near the city, but both were experienced frontiersmen and knew how to find and use any shadows or other available cover. Many times their lives had depended on being able to get from one place to another without being seen.

Soon they were inside the lost city, creeping through alleys between the stone buildings. Their general destination, Audie decided, would be the giant pyramid at the far end of the main avenue. That was where Preacher had been staked out to suffer the torments of the damned. That was the likely center of the Aztecs' religion. It made sense that the high priest's quarters, as well as those of the high priestess Eztli, ought to be somewhere not too far from that looming edifice.

A faint rumble of anger sounded deep in Nighthawk's throat as they passed the squat building where they had been imprisoned for so long. The big Crow didn't make his usual pungent comments, but he didn't have to for Audie to understand how his old friend felt about that place.

Shouts suddenly rang out up ahead. Audie wasn't the least bit surprised. If anything, he had expected the city to be in a much bigger uproar than it was. Preacher had that effect on places.

"Come on," Audie whispered. His short legs carried him quickly toward the disturbance with Nighthawk striding along beside him.

What they were hearing didn't sound like the noises of a battle, thought Audie. He could understand quite a bit of the Aztec language, thanks to his long conversations with Nazar, so as the words became clearer he realized that the men running to and fro in the streets were looking for someone.

He had no doubt who that someone might be and put out a hand to signal a halt as he heard a frantic yelp somewhere nearby. It was like the sound a small animal might make if it found itself caught in the talons of a swooping hawk or eagle, but Audie thought it came from a human throat.

He signaled to Nighthawk and they drew back deeper into the shadows as a group of warriors appeared, dragging along a prisoner. Audie recognized Nazar. His heart sank a little at the thought of the turtle-like priest being a captive. Did that mean the warriors had captured Preacher, too?

Watching from the thick gloom, Audie spotted Tenoch with a crude, darkly stained bandage around his neck. He had been wounded. Probably by Preacher, Audie thought.

But where was the mountain man? That seemed to be the question on Tenoch's mind, too, as Nazar's trembling form was dragged before him.

Tenoch spoke too rapidly for Audie to follow everything the high priest said, but he could tell that Tenoch was questioning Nazar about Preacher. From the sound of the interrogation, Preacher and Nazar had penetrated into Tenoch's chambers and attacked him. Tenoch had been wounded, but Preacher had failed to kill him. Then Preacher and Nazar had gotten away.

Tenoch demanded to know if Preacher still had Eztli with him, and that angry question brought a smile to Audie's lips as the former professor listened in the shadows. He knew that Preacher must have taken Eztli with him when they fled in order to use her as a hostage. Knowing his old friend as he did, Audie suspected that treating a female that way had bothered Preacher somewhat. But the mountain man would do whatever was necessary in order to achieve his goals.

Stammering in fear, Nazar confirmed that Eztli was still Preacher's prisoner the last time he saw them. Then Tenoch reached out, closed his hand around Nazar's throat, and asked where that had been.

The choking pressure prevented Nazar from answering. His eyes grew wide and bulged out. His tongue protruded between his lips. When Tenoch finally let go of him, he sagged in the grip of the men holding him up and seemed to be only half-conscious as he gasped for precious breath to fill his starving lungs.

After a long moment, Nazar looked up at Tenoch and mumbled something. Tenoch forced him to repeat it, then snapped orders at his men. Several of them rushed off.

Tenoch and the rest of the group followed at a slower pace, dragging Nazar along with them.

Nighthawk leaned closer to Audie and made that rumbling sound in his throat again.

Audie whispered, "I know. I would have liked to jump right in the middle of them, too. But there were too many of them. We can't help Preacher if we get ourselves killed or captured."

Nighthawk just grunted, clearly not happy with Audie's answer but recognizing the wisdom of it.

Unknown to the Aztecs, the two of them

joined the procession, following Tenoch and the others but staying well back, out of sight. After a few minutes, the group of warrior-priests entered one of the blocky buildings. Audie and Nighthawk, knowing that inside the cramped, unfamiliar confines they would be at a potentially fatal disadvantage, waited to see what was going to happen next.

The thing that Audie worried about the most was what happened.

The Aztecs emerged from the building again. And Preacher was their prisoner.

The mountain man wasn't nude anymore. He wore a pair of buckskin leggings, but that was all. He didn't appear to be injured, at least no more than he had been when they had all escaped from the prison earlier that evening.

He wasn't the only captive. Tenoch's men still had Nazar, of course, but there was another prisoner, alive but apparently unconscious, a man Audie had never seen before.

A frown creased the little man's face as he studied the third captive in the light of a torch. At first glance, the man appeared to be one of the Aztecs, but there were subtle differences, Audie realized. After a moment, he realized what they meant.

The third prisoner reminded Audie very much of Blackfoot warriors he had encountered outside the hidden valley.

That thought made the wheels of his brain speed up. He remembered what Nazar had told him about the legends of how the Aztecs had come there hundreds of years earlier and first conquered and then assimilated the Indian tribe they had found living there. Clearly, the degree of intermarriage had varied among the population. Tenoch and Eztli, for example, appeared to be almost pure Aztec in their heritage. The rest of the priests were predominantly Aztec as well.

It was possible that some of the conquered Blackfeet had tried to maintain their bloodlines, too. From the looks of the man captured along with Preacher and Nazar, he seemed to come from such a background. Audie wondered if the man had tried to help the two fugitives, and that was why he had incurred Tenoch's wrath.

Tenoch and Eztli came out of the building. Eztli was nude but seemingly not bothered by that fact. Tenoch looked shakier, but Eztli was beside him to steady him. He barked some orders, and most of the warriors started off in one direction, taking Preacher, Nazar, and the other prisoner with them.

Tenoch and Eztli and a couple guards headed another direction. Audie suspected they were returning to Tenoch's quarters so he could rest. Clearly, he'd had some damage done to him.

Audie had no doubt about the identity of the one who had dealt it out.

Preacher.

Tenoch would hate Preacher more than ever. Only the mountain man's death would satisfy Tenoch's need for vengeance and he wouldn't waste the opportunity for a spectacle. He might wait at least until the next sundown and stage another sacrifice. Perhaps even a triple sacrifice . . .

"Umm," Nighthawk said softly.

"We'll follow them," Audie replied, "just to make sure where they're taking Preacher. Before it's too late, we'll start thinking about ways to get him out of the hands of these devils. I've lost count of how many times Preacher has saved our lives. It's our turn to rescue him from a horrible death."

Any death Tenoch had in mind . . . was bound to be horrible.

Chapter 40

Audie knew that he and Nighthawk, despite their formidable skills, wouldn't be able to accomplish much if they tried to rescue Preacher by themselves. They would stand a much better chance if they had help of some sort, and once Audie thought about it for a while, he realized where they might be able to locate such assistance.

"Do you think you can find your way back to that building where they captured Preacher?" he asked Nighthawk in a whisper.

The big Crow gave him a slightly offended frown as if such a question was ridiculous and shouldn't have been asked in the first place.

"Yes, of course you can," Audie said quickly. "I should have known better. I believe I could find the place, but I trust your instincts more than my own, old friend. Lead on."

"Umm," Nighthawk said.

"You saw the third prisoner Tenoch and his men took out of there with Preacher and Nazar. I thought he had the look of a Blackfoot about him."

At the mention of the rival tribe, Nighthawk turned his head and spat on the street. The Crow and the Blackfeet were hereditary enemies. They had been raiding, killing, and enslaving each other for countless generations. He said, "Umm," again.

"Yes, I know. You can go on all day once you get started vilifying them. But remember, if these people are indeed of Blackfoot heritage, they're not like the ones we've known outside this valley. They've been cut off for hundreds of years and have had no interaction with other tribes except the Aztecs, who conquered and oppressed them for all that time. My hope is that they'll be willing to help us, especially since it seems that one of their own is destined to face Tenoch's sacrificial knife."

Nighthawk still wore a dubious expression. Clearly, it was difficult for him to place his faith in any sort of Blackfoot, even those who hadn't grown up hating the Crow.

After a moment he nodded, and with no further delay, he and Audie started through the dark alleys, back toward the building where Preacher had been recaptured.

Not surprisingly, Nighthawk had no trouble finding the place again. Once he had been over a trail — even a "trail" that consisted of a winding path through dark alleys — it was etched into his brain forever, an ability he shared with Preacher. Audie was almost as good at finding his way around, but with those two the trait bordered on supernatural.

Tenoch hadn't left any guards behind, relying on the fear of him and his men that gripped the populace to keep them under control as much as anything else. All Audie and Nighthawk had to do was open the door and walk in.

Nighthawk hesitated.

Audie said, "I know what you're feeling. You don't want to be shut up behind stone walls again. I understand. We're meant for the great outdoors, you and I. I felt the same way in the cloistered halls of academia. That's one reason I left it all behind and came to the mountains. But we have to go in there if we're going to find anyone to help us in our quest to free Preacher."

"Umm," Nighthawk said in acceptance. He lifted the spear he had taken from one of the guards earlier and held it across his chest as an even grimmer expression than usual settled over his rugged face. He marched forward.

Audie hurried to keep up with him.

Nighthawk opened the door and they stepped into darkness.

But it wasn't complete darkness, Audie realized after a moment. A faint glow up ahead served as a guide as they moved stealthily along a corridor.

They turned a corner and saw a doorway through which the light slanted, its flickering quality coming from a candle. Stealing forward, they reached a point where they could look through the doorway and saw a woman kneeling and weeping beside the body of a man. He had a bloody wound in his back, but whatever had caused it had been removed.

Nighthawk suddenly stiffened and began to turn. Audie knew his friend had sensed some sort of danger, so he followed suit. Neither had done more than start to move when the sharpened heads of spears pressed into their backs.

A harsh voice barked a command for them not to move. Audie understood the words, even though a couple seconds passed before he realized they were a blend of Aztec and Blackfoot.

Language, like most things, evolved over

time, and those people had had approximately four hundred years to develop in different ways from their cousins in the outside world. Still, most of the words had common origins, so Audie was able to recognize them. It was actually easier than if a contemporary American had tried to understand someone speaking in Olde English.

"Friends," he said in a firm voice, using the Blackfoot word. "Nighthawk and I are friends to your people."

Stunned silence greeted the declaration. Audie glanced over his shoulder and saw four men gathered in the corridor behind him and Nighthawk. Two pressed their spears against the intruders, and the other pair stood ready to strike if they needed to.

It was likely they knew about the prisoners escaping several hours earlier. Even if they didn't, all they had to do was look at Audie and Nighthawk to know they didn't belong. They could curry favor with the priests by turning the two fugitives over to them.

Audie was counting on what he had just seen to mean that they wouldn't do that. He pointed at the dead man and the woman who had turned a tear-streaked face toward the doorway and went on. "The ones who did this are our enemies."

The men didn't say anything right away. They prodded Audie and Nighthawk deeper into the room filled with yellow candlelight and surrounded them with leveled spears.

"You are from beyond the Wall of the Gods?" a man asked.

Audie knew he meant the cliffs that closed off the valley on the east. He nodded. "Yes, we are from the land beyond that wall. We were brought here as prisoners by Tenoch and his men, but we have escaped. We came to look for our friend, but Tenoch has him."

"Preacher," the man said.

"That is what he is called. We watched while Tenoch's men took him and a priest called Nazar and another man from this place as prisoners."

"Elk Horn was the other man." The spokesman added bitterly, "Our brother. His wife was struck down by the priests, as was the husband of this woman."

The speech was strange and archaic, but Audie had no trouble grasping everything the man was saying. He'd always had a knack for languages, prompted by his study of Latin at an early age. Given the hostility and contempt with which other children had treated him because of his size, there hadn't been much for him to do *except* study.

"You do not have to threaten us," Audie said. "We mean you and your people no harm. In the world beyond the cliffs, we are friends with the Blackfeet, the people from which you came."

Nighthawk grunted. Audie gave him a quick warning look, then went on. "I can tell by the words you speak and the clothes you wear that your people have tried to keep their ways alive, despite being conquered by the Aztecs."

"There were too many of them!" the spokesman spat out. "The old stories tell of how they came here, to this rich valley where our ancestors lived, and brought death and destruction with them. They burned the lodges of our people. They killed women and children. Our warriors fought valiantly."

"I'm certain they did," Audie said quietly.

"But there were too many of the outsiders. They were too brutal. In the end, our people could not stand before them."

Audie nodded. It was quite a telling observation that Blackfoot legends spoke of how brutal the Aztec invaders were. The Blackfeet were feared from one end of the frontier to the other as fierce fighters. To think that the Aztecs were even worse . . .

Well, Audie mused, that explained how

they had been able to establish an empire in what was now Mexico, didn't it? But like all empires, eventually it had been brought low.

"There is no shame in what happened here," Audie said. "The Aztecs conquered many tribes over time. But now" — he swept a hand around him — "this is the only Aztec city that remains anywhere in the world. In all the others, the people are gone and the buildings fall into decay. The Aztecs have come to the end of their rule . . . and so should it be here. Tenoch should be the last high priest to stain his hands with the blood of innocents."

Audie knew he was fomenting revolution. If he could convince the Blackfeet who clung to their ways to rise in rebellion, that would be the best distraction he and Nighthawk could ask for as they tried to free Preacher.

At the same time, Audie felt a pang of regret deep inside him. He was asking these men to risk their lives, as well as the lives of their families, in a cause that might be hopeless. Tenoch's men might crush any sort of rebellion and then mete out a cruel vengeance on those who'd dare to defy them.

Even as that thought crossed his mind, Audie remembered how few the priests really were, compared to the rest of the population. They ruled with an iron fist, backed up by knives, spears, war clubs, and their merciless nature, but if enough of the people rose . . .

It was impossible to predict. Best to concentrate on smaller goals, he decided, like freeing Preacher and getting out of the blood-drenched valley. "Do you know what Tenoch plans to do with our friend, the one he took from here along with Nazar and Elk Horn?"

The spokesman hesitated, then said, "I heard him tell Eztli that they would all be sacrificed the next time the sun goes down."

"Will you help us save them? We will free Elk Horn as well, and kill Tenoch."

It was a bold promise, but fortune favored the bold, Audie reminded himself.

"The place where they are being held will be heavily guarded," the man said with a frown. "But when they bring the prisoners out, to take them to the Bowl of the Gods, there might be a chance . . ."

Audie nodded. "Then that is when we should strike. That will give time, as well, to spread the word among the rest of the people. When Tenoch dies, everyone who wants to throw off the yoke of Aztec rule should rise against them."

The man frowned again. "Many will be killed."

"The tree of life must often be watered by the blood of free men," Audie said, shamelessly paraphrasing Thomas Paine.

The Blackfoot looked at him solemnly for a long moment, then finally nodded. "I am called Bearpaw."

"I am Audie, and this is Nighthawk."

"Umm," the big Crow said.

"Bearpaw, my friend," Audie went on, "I believe that together, we are on the verge of doing great things."

CHAPTER 41

Preacher had been awake for a long time, so after he was strung up in the cell again, he did the only sensible thing, the thing that most frontiersmen learned to do whenever they got the chance.

He fell asleep.

Granted, his position wasn't very comfortable, but he knew it wasn't likely to improve any time soon. He leaned his head back against the wall, ignored the soft, terrified whimpers coming from Nazar, and dozed off.

When he woke up, sunlight was sifting down through the ventilation openings in the roof. He didn't know exactly how long he had been asleep, but his head had drooped forward and the muscles in his neck were stiff. He rolled his head and shoulders around as best he could to loosen them up.

A few feet away, Nazar hung from his

bonds. He seemed to be more asleep than awake, although he was still mumbling softly. Preacher supposed exhaustion had finally caught up with the little priest.

Beyond Nazar was Elk Horn, awake and glaring at Preacher.

Not pure-blood Blackfoot, the mountain man reminded himself, but it was easier to think of him that way. He met Elk Horn's hostile stare and said in the man's native tongue, "I'm sorry, old son. I reckon I know what you're thinkin' right now."

"If not for you, my woman would still be alive," Elk Horn rasped.

"Yep, that's it," Preacher agreed. "There's some truth to it, but Tenoch and his men bear most of the blame. They're the ones who figure they can go around killin' anybody who gets in their way. They've gotten away with that for a long time, haven't they?"

Elk Horn had no answer for the question. He turned his head to look away from Preacher.

Their conversation had penetrated Nazar's stupor. The little priest raised his head and blinked slowly as he peered around the squalid cell, making him look more like a turtle than ever. "They are going to kill us," he said in English.

"Everybody dies sooner or later," Preacher said. "I've always figured how a man dies ain't as important as how he lives."

Nazar snorted contemptuously. "Those are noble words, but they will mean nothing when Tenoch starts to cut your chest open with a flint knife. Then you will scream and beg for death."

"Not likely," Preacher snapped. "I don't plan on givin' him that much satisfaction. I don't expect it'll come to that, though."

"Oh? Do you think the gods themselves will come back and rescue you?"

"Nope. I'll go out fightin', though. I'll make those varmints kill me before they ever get a chance to sacrifice me."

"Again, noble words. Empty words."

Preacher didn't want to waste any more breath arguing with Nazar and leaned forward a little to look past the priest. "How about it, Elk Horn? As soon as they cut us loose to take us outta here, we jump 'em and fight to the death?"

"It is the way of men," Elk Horn replied grudgingly.

Nazar said, "You are both mad. I will cling to life as long as I can and beseech the gods for a miracle."

"You do that," Preacher said.

The three men fell silent again. Preacher

wondered if their captors were going to bring them any food or water. It seemed unlikely, since they were fated to die before the day was over.

Eventually, the bar was removed and the door swung open. Eztli strode in, followed by several guards. She was clothed again, if you could call it that. The outfit was so skimpy and revealed almost as much flesh as when she'd been nude. The huge feathered headdress she wore would have done a better job of covering her if she'd held it in front of her. Modesty obviously meant nothing to her.

She went over to Preacher, the sandals she wore making soft sounds on the stone floor. Stopping in front of him, she regarded him up and down with the same sort of haughty, arrogant gaze he had come to expect from her.

When she spoke, her voice was as musical as ever, as pretty as the rest of her. Too bad it all went with such a dark soul, Preacher thought.

"You know, I'm pickin' up a few words of your lingo," he told her. "If I was to stay around here long enough, I might learn to speak it. I got a hunch you and your beau don't intend for me to be around that long, though."

She turned her head and barked something at Nazar. He sighed. "The high priestess wishes me to serve as a . . . a messenger?"

"She wants you to tell me what she's sayin', and you'll tell her what I'm sayin'," Preacher explained.

"Yes. That is it."

"So go ahead. What was she jabberin' about?"

Nazar said, "She would have you know that your attempt to kill Tenoch failed. He is as healthy as ever."

"Don't reckon I believe that. I stabbed the son of a gun in the neck, and he lost a lot of blood. He may be alive, but he ain't hale and hearty."

Nazar frowned as he puzzled over how to translate Preacher's response. After a moment, he spoke to Eztli, whose glare darkened. She spewed out some obviously angry words.

"She says you will see for yourself when Tenoch carves out your heart and offers it to the great god of war Huitzilopochtli when the sun touches the Bowl of the Gods this evening. But you will suffer before then."

"I'm sufferin' now, just listenin' to her."

Nazar shook his head. "I will not say that to her."

"I don't care whether you do or not, old son." Preacher met Eztli's cold stare. "I reckon she's got a pretty good idea of what I'm sayin'. The two of us seem to understand each other. I understood just fine when she stretched out on a pile of furs and offered herself to me."

Eztli stepped closer to him and bared her teeth in a feral grimace.

"You see?" Preacher said with a grin. "She knows what I'm gettin' at."

Another torrent of words came from Eztli. Then she stepped back and motioned the guards forward.

Were they taking him out of here? Preacher wondered. Was it already time for him to put up such a fight that they would be forced to kill him? He glanced at Elk Horn, saw the Blackfoot straining at his bonds. Whatever was about to happen, he wanted to be free so that he could be part of it.

That wasn't going to happen. The guards wrapped several lengths of braided rope around Preacher's arms and legs, binding him so tightly that he couldn't put up any sort of struggle when they cut him down from the wall. He seethed inside as they lowered him, then picked him up by the ankles and wrists and carried him out of the cell.

Eztli snapped an order over her smooth, bare shoulders, and more guards freed Nazar and forced him to come along with them. The little priest didn't put up any fight.

The group marched through the streets until they reached a large sunken area surrounded by sheer stone walls ten feet high. Preacher's captors perched him at the edge of the pit. At Eztli's orders, some of the ropes around his arms and legs were cut, but not enough so that he could get loose easily, then one of the guards gave him a hard shove in the back.

Preacher couldn't stop himself from falling forward. He twisted in mid-air so that he would be less likely to break any bones when he landed, but the impact was still enough to jar him when he smashed down on the pit's stone floor. Three warrior-priests armed with war clubs stared at him.

Eztli said something in a loud, clear voice. Nazar translated, "You will be given a chance to free your hands and feet. Then you will fight these three men, who have been told they may not kill you no matter what you do. Their job is to break your arms and legs in several places, so that you can cause no trouble when you go to be sacrificed to Huitzilopochtli."

"How come she didn't just go ahead and have 'em do that while I was hangin' on the wall in that cell?" Preacher asked as he started working at the bonds on his wrists and ankles, wondering how the men had gotten into the pit . . . and how they might get back out after their work was finished. Ladders that had been pulled up?

"Because there are visitors to the city, and Eztli wishes to entertain them."

Preacher glanced up. The pit was surrounded by the warrior-priests and strangers whose garb was different from the Aztec garments. His eyes narrowed as he realized he was looking at actual Blackfoot war chiefs from outside the hidden valley. He thought he might have even laid eyes on a couple.

One of them spat out a familiar name in Blackfoot. "Ghost Killer!"

Preacher grinned at the man. He'd freed his ankles, so he lifted his wrists to his mouth and began using his teeth to untie the bonds around them. Tied so tightly, it took a while, but eventually he loosened the ropes enough to twist out of them. He put a hand on the stone and pushed himself to his feet.

He figured the Blackfoot chiefs being

there had something to do with Tenoch's plans to expand a new Aztec empire beyond the valley. Tenoch and Eztli wanted to impress their visitors by having Preacher crippled right in front of them.

Preacher didn't care about the odds. He was free and had another chance to put up a fight, which was more than he had expected when he was recaptured. With a fierce smile of anticipation on his face, he turned toward the three men in the pit with him.

For a second, they all looked a little doubtful about the wisdom of being there then Eztli shouted a command and they charged at Preacher, lifting their war clubs to strike him down and break his bones.

CHAPTER 42

Preacher didn't retreat. For one thing, there was nowhere for him to go. The pit was a square about twenty feet on each side. For another, the Good Lord hadn't put any backup in him. He had always believed it was better to go on the attack whenever possible.

Instead of waiting for the warriors' charge to reach him, he went low and launched himself in a diving tackle at the legs of the man in the middle of the trio. His arms closed around the warrior's knees and drove his legs out from under him. With a startled yell, the man fell forward over Preacher, hitting his face on the pit's stone floor with stunning force.

Preacher rolled away as the momentum of the other two men carried them past him. He came nimbly to his feet and struck as they stopped to turn toward him. Leaping high, he crashed a kick into the small of one man's back. He hoped the blow would break the warrior's spine. At the very least, it knocked him down, so as Preacher landed on his feet again he faced only one opponent.

That one was big and burly and surprisingly fast. With a yell, he darted at Preacher and swung the club in his hands. He didn't aim the blow at Preacher's head but rather at his shoulder, and as the mountain man twisted aside, he remembered what Nazar had said about the men being under orders not to kill him.

That gave Preacher an advantage. He didn't care if he sent all three varmints west of the divide.

As the third man tried to catch him on the backswing, Preacher stepped in and grabbed his arm with one hand while he used the other to pound a punch into the warrior's ribs. The man grunted but it didn't really seem like the blow shook him much. He bulled forward, lowering his shoulder and driving the mountain man toward the closest wall. Preacher knew that if he was caught between the warrior's weight and the unyielding stone, his ribs might snap, so he let himself fall, grabbed the front of the man's buckskin shirt, and heaved. A foot planted in the man's stomach levered him up and over.

The move took the warrior by surprise. He was unable to stop himself before the top of his head slammed into the wall. Preacher heard a sharp crack like a branch breaking, and when he rolled over and came up on one hand and one knee, he saw that the man had dropped to the bottom of the pit in a limp sprawl that signified death from a broken neck.

The other two were back on their feet, not out of the fight like Preacher had hoped. The one who had fallen on his face had blood smeared across his features from an obviously broken nose.

They began to proceed in a more strategic fashion, separating and slowly circling him so they could come at him from two different directions at once.

Preacher knew that if he waited for them to make the next move, he would be playing into their hands. Again he went on the offensive, charging one of the men as he shouted at the top of his lungs.

The warrior slashed at him with the club, but Preacher went under the swing and grabbed the man around the midsection in a bear hug. Hearing feet slapping the stones behind him, he twisted, taking the man he had hold of with him. His head was in the way when his companion's war club came down in a stroke originally aimed at Preacher.

With a crunch of bone, the war club smashed into the back of the man's head. His eyes opened wide and blood shot from his nose. He fouled himself as he died. Preacher shoved the body at the remaining warrior, who stumbled as he tried to get out of the way.

Preacher took the war club from the man whose skull had been crushed, leaped over the corpse, and went after the third man, who frantically blocked the mountain man's swings as he tried to back away. When he hit the wall, he couldn't go anywhere else.

Rather than boring in, Preacher backed off a little. His bare chest rose and fell as he breathed heavily. The sleep he had gotten in the prison cell had helped him some, but he was still far from being in top fighting shape.

Good enough to kill two Aztec warriors and put the fear of God in a third one, he thought grimly.

He glanced up at the people surrounding the pit. The Aztecs had cheered as the warriors attacked, but now that Preacher had killed two of the trio, they had fallen silent. Eztli looked mad enough to chew nails.

The visiting Blackfoot chiefs were silent,

but that was to be expected. They looked on with great interest, but they weren't going to cheer one way or the other, despite the intense hatred they felt for Preacher. He couldn't help but grin at them, which made their expressions turn sour.

As always, though, there was a shadow of respect in their eyes for the man they knew as Ghost Killer.

Eztli snapped an order at the lone remaining warrior-priest. He looked like the last thing he wanted to do was follow it, but he screwed up his courage and charged Preacher again, yelling harshly.

He swung the war club, aiming the blows at Preacher's head. Tenoch might have wanted the mountain man crippled but kept alive for the sacrifice at sundown, but from the looks of it, Eztli had abandoned that plan and wanted Preacher dead.

The clubs flashed back and forth as Preacher parried the blows each time one fell. A while back, he had fought a duel with swords, and this battle reminded him of that clash even though the weapons were much more crude.

The warrior fought with a desperate, manic intensity. He had seen Preacher slay his two companions and knew the same fate was in store for him unless he killed the mountain man first. When all was said and done, only one man would be left standing alive in the pit.

His haste caused him to be careless. After one particularly hard, out-of-control swing, he found himself wide open and couldn't bring his club up in time to block Preacher's counterattack. The warrior tried to jerk away, succeeding only in causing Preacher's club to glance off his jaw.

The blow shattered bone. The warrior stumbled back a couple steps with his mouth hanging open as blood welled from it.

The terrible pain drove him to attack again as a choked cry escaped from his ruined mouth and jaw. Preacher darted out of the way of the clumsy charge and swung his club with such ferocious power that the third warrior's head was literally torn from his shoulders as the blow landed. The head flew across the pit and bounced off the opposite wall as the blood-spouting torso took another step and then collapsed. The crimson pool around the body spread rapidly as the blood continued to pump for several seconds.

Surrounded by dead men, Preacher held the club and glared up at the men around the pit. None looked like they had the least bit of desire to climb down in there with him.

Eztli let out a scream of what sounded to Preacher like pure frustration. She rained words down on him then turned to Nazar, still held by two guards, and jabbered at him for a few seconds.

When the high priestess fell silent, Nazar swallowed hard and said, "You will be left here until the time comes for your sacrifice. The dead . . . the dead will keep you company."

"Better company than some I could think of, I reckon," Preacher drawled. "At least they died fightin', like men."

Nazar flushed. "I risked my life to help you, and now I will lose it. What more can I do?"

Preacher shrugged. "Reckon you've got a point." He turned to the Blackfoot chiefs, lifted his arm, leveled a finger at Eztli, and went on in their language. "This one is treacherous, despite her beauty. She cannot be trusted. None of them can. Before you make any treaty with these people, you should think about that. You know me. You know the Ghost Killer does not lie."

He didn't know how much of the Blackfoot tongue Eztli understood. The way it was spoken in the valley was different from the outside world, anyway. As a priestess, it was possible that she didn't speak anything except pure Aztec.

Eztli shrieked at him, realizing that he was trying to undermine her with the visiting chiefs. She didn't like it, hurried over to the Blackfeet, and began hustling them away from the pit. They didn't take kindly to that, especially from a woman.

One of the men turned away from her and looked down into the pit at Preacher "The Ghost Killer does not lie, but neither is he a friend of the Blackfeet. It will be good to see you dead." With that, he stalked away from the pit.

The others of his tribe went with him. Eztli's guards dragged Nazar away and the other warriors drifted off, as well.

That left Eztli standing alone on the rim of the pit, scowling down at the mountain man. Preacher tossed the war club aside, crossed his arms over his chest, and stood gazing up at her with a faint smile on his face as he waited to see which of them would break first.

He had a pretty strong hunch it wouldn't be him.

He was right. Eztli made an angry noise and looked so exasperated he halfway expected her to stomp a sandal-clad foot at him.

She turned away and disappeared.

That left him with the three corpses. The coppery smell of freshly spilled blood filled the air, and flies were already starting to buzz around the limp, motionless forms.

Preacher went over to a corner as far from the bodies as he could get and sat down with his back against the stone wall. "Well, fellas, looks like we're gonna be spendin' the day together."

CHAPTER 43

About fifteen miles to the east, on the other side of the Sawtooth Cliffs, a group of men made their way along one of the creeks that meandered through Shadow Valley. Even though the sun was shining, the usual air of gloom hung over the valley. It had been that way ever since Miles O'Grady and his companions had come to trap beaver along the fast-flowing streams. It always seemed like the sun might disappear without warning at any moment, never to return.

Working in Shadow Valley for the past couple weeks, they had done fairly well, despite O'Grady's constant misgivings. They had worked out a system in which some of the men worked the trap lines while others stood guard and still others scouted ahead of the main party.

But not alone. Never alone. No man wanted to be by himself in that haunted place.

So far, they hadn't lost a single man. O'Grady considered that an accomplishment. True, the young man named Boone Halliday had gone off on his own despite practically ordering him not to do so. O'Grady had no real authority to enforce it, despite being elected the captain of the group, and anyway, he suspected that Boone had gone after Preacher. O'Grady had seen the hero worship in Boone's eyes when he looked at the legendary mountain man. If Boone had found Preacher, he was in the best possible hands.

If he hadn't . . . well, it had been the youngster's choice to take off on his own, although at times O'Grady was touched by pangs of regret that he hadn't been stronger in his insistence that Boone stay with them.

During the time they had been in Shadow Valley, they hadn't seen another human being or heard any gunshots or shouts in the distance. It was like they were the only people within a hundred miles.

The only ones who didn't have enough sense to stay far away from Shadow Valley, O'Grady thought wryly as he called a midday halt.

Some of the men stretched out on the creek bank to drink or hunkered on their heels and chewed jerky or pemmican. Others stood guard, peering around at the countryside through narrowed eyes as they stood tensely with their thumbs looped over the hammers of their flintlock rifles, ready to cock and fire.

O'Grady was among those standing watch. They would have their turn to eat and drink when the others were finished. The group was a strong one. It had grown to two dozen men before they'd ventured into Shadow Valley. Their profits might not be great once the money from the furs was split up into that many shares, but at least they would make *something* . . . and they would come out alive and with whole skins, or so O'Grady hoped, anyway.

Suddenly, one of the other guards whipped his rifle to his shoulder, eared back the hammer, and pulled the trigger. The weapon went off with a loud boom as powder smoke gushed from the barrel. The heavy lead ball tore into a stand of brush about twenty yards away.

"What the bloody hell!" O'Grady exclaimed. "What are you shooting at, Dixon?"

"I thought I saw somethin' movin' around in the bushes over there," Dixon replied in an excited voice. "A redskin, maybe!"

"Or maybe not," O'Grady said. " 'Tis usually a good idea to know exactly what you're shooting at before you pull the trigger."

Dixon scowled resentfully. "If you want to stand around and let some bloodthirsty savage sneak up on us, that's up to you, O'Grady. I see somebody skulkin' around, I figure they're up to no good."

"But that's just it," O'Grady said. "You didn't really *see* anything, did ye? You just thought ye did. Now we have to find out, and hope that your shot doesn't bring any unnecessary trouble down on us."

All the men were on their feet. The blast of Dixon's rifle had brought them upright, food and drink forgotten at the prospect of danger.

O'Grady nodded to two of them. "Holcomb, Stanton, you fellas come with me and Dixon. The rest of you boys stay back, but be ready for trouble."

He could tell from the grim faces of the men and the way they held their rifles that they were ready, all right. If anybody tried to jump them, be it Indian war party or — *something else* — they'd be in for a fight.

"Come on," he snapped at Dixon. "Let's see what you shot at."

"I'm pretty sure I hit it," Dixon said in a surly voice.

"We'll find out."

O'Grady advanced cautiously toward the brush with the other three men right behind him. He supposed that was what he got for agreeing to be their captain. His nerves were stretched taut as cables as he reached out with his rifle and used the long barrel to part the brush. He had already pulled back the hammer, and his finger hovered over the trigger.

The groan that came from inside the thicket was almost enough to make him fire. He held off at the last second as he realized the noise didn't sound threatening.

It sounded hurt.

It didn't sound like an animal, either. That groan had come from a human throat.

Maybe it was a trap, O'Grady thought wildly.

Maybe savages lurked in there, trying to lure the trappers deeper into the brush by pretending that one of them was hurt. But the sound of pain had seemed genuine. O'Grady, despite his hardened frontiersman's exterior, had a soft heart.

"Be ready," he snapped at his companions as he forced the brush aside and stepped through the gap. He stopped short in surprise as the sight of an Indian woman lying huddled on the ground, apparently only half-conscious.

She didn't look exactly like any Indian woman he had ever seen, O'Grady realized as he lowered his rifle. She wore a buckskin dress, but the decorations didn't belong to any tribe that he was familiar with. She lay on her side and he could see her face. Her features had a slightly different cast to them, as well.

His eyes were drawn to the big, dark bloodstain on her side. She was hurt, all right, and as far as O'Grady could tell, she was alone.

He lowered the hammer on his rifle, dropped to a knee beside the woman, and placed the weapon on the ground. Dixon, Holcomb, and Stanton crowded up behind him.

Dixon blurted out, "Hell! It's a squaw!"

"Looks like you shot a redskin woman, Dixon," the gray-bearded Stanton drawled. "That's a mighty good way to bring hellfire rainin' down on us, when her menfolk find out what you done."

Dixon licked his lips nervously. "Maybe they won't find out. If we bury her —"

"She's not dead," O'Grady broke in. "Anyway, you didn't shoot her, Dixon. That blood on her dress isn't fresh. You missed — and I, for one, am thankful for that."

"What do you mean, I missed?" Dixon

sounded almost offended, even though in reality it was probably a stroke of luck.

O'Grady pulled his knife from its sheath and cut away some of the blood-soaked buckskin to expose the wound. "She's been stabbed or cut by something. Looks pretty bad, but if we take proper care of her, she might have a chance. Help me pick her up and carry her back to the creek. We'll make camp there. Careful now!" he added as they moved in to lift the wounded woman.

"Say," Holcomb said, "what sort of Injun is she? I don't recollect seein' any who look just like this."

"I wondered the same thing," O'Grady said. "Maybe if she wakes up, she can tell us."

The other men were just as surprised when they emerged from the brush carrying the wounded woman. O'Grady told one of the men to spread a blanket on some thick grass. They placed her on it as gently as possible.

"Half of you back on guard," O'Grady barked as he knelt beside her to patch up the wound. "If anybody comes looking for her, I want us to know about it before they find us."

He used water from the creek and a piece of cloth cut from a spare shirt to clean away as much of the dried blood as possible. The wound in the woman's side was long and jagged, but not as deep as he had thought. She had lost quite a bit of blood and was weak from that, but he thought she stood a good chance of recovering if the wound didn't fester.

To that end, he made a poultice of leaves he knew would be good for that purpose and bound it in place with a strip of cloth cut from an extra shirt. He got a cup, filled it with water from the creek, and lifted her head and shoulders to try to get her to drink a little.

"Where do you reckon she came from?" one of the trappers asked.

"I have no earthly idea," O'Grady said. "She either crawled up in the brush or else she'd been lying there for a while and tried to get up when she heard us talking. When she moved around a little, Dixon got trigger-happy."

"Hey, if she'd been a murderin' redskin, you'd be happy I shot her," Dixon protested.

"But again, ye didn't shoot her. Your impulsiveness wouldn't have done us a bit of good, lad."

Dixon muttered something and walked off. O'Grady kept trying to coax the woman to drink, but she was barely conscious.

Finally, he managed to trickle some of the water between her lips and into her mouth. She swallowed, and her eyelids fluttered as she seemed to get a little stronger. O'Grady got her to drink more.

At last her eyes opened. O'Grady expected her to be frightened as her gaze focused on him, since he was a stranger and white, to boot, but she didn't flinch or try to pull away from him.

"Don't worry, lass," he told her, trying to sound reassuring. He didn't know if she spoke any English, and although he had a smattering of Indian tongues, he wasn't sure which one he ought to try first. "We'll take care of ye. Can ye tell us who ye are and where ye came from?"

The words that came from her mouth couldn't have shocked him any more if they had been uttered in Russian or Chinese.

"Boone Halliday!" she cried. "Boone Halliday!"

CHAPTER 44

Not surprisingly, the three dead men in the pit started to stink before the day was over. The flies got worse. Dark clouds of them buzzed around the corpses. The pool of blood around the body of the decapitated man turned black because so many of the filthy little creatures settled on it.

Preacher had nothing to do, so he moved around the pit, following the little shade and dozing when he could. Every moment he slept was spent regaining his strength.

He would need it. He still planned to put up such a fight that his captors would be forced to kill him before they could sacrifice him on that bloodstained altar in the amphitheater they called the Bowl of the Gods.

From time to time, children came up to the edge of the pit and peered into it with wide, frightened but curious eyes.

To them he was probably some sort of devil, he thought, smiling at them in an attempt to make them see that wasn't the case. That didn't really work and they just scampered off.

A few adults came to gawk at him, too, but the guards Eztli had left behind ran them off pretty quickly.

Preacher was surprised when a woman with a water skin showed up. He had figured that Eztli wouldn't allow him to have anything to drink.

The guards stopped the women from going too close to the pit. They had a long, animated discussion while one of the guards examined the water skin.

Preacher thought the woman looked like one of the group that was almost pure Blackfoot and wondered if she had been there the night before, during the battle in which he'd been recaptured.

Finally, the guard handed the water skin back to the woman and jerked his head toward the pit. Whatever the woman's argument had been, she had convinced him. As she stepped up to the edge, Preacher got to his feet. She tossed down the water skin.

He had no trouble catching it. "Much obliged, ma'am," he drawled.

Most of his attention was focused on a small piece of paper that fell into the pit when the woman threw him the water skin.

It must have been hidden in her hand the whole time and she had used the water skin as an excuse to drop it into the pit.

Why would one of the women from that lost city try to get a note to him?

The answer was simple, Preacher thought — she wouldn't. She was passing along a message from someone else.

He nodded to her, to let her know he had seen the paper, but she ignored him, turned, and scurried away.

Preacher didn't go after the note right away. He didn't want to draw the guards' attention to it. He lifted the water skin to his lips and drank.

The smell in the pit had kept him from being very hungry, although in truth he would have had a hard time remembering the last meal he'd eaten. But he was thirsty, and even though the water was brackish, it tasted good to him. He lowered the water skin, leaving some for later, and wiped the back of his hand across his mouth. He didn't want it to make him sick.

The note lay close to the wall. As he drew near, he was able to confirm that it was indeed a small, folded piece of paper.

Lowering himself to the floor of the pit, he sat once again with his back against the wall. The note was under his leg. Carefully, he slid his hand along and retrieved it. Working by feel, he unfolded it and then held it where he could see it.

Written in brown letters — it looked to Preacher like dried blood, of all things — were two words. *Have hope,* followed by the letter *A.*

Only one person could have written that, Preacher thought as his heart began to slug harder in his chest. The note had to be from Audie.

Preacher had told Audie and Nighthawk to get out of the hidden valley along with the others, but if they had turned back to help him — probably after making sure that Boone, Zyanya, and the rest of the fugitives reached the passage through the cliffs safely — that wouldn't have surprised him a bit.

After all, he wouldn't have gone off and left them behind.

He closed his hand around the note and slipped it into the waistband of his leggings as unobtrusively as possible. In an instant, his plans had changed. Instead of dying on his feet putting up a fight, he knew he needed to stay alive until Audie and Nighthawk made their move, whatever it might be. *Have hope,* Audie had said, and that was exactly what Preacher intended to do.

Hope that he might get out of the valley alive.

Hope that he would get the chance to settle the score with Tenoch and Eztli before he went.

To Boone, the journey through the cliffs and on to the Aztec city seemed to take forever. Hanging from a pole, he was in pain with every step his captors took. His arms, shoulders, legs, and hips ached intolerably because of the weight hanging from them.

At long last the hellish trip ended. The party reached the same squat building where the three white men had been imprisoned earlier. The warriors took them inside and dumped them on the stone floor.

Boone looked over and saw a single prisoner tied to the iron rings on the wall. He didn't recognize the man, whom he took to be one of the Aztecs. He certainly wasn't a white man.

There were subtle differences in his appearance, though. Boone was so uncomfortable that it was difficult to concentrate, but thinking was a welcome distraction. After a moment, he decided that the other prisoner was one of the inhabitants of the city who had only a little Aztec blood. More than likely, he was descended mostly from the

Indians who had lived in the valley when the Aztecs conquered them.

The warriors removed the poles, lifted the captives against the wall, and tied them to the rings with their arms stretched uncomfortably over their heads as before. Without a word, the warriors went out, slammed the door behind them, and dropped the bar in its brackets.

Boone was right back where he had started, and Zyanya was dead, having given up her life for nothing. He struggled not to let despair and grief overwhelm him. Maybe it would be easier to just give up. . . .

A short time later, the door was unbarred and opened again. Two spear-carrying guards came in, dragging a stumbling figure between them. Boone recognized the short stature and the large, bald head on the thin neck. He bit back a groan.

The last time he'd seen Nazar, Preacher had been with the little priest. The sight of him caused Boone's heart to sink. He had hoped that Preacher had gotten away.

Nazar didn't seem any happier to see Boone. As the warriors strung him up on the wall, he stared at the young trapper, then asked in a croaking voice, "My niece . . . ?"

"I'm sorry, Nazar," Boone said. "We ran

into trouble —"

Nazar interrupted him with an outburst of words that made no sense to Boone, but he had a strong hunch Nazar was cursing him.

That was all right, he thought. He deserved it for what had happened to Zyanya.

Finally Nazar ran out of angry words. He moaned and let his head droop forward.

"I'm sorry," Boone said. "I didn't mean for her to be hurt. I really didn't."

"I wish you and Preacher had never come here," Nazar said bitterly. "It would have been better to go on suffering under Tenoch's yoke."

"What about Preacher?" Boone ventured to ask. "Where is he? Is he . . . ?"

"Alive?" Nazar laughed humorlessly. "Yes, he is alive . . . for now. He is a prisoner in a fighting pit, waiting to be sacrificed at sundown along with me and this man, who tried to aid him." Nazar jerked his head toward the prisoner who had been in the cell when Boone and his two companions were brought in. He frowned speculatively at Boone. "I wonder if now there will be six sacrifices, instead of three."

Boone didn't know the answer to that, but he was glad to hear that Preacher was still alive. The mountain man might be in a bad fix, but as long as he was drawing breath, there was a chance he might turn the tables on his captors.

Boone thought of something else and started to ask Nazar if he'd seen any sign of Audie and Nighthawk, but he closed his mouth before any words could come out. He didn't completely trust the little priest not to sell them out in an attempt to save his own life.

With Preacher still alive . . . and with Audie and Nighthawk maybe on the loose somewhere in the city . . . there was reason to hope that things could change. If nothing else, Boone wanted a chance to go down fighting, rather than being sacrificed as a helpless victim.

He would bide his time and not say anything.

After a few minutes, Nazar asked grudgingly, "What happened when you tried to escape? Did you make it through the cliffs?"

Boone told him about running into the party of Aztec warriors bringing the Blackfoot chiefs to the hidden valley. He didn't mention that Audie and Nighthawk were no longer with them at that point.

"I know about the Blackfeet," Nazar said, nodding. "They were taken to the pit where Preacher fought three men. They know

Preacher from the world beyond the Wall of the Gods."

"Yeah, from the stories I've heard, Preacher's had plenty to do with the Blackfeet. They helped him get his name." He didn't elaborate on that story. It might not be a good idea to mention that Preacher and the Blackfeet were mortal enemies everywhere except in the valley.

Nazar already seemed to have gathered that. "They called him Ghost Killer."

"It's a good name for him, I reckon."

"No more. Before this day is over, he will never kill anyone again. He will be the one claimed by the gods."

"We'll see." All Boone could do was mourn Zyanya . . . and wait.

Chapter 45

Nothing had ever yet been found to stop the sun from wheeling inexorably through the sky. It continued its merciless pace, sliding steadily toward the mountains to the west of the valley, with their notch that would soon throw slanting rays of hellish light into the Bowl of the Gods.

With only the three corpses to keep him company, Preacher had nothing to do but think. He figured that Audie and Nighthawk would strike when it came time to take the prisoners to the amphitheater. Preacher, Nazar, and Elk Horn would all be out in the open then, and a swift, unexpected attack might free them.

Whether or not they could battle their way free of the city if they got loose, Preacher didn't know, but his fists clenched in anticipation of trying.

At the same time, he mused about the hidden valley and its very existence. He had been in Shadow Valley before and had never dreamed that the lost outpost of a barbaric empire lay right on the other side of the Sawtooth Cliffs. How long might it have remained so, completely unknown to the outside world, if it hadn't been for the earthquake that had reopened the long-closed passage?

How many other bizarre things were hidden away in the vast sweep of the Rocky Mountains? Preacher had seen probably more of the frontier than any other man alive, and yet he had scarcely set foot in even half of it. There was no telling what else was out there.

He remembered something Audie had said once, when the former professor was quoting one of the plays old Bill Shakespeare had written. *There are more things in heaven and earth, Horatio, than are dreamed of in your philosophy.* Preacher shrugged his shoulders. "Something like that, anyway." He didn't recall who that Horatio fella was, but the sentiment was sure true, especially when it came to the frontier.

He had paced himself with the water the woman had brought him, to make it last, but when the sun was just a hand high over the mountains there didn't seem to be any point in worrying about that anymore. He drank the rest of the water and tossed the skin aside. It wouldn't be much longer.

That prediction proved to be accurate. A few minutes later, several guards appeared at the rim of the pit. One of them dropped the end of a rope down to Preacher. They were going to make him climb out.

He didn't mind, as long as he got out of there. While some of the warriors held the other end of the rope, Preacher took hold of it and began to climb, using his feet to walk up the rough stone wall.

When he got to the top, other guards grabbed his arms and jerked him out of the pit. He thought of throwing a couple into the pit to start a ruckus, but he remembered the note the woman had dropped. If he made a move, it might ruin any plans Audie and Nighthawk had made. He had faith in his friends. They had never let him down.

With spears ringing him and sometimes poking him hard enough to break the skin, he was prodded along the street toward the amphitheater where the Aztecs intended to sacrifice him. Another group of guards and prisoners came out of a side street to join them.

Preacher wasn't surprised to see Nazar and Elk Horn, since he knew the two of them were scheduled to die along with him, but he was disappointed when he recognized Boone Halliday and the other two prisoners. Their legs were free, but their hands were tied. Their presence meant the fugitives who had fled the city hadn't gotten away after all.

"Preacher!" Boone exclaimed.

"I'd say I'm glad to see you, boy, but I sure ain't," the mountain man replied. "I'd rather you and those other fellas and that gal o' yours were a long way off by now."

At the mention of Zyanya, Boone's face fell.

Preacher saw the reaction and knew what it had to mean. "Aw, hell. The little Aztec gal . . . ?"

"She . . . she didn't make it," Boone said as they were all marched along the street toward their appointment with destiny. "She was killed when we ran into some of Tenoch's men who were bringing a bunch of Blackfoot chiefs to the valley."

Preacher nodded. "I saw those fellas. Tenoch plans on makin' a treaty with 'em, I reckon. I warned 'em not to trust the varmint, but I don't know if it did any good. Probably not."

"They're going to have a . . . a mass sacrifice, aren't they?" Boone swallowed hard. "They're going to kill all six of us?"

"That's what they're plannin', looks like," Preacher said. "Whether or not they actually succeed in it . . . we'll have to wait and see about that."

The mountain man's words were enigmatic enough to make Boone glance sharply at him. "What do you mean by that?"

Preacher just shook his head slightly to indicate that he didn't want to explain.

After a moment, Boone nodded slowly. "I think I know what you mean, Preacher. The same idea occurred to me."

Preacher kept his eyes open as the procession trooped along the street. He wanted to be able to make a move of his own as soon as he had the opportunity. But as they neared the amphitheater he began to frown. What if he and Boone were both wrong about Audie and Nighthawk?

What if no help was coming, after all?

In that case, all they could do was die as well as possible, Preacher thought grimly, and that meant with the blood of their enemies on their hands.

They could see the amphitheater ahead of them. Nazar began to make frightened noises. He dragged his feet, and the guards flanking him solved that problem by taking hold of his arms and lifting, so that they were half-carrying him. Nazar had to pump his legs quickly just to keep from tripping and falling. If he had, the warriors would have just dragged him on to his fate.

Quite a few of the Aztecs were waiting in the amphitheater, Preacher noted, but not as many as had been on hand for the sacrifice he and Boone had watched when they'd first arrived in the lost city. The spectators on hand didn't seem to be as enthusiastic as that earlier crowd, either.

But the two most important figures were on hand, Preacher saw as they reached the tiered steps leading down to the blood-stained stone altar. Tenoch and Eztli waited by the altar, along with the wizened little shaman whose job would be to hand the sacrificial knife to Tenoch.

Tenoch raised his arms in triumph, and the cheers from the crowd grew louder. A much smaller bandage was tied around his neck, and he certainly appeared healthy.

Maybe the war god Huitzilopochtli had healed him of his injury, Preacher thought dryly — although the mountain man didn't really believe that for a second.

Spear points prodded him again. Preacher began walking down the tiers. They were wide, too wide to take with one step each. Two strides were required to cross them. As Preacher descended first, followed by Nazar, then Elk Horn, then Boone and the other two trappers, he thought about how his hands were free while the others were still tied. If anybody was going to start a ruckus, it would have to be him.

That would just get him run through with several spears, more than likely, but that was better than giving Tenoch the bloody satisfaction of sacrificing him.

He had tensed his muscles to do that when he saw something that made him pause. One of the Aztecs he was passing in the crowd looked around at him — but it wasn't an Aztec at all. Nighthawk was dressed like one of them, slumping to conceal his great size. A faint smile tugged at the big Crow's mouth as his eyes met Preacher's. Nighthawk hardly ever smiled, and when he did it meant only one thing.

All hell was about to break loose.

CHAPTER 46

Preacher's eyes searched among the crowd for Audie, but he didn't spot the former professor. He was willing to bet that since Nighthawk was there, Audie wasn't far away.

As he searched among the faces in the amphitheater, Preacher noticed that many of them seemed to be more Blackfoot than Aztec in appearance. Had they come because Elk Horn, one of their leaders, was going to be sacrificed — or did they have something else in mind?

It was hard for Preacher not to grin when he thought about what the next few minutes might bring. That expression would have looked out of place on the face of a man going to his death, though, and he didn't want to tip off any of the guards.

However, he said quietly to Boone in English, "Be ready for whatever happens."

"Really?" Boone whispered back.

"Umm," Preacher said.

Understanding flashed in Boone's eyes.

They had reached the bottom of the tiered steps. The guards forced them toward the altar. Tenoch and Eztli wore self-satisfied smirks as the prisoners were brought before them.

At a snapped command from Tenoch, the guards pushed Nazar up next to Preacher.

Tenoch jabbered at him for a moment, then Nazar said in a trembling voice, "The great high priest commands me to tell you that you will be the last to die. You will watch while . . . while the rest of us are" — he stopped and swallowed hard before he could go on — "sacrificed to the great god Huitzilopochtli."

Eztli pointed at one of the trappers who had been brought back with Boone.

"That one first," Nazar said.

The man started to curse and struggle, but he was no match for the guards who had hold of him, especially with his hands tied. They forced him toward the altar.

Somewhere in the crowd, a powerful voice bellowed in the Blackfoot tongue, "Now!"

Despite his size, Audie had learned how to project his words to the back of large lecture halls when he was still a professor. The order he had given rang out clearly, filling the whole amphitheater.

As the echoes of the shout began to roll away, men throughout the crowd leaped at the warriors, wrestling spears and clubs away from them and striking with all the pent-up fury of men who had been enslaved all their lives, men who had seen their families suffer under that same iron heel.

The amphitheater erupted in bloody chaos.

Preacher struck with all the speed he could muster, leaping at the high priest and swinging a punch that smashed into Tenoch's jaw and knocked him sideways into Eztli. While they were tangled up with each other, Preacher chopped the edge of his hand down on Tenoch's wrist. Tenoch dropped the sacrificial flint knife the old shaman had handed him.

Preacher caught it in mid-air and slashed at Tenoch's throat, but the man twisted out of the way in time to avoid the deadly blade.

Guards crowded between Preacher and the high priest and priestess. He couldn't see them anymore, and he had his hands full fighting off the attackers and avoiding the spears they thrust at him.

Nighthawk swooped toward the altar like a giant bird of prey. From behind, he caught hold of two warriors by the neck, lifted them, and smashed their heads together with such force their skulls cracked. They dropped like rag dolls when he let go of them.

He repeated the maneuver twice more, killing six warriors before they realized that death rampaged among them.

Audie emerged from wherever he had been concealed and dashed among the prisoners, wielding a knife as he cut their bonds and freed them. As soon as Boone was loose, he bent, grabbed a fallen spear, and rammed it through one of the warriors. He let out a fierce whoop as he fought to avenge Zyanya.

Nighthawk had gotten hold of a club. He laid out enemies around him like a man scything through a field of wheat as he battled his way to Preacher's side. The mountain man had tucked the flint knife inside his leggings and had a war club, too. Fighting back to back, the two men were soon the center of the melee around the altar.

The uprising was going on all around the amphitheater, with heavy casualties on both sides. From what Preacher could see of the clash, he wasn't sure there were enough Blackfoot descendants to overwhelm Tenoch's followers. But if he could kill Tenoch — cut off the head of the snake — maybe that would be enough to swing the tide.

With that thought in mind, he looked for Tenoch, but he didn't see the high priest . . . or Eztli, either. Maybe they were hiding, waiting for the warriors to take care of the unexpected rebellion.

Gradually, Boone and the other trappers, along with Elk Horn and several more of the Blackfoot descendants, formed a ring around the altar with Preacher, Nazar, Audie, and Nighthawk. The Aztecs withdrew a little, creating a lull in the battle. Preacher scanned the rows of the amphitheater and saw that most of the fighting was over — and their allies hadn't won. More and more warriors were turning away from the bodies of their vanquished foes and coming down to join the forces surrounding Preacher and his friends.

Looked like this might be their last stand, the mountain man thought.

Sure enough, to make sure they were there for the finish, Tenoch and Eztli appeared again, striding forward through the ranks of warriors with looks of smug arrogance on their faces.

As the sun almost touched the western mountains, splashing garish red light over the scene, Tenoch spewed some words.

Preacher glanced over at Nazar, who said,

"We are no longer worthy of giving our hearts to the great god Huitzilopochtli. We are to be slaughtered like animals, and our insides will be taken out and strung along the streets."

"Let him come and try," Preacher growled.

Tenoch snatched a war club away from one of the men. He thrust it in the air over his head and opened his mouth to shout the command for his men to close in and kill them.

A rifle blasted, and the war club flew out of Tenoch's hand as a heavy lead ball slammed into it, breaking it in half.

Preacher had never been more surprised to hear a gunshot in his life.

But he had never been happier to hear one, either.

While the boom of the shot still filled the air, a familiar voice yelled, "Let 'em have it, boys!"

More shots rang out. The Aztec warriors began to fall. Preacher looked toward the top of the steps and saw Miles O'Grady and several other trappers firing into the Bowl of the Gods. Other men were spread out around the amphitheater, and their rifles began to roar, as well.

Like a wave, trappers came down the

steps, emptying their rifles, hauling out pistols and firing them, tearing into the warriors with knives and tomahawks. Some stayed where they were to reload and pick off more warriors.

The first volleys had cut down at least half of Tenoch's men, and the others stood no chance against the fierce attack by the men from the outside world. The warriors were falling right and left.

Preacher and his companions joined the fight. He had no idea how O'Grady and the other trappers had appeared just in time, but he wasn't going to wonder about it just yet.

He lunged toward Tenoch and swung the war club, hoping to cave in the high priest's skull.

Tenoch darted out of the way and grabbed the club before Preacher could pull it back. In a heartbeat, the two men were locked in a deadly, close-up struggle as they wrestled over the weapon.

A few yards away, Nazar was trying to stay out of the way as much as possible when Eztli suddenly appeared in front of him and thrust a spear at him. Nazar couldn't avoid the attack. He grunted as the spear point sank into his body. He fell to his knees. Eztli pulled the spear out and spat on him as blood began to well from Nazar's chest. She laughed and turned away contemptuously.

Somehow, Nazar found the strength to get back to his feet and throw himself at Eztli's back. He tackled her from behind, knocking her forward onto the bloodstained altar, got an arm around her neck, and hung on as she tried to buck him off. He pressed down harder and harder on her throat until she finally stopped struggling.

Nazar's head dropped forward, and the two of them lay there on the grim stone slab, still as death.

Preacher had his hands full with Tenoch. The high priest succeeded in ripping the club away, but before he could use it, Preacher punched him in the throat. Tenoch gagged and hesitated. Preacher bulled against him, forcing him back, and Tenoch sprawled on the altar, lying across it, near the heads of Eztli and Nazar. Preacher snatched the flint knife from his leggings and brought it up, then drove it down with terrific speed and force.

The blade went into Tenoch's chest, all the way to the carved handle.

Preacher kept the pressure on as he used his other arm to bat the war club out of Tenoch's suddenly weak grip. Tenoch's eyes widened with pain and shock as Preacher leaned over him.

"How's it feel, old son?" Preacher asked as his lips drew back from his teeth in a savage snarl. "How's it feel to have that knife in your chest for a change? I reckon I could carve your heart out . . . but I wouldn't want to touch the filthy thing."

Even though he knew it wasn't possible, Preacher would have sworn that Tenoch understood everything he said. The realization that he had lost, that he was about to die, shone brightly in the high priest's bulging eyes.

Then the light of life went out of those eyes.

Preacher let go of the knife, leaving it buried in Tenoch's chest, and straightened to see that Nazar and Eztli were dead, too.

But Audie, Nighthawk, Boone, Elk Horn, and most of the trappers were still alive. The fight was over. The few warriors who hadn't been killed were being guarded by Miles O'Grady's men.

O'Grady himself strode up to the altar and exclaimed, "Preacher! Thank the Lord we got here in time. Are ye all right?"

"Yeah, I reckon I will be, Miles," Preacher replied. "How in blazes did you wind up in this valley?"

O'Grady grinned. "A girl told us how to

find ye and said ye needed help. I believe her name is Zyanya, or something like that, although at first she wouldn't say anything except to call out the name of our young friend here."

Boone had let out a stunned, inarticulate cry at the mention of Zyanya's name. He grabbed O'Grady's arm and babbled, "Is . . . is she all right, Miles?"

"Well, she was wounded and had lost some blood," O'Grady said, "but I left a couple men to take care of her, and I expect she'll be fine by the time we get back. She really perked up when I promised her we'd come here and find ye. I'm mighty glad I don't have to disappoint her."

"Take me to her," Boone said. "You've got to take me to her!"

"First thing in the morning —"

"No. Tonight. We'll take torches to light our way through the cliffs." Preacher looked around. The sun had slipped behind the mountains, but the sky above them still seemed to drip with blood from the red glare. "I want to put this damned place behind me."

Chapter 47

There was no sign of the Blackfoot chiefs from the outside. They hadn't been at the sacrifice, and Preacher figured they must have slipped out of the valley and headed home when they heard that Tenoch and Eztli were dead and their followers' hold on the city was broken.

Just as well, Preacher thought. They might have turned Elk Horn against him — and he was happy to call the man a friend, even though the valley was the only place in the world where it would be true.

Elk Horn was sort of in charge, but it was possible some other bunch of priests, followers of some other Aztec god, might wangle their way into power. Preacher hoped not, but it wasn't for him to work out. He shook hands with Elk Horn, wished him well, and left with Audie, Nighthawk, Boone, Miles O'Grady, and the rest of the party.

With torches blazing, they entered the passage through the cliffs. Preacher, Audie, and Nighthawk hung back to bring up the rear. As they paused, they turned to look back at the valley, shrouded by night.

"I wish there was some way to call up another earthquake once we're outta here and close off this place forever," Preacher said. "I hate to think about the evil that's in there slitherin' out like a snake again."

"I don't think that will happen," Audie said. "I know from talking to Nazar that with each generation, the number of people with almost pure Aztec blood drops significantly. Now that the Blackfeet outside the valley know they're here, there's a good chance that some of them will move in and dilute the Aztec bloodlines even more. Give it thirty years and these people will be Blackfoot, not Aztec." A slightly wistful tone came into the former professor's voice. "In fifty years, no one will know the Aztecs were ever here. People will look back from a more civilized time, and they'll have no idea of the terrors and wonders that were once hidden in these mountains."

"Umm," Nighthawk said.

With torches held high, the three men turned and disappeared into the great slash leading through the cliffs, heading back toward the life on the wild frontier they all knew and loved.

The employees of Thorndike Press hope you have enjoyed this Large Print book. All our Thorndike, Wheeler, and Kennebec Large Print titles are designed for easy reading, and all our books are made to last. Other Thorndike Press Large Print books are available at your library, through selected bookstores, or directly from us.

For information about titles, please call:

(800) 223-1244

or visit our Web site at:

http://gale.cengage.com/thorndike

To share your comments, please write:

Publisher
Thorndike Press
10 Water St., Suite 310
Waterville, ME 04901